# Uncle Kenny's Other Secret Agenda

by Lawson Reinsch

Print ISBN: 978-0-9961600-3-2
.mobi ISBN: 978-0-9961600-4-9
.epub ISBN: 978-0-9961600-5-6

PH1.3_v09u

For Judy. Again. Always.

Seattle, July 2<sup>nd</sup>, 1990

Act casual, I tell myself. Get in. Get out. I hover my knuckles over Sam's bedroom door, but I can't make myself knock. I bounce my weight from foot to foot, wipe my hands on my jeans. (They're baggy, but too short. Only my new go-to-church-because-Dad's-in-town suit fits, but that's only so I don't reflect poorly on Senator and Mrs. Senator.) I turn around to face the giant antique silverback mirror across the hall from Sam's bedroom. I check my hair, check my shirt, check myself for obvious signs of weakness. I try out a few smiles until I find one my brother may not see through. The settee beneath the mirror calls my name, but if I sit I'll be planted. And I'm not supposed to sit there anyway. Mom doesn't want me to because it's older than the United States of America. Sam doesn't want me to because he doesn't want me around, much less camped out in front of his door. That's fine. I don't really want him around either. But I'm stuck with him until summer's over and he goes back to Ye Olde Fightin' Academy. Sam got out. But military school would eat me alive so I'm stuck as fuck until I turn 18. Five years, hard time. Get out. Get. Out. Getoutgetoutgetout.

I raise my hand to knock.

I don't knock.

I'd call Sam's name but my voice is changing and I know it'll break. I still don't knock.

"Go away, Paul," he says from inside. A barbell clangs on the holder thingy attached to one of Sam's machines. The metallic clunk jolts up my spine, killing the signal my brain sent down to my legs to scramble out of here. Sam eases open the door part way, drops a shoulder against the jamb, and looks up at me. Sam at 20 is the same 5'10" he was at 19 and at 18. At 13, I'm already 6'2". I have to fight myself not to spin out again with math projections, extrapolating my 99th percentile up the curve seven more years, past tall, past really tall, past too tall, up, up, up. Maybe I should start smoking.

"What did I tell you about loitering?" he says. Yes, there's a question mark at the end of his sentence, but there's zero question in Sam's tone. Gripping the edge of the door, his knuckles pulsate white, red, white, red as he squeezes the oak. I watch that as long as I can before I look him in the eyes. Sam's eyes are silver-gray like the skin of a shark. And through these windows to his soul, I don't see anything at all, just my own murky reflection from the impenetrable surface, like looking in the hazy antique mirror.

My voice only cracks a little when I ask, "Have you seen Terry?"

"She's your dog," Sam says, then just stares at me, his knuckles flashing like warning lights.

Did you kill my dog? I want to ask him that. I can't bring myself to ask him that. He might just say yes. Then what? Oh, okay, just checking. See you at dinner. Wow, even that wouldn't make Stockton family dinners more awkward.

Sam eventually lifts both eyebrows to ask, anything else?

I blink. I swallow. He closes the door in my face. Slowly. He keeps his unblinking eyes targeted on mine until the door obscures his face. And he closes the door so slowly that the usual compressed thunk is spread out into distinguishable sounds: tick of latch hitting strike plate, metal-on-metal scrape across the plate, crisp tock of bolt springing into the hole in the jamb. I can't hear Sam cross his bedroom, but I hear the weights rattle, then start clinking in rhythm.

Clink, clink, clink, clink.

I call through the door. "Do you know where Monique is?"

Her car's here, but she's not in her room.

Clink, clink, clink, clink.

My pattern thing kicks in hard and my eyes start scanning around the raised panels of Sam's bedroom door, my gaze tracing the nested rectangles in quick succession, then resetting and starting again. Edge of the panel's flat center, trough of the first carved valley, inside edge of the trim piece, outside edge of the trim piece.

Clink, clink, clink, clink.

Never mind. Monique will be in one of the kitchens.

Trace, trace, trace, trace. Four corners, eight, twelve, sixteen.

Clink, clink, clink, clink.

Abigail. Sam still calls our sister Abigail, siding with our parents. Well, Sam sides with Sam. But instead of asking for Monique, I should—

Clunk.

And my nervous system short circuits again and I'm frozen, though I hadn't really thawed. Seattle is glorious in the summertime, but it's always chilly with Sam in the house. My eyes follow the wood grain running down the panel in front of me. Sam doesn't answer as I trace the lines, faster and faster. There's enough time for him to sit up and wipe his forehead with a towel, maybe stretch out whatever wiry muscle he's been torturing. Using a muscle tears the fibers, then they repair themselves, stronger. Destroy, rebuild, destroy, rebuild. According to Sam, pain is weakness leaving the body.

Finally—just loud enough for me to hear—he says, "She's your sister."

And now I have to add Monique to my Worry List of loved creatures who Sam may have buried in the backyard. The many flight responses that had log-jammed along my spine break free, hitting my legs all at once. Even though it'll hurt my knees—achy and sore like the rest of me from growing too fast—I break into a run down the hallway, rattling fine dustables in display cases and vases on tables. If I've learned anything from Sam, it's that I'll never learn anything from Sam.

Well, nothing I wouldn't rather forget.

I pop into the old kitchen to ask Antonia if she's seen Monique and to filch some chocolate milk. My stash is undisturbed. While I pour, Antonia rattles Portuguese at Marisa and a young woman I've never met before who's stirring a giant pot of what smells to be risotto.

Antonia asks Marisa and New Girl, "Blah blah blah have knowledge blah blah Monique?"

I don't speak much Portuguese.

Marisa asks, "Blah blah Monique?"

Antonia says, "Abigail blah blah Monique now, blah Abigail blah blah furious hatred of mother and father."

The woman I don't know says, "If blah blah blah Abigail blah blah-blah," and Marisa laughs.

Antonia frowns at Marisa, tells me, "No, we no see Monique."

I rinse my glass and put it in the top rack of the dishwasher. Ducking my head around the pots and pans hanging over the island, I address the young lady I haven't met. "Hi, I'm Paul." She looks at me and says nothing until Marisa translates.

There's some blah-blah back and forth until New Girl looks at me, dips a little curtsy, and says, "Sou Corina," while she presses her palm where her collarbones meet.

"Nice to meet you, Corina." As I head to the door, I add, "Welcome to hell," but stop the door mid-swing and turn to Antonia. "Don't translate that part." Antonia grimaces at me. I nod. She nods. "Obrigado for the milk." As I step into the hall, the room behind me explodes into the various permutations of two voices at once blah-blahing, the volume rising and falling as the kitchen door swings back and forth and finally settles to a close. In my head I repeat Corina's name until I think I'll remember it. But Mom hiring Corina means I can forget Marisa now. She's as good as gone as soon as Corina gets the risotto right. Atelogo e boa sorte. Goodbye and good luck. Nice almost knowing you.

Monique's not in the new kitchen either. Janelle is making clam chowder, which means Uncle Kenny is already here. There's more English in the new kitchen, but no more information about my missing sister (or my missing terrier), so I head up the back stairs to try Monique's room again.

I knock, say, "Monique?" and there's a scrape of wood on wood and the door's open before I can say "just me" so she knows I'm alone.

Monique, standing in bra and panties, holding a wooden chair lion tamer style in one hand, waves me in with the other. As I step past her, she closes the door and jams the chair under the doorknob, kicking the chair's feet into the parallel gouges in the cherry floor.

There are clothes everywhere, flung over dressers, filling the couch, piled in the window seats high enough to obscure the Seattle skyline to the westish-southwestish and Mount Rainier to the southeast.

"Any chance Terry's asleep under one of these piles?"

"Mom."

Meaning Mom kenneled my dog, or rather, had the chauffeur kennel my dog, which at least means she's not dead yet.

"Can I move this?" I ask, picking up a gown draped across the corner of the bed where I always sit. It's light blue, silk, weighs about six grams. Silver threads woven into the spaghetti straps continue through the delicate piping along the neckline. "If you're wearing this tonight, you have to let me give you your birthday present early." Dangly earrings. Platinum with sapphires that match her eyes, like this dress.

"I'm not wearing that," she says. "Uncle Kenny's here."

While Monique climbs into what looks like a burlap bag, I hold the flimsy blue dress at arm's length suspended on two index fingers. Yeah, even with her modest chest, the décolletage would be . . . problematic. I lay the dress on top of the pile covering the back of her couch. Monique twists her long black hair into a rope, pulling it over one shoulder as she turns her back to me.

"Zip."

I zip. She turns to the standing mirror in the corner, sweeps a hand down her abdomen then twists around and rotates her hips to look at her butt. I stand to look over her shoulder, but she turns to me, arms down but away from her body—What do you think? Like Sam, Monique is also 5'10", but has a leaner build, a runner's build, sinewy. She doesn't look sick like the emaciated models, just trim and fit. Which means she has the problem of looking good in everything. Even this shapeless bag drapes on her frame in a way that is zero percent androgynous. It hides her long legs, but suggests or accentuates every other nubile curve.

"Nope," I say and she's already out of it.

"Pant suit," she says. "Boy clothes."

"Play his phobia off his philia."

Monique, by any other name, is jailbait for four more days. She grabs one of the navy blue jackets from the hook on her bathroom door, puts it on without a blouse. The narrow waist and flare at the hips are working against her.

"Too tailored," I say. Also, silk. That glimmer and liquid flow draw the eye. She takes it off, hangs it on the back of her desk chair, and takes another from the bathroom door.

"How did you know it was me at the door?"

"You thump."

"When I walk?"

Monique pulls the lapels together at the top button with one hand and twists to check the mirror again. Twist, arch, twist, shoulders back.

"It's why your knees hurt." This jacket works, in that it doesn't quite work. She finds the matching pants and pulls them on. Sub-optimal. Monique's legs, they're never going to not look good. But the longish jacket boxes up her shape and the look is as bad as it's going to get outside of a Harry the Husky mascot costume or a full body cast.

"You should get changed," she says, taking off the jacket and handing it to me. In what seems to be a single smooth motion, she slips a high-neck blouse off a hanger in her closet, spins it around herself and ends up with both arms through the sleeves. She starts buttoning in the middle, works one hand up and one hand down.

"Too early," I say. "I'll get grubby."

"Dinner's at six."

"Sam said—" Monique stops me with a look. I know not to believe Sam when he tells me casual dress, but— Oh, he didn't tell me directly. He mathed me. Out in the yard, right at 3:30 he said, "Three hours to dinner. Don't be late." He petted my dog, asked me the time to fix my crazy brain on the number, then he mathed me. "Crap."

She's done buttoning, so I hand her the jacket as I head for the door. Holding it by the collar, she flips it over her shoulder as I turn back to her.

"Sorry, Monique, but you look really nice."

"Yaaahhh," she says, resigned. With her other hand, she opens her top desk drawer, slides an only-semi-frilly purple garter across the desktop into the drawer before closing it again. I've learned that women's clothes often don't have pockets, especially dresses. From atop the desk, next to where her garter had lain, Monique retrieves her stiletto and drops it into the front pocket of her slacks.

Does *Seventeen* magazine do stories on carrying defensive weaponry? Concealment, it's not just for pimples! Home safety quiz: what's more dangerous than hot burners on the stove or your wet bathroom floor? Happy Birthday, Cancer. The stars are aligned for your horror-scope. Someone's planning a birthday surprise for a special young lady. Watch your fucking back.

Monique stands before me. Still, but not placid. Coiled. Ready. She's pretty enough to scare off a lot of guys her age, and pretty enough to attract a bunch of the wrong guys for the wrong reasons. The challenge. The conquest. Nothing about Monique as Monique. She's said before there are worse problems to have, but she doesn't say that this time. Not here. Not now.

"Go change," she says.

I nod. Turn. But as I reach for the chair to unjam the door, a clanging, rattling, rhythmic thumping builds in the hall and stops outside Monique's bedroom door. Her head twitches once before she looks from the door to me, like she's doing a double take. I think our brother just impersonated my thumping approach—spot on, I'm guessing from Monique's look. That's a trick that will only work once. We look from each other to the door, asking in unison, "Sam?"

"Back away from the door," he says. A wooden yardstick

shoots through the crack under the door, swatting at my feet. I hop back as the yardstick retracts. "Don't open it." He uses the yardstick to push some cloth—no, a folded-over T-shirt—under the door, jab, jab, jab until only a little bit must be left on his side. The yardstick slips out of the wad of T-shirt, comes back naked, sliding deeper into the room and finally finding purchase up against the foot of the chair Monique had levered under the doorknob. I don't know if he smacks the yardstick or just pushes, but the chair foot jerks out of the gouge in the floor and slides away from the door as the chair topples over backward. The hard wooden back makes surprisingly little noise when it lands on the folds of T-shirt.

Like a magician whipping a tablecloth out from under plates and glasses and candelabras, Sam yanks the T-shirt out from under the fallen chair. The garment disappears under the door. In about four fast heartbeats, the knob turns, the door cracks open, Sam's hand picks up the chair, rights it. Sam closes the door as he slips into the room, already wearing the T-shirt he shoved under the door. The end of the yardstick dangles from the hand he's using to make the "Shh" sign in front of his lips.

"Window," he says, lowering the index finger into a pointing gesture and following it across Monique's bedroom. Monique and I follow. When we arrive at the window that Sam's already got unlatched and swung open, he again gives me the "Shh" sign, even though I haven't said anything. I'm actually about to say out loud that I haven't said anything when I hear voices below us outside. Dad and Uncle Kenny.

I do the "Shh" sign back at Sam until he lowers his hand. He lays his other hand onto a pile of Monique's clothes filling the window seat. We three listen. Sort of. They're not that hard to hear, but apart from the occasional number, holy crap, Snoozetown. Tributes and transfers and taxes and tithing. Bonds and banks and borders and bullshit. Distractions fall upon me.

One of Monique's overhead lights is about to burn out and the resistance whine from the disintegrating filament is piercing, at least to me and my dog, wherever she is. Warm air pours in through the open window. I notice the clothes under Sam's hand are all blouses, a mix of fancy and casual, but all carefully folded and stacked. The adjacent mound is a mix of discarded skirts and sweaters and dresses. This pile lacks structural integrity because nothing's folded, even though some of the garments' tags are still on. The heap that threatens to topple over onto Monique is comprised exclusively of stuff that Mom picked out for Monique. The neat pile is shirts Monique bought when I was with her.

Sam eases the window closed and latches it.

"I didn't say anything," I say.

"Good for you, Paul," Sam says. "Way to miss the point." Sam grabs my wrist. "Don't make a fist like that. Keep your thumb outside or you'll dislocate it when you hit something." *When* you hit something, not *if.* I choose to take that as Sam believing in me rather than focusing on how hitting something or someone seems somewhat of an inevitability with Sam. I hadn't even known my hands were clenched.

"They're stealing," Monique tells me.

"Stealing what?"

"Is he even here?" Sam asks Monique. It's so much fun to be talked about like I'm not in the room.

"Campaign contributions," Monique says. "Moving money offshore."

Sam turns his attention back to me, which, I have to say, does not make me feel better. "Seriously. What are you paying attention to?"

If I flicked the lights off and on, the bulb above our heads would not come back on. I wonder if it's worth explaining this to Sam, or demonstrating, but his was a rhetorical question and Sam's moving on.

"Uncle Kenny has another secret agenda," he says.

"You can't be surprised they're crooked," Monique says, crossing her arms.

"The scale," Sam says, shaking his head before reengaging me. "What's compound interest on twelve million dollars?"

"I'd need to know the rate and frequency of compounding?" I get about halfway through "frequency" before Sam waves me off, turns back to Monique and crosses his arms like hers. The yardstick still poking out of his fist now extends horizontally, nearly touching my chest. We're twenty-one inches apart. Three times seven. Prime times prime. The end of the stick rises and falls before me as Sam breathes calmly, staring at Monique.

"Police? Media?" Monique says with enough doubt in her tone that Sam doesn't bother to shake his head. "FBI? Who oversees campaign financing?"

"Probably Dad," Sam says. "Or Uncle Kenny, or someone they own."

"Five percent APR," I say, "compounded monthly is about six-hundred-thousand a year."

Sam turns to me, looks me up and down.

"Fifty thousand per month," I say. "If they start with exactly twelve million."

"Your thing?" he asks, but "you" isn't me. Now I'm being talked over because I *am* here.

"Still good," Monique says.

Sam looks out the window, then at Monique and me in turn, and finally rests his gaze outside on some point in space that I can't see. A defeated quiet permeates the room, the silence broken only by the whine of the dying light bulb above us.

I cross the room to the switch by the door, point to the ceiling above their heads until they look up. Ninety percent of the energy used by an incandescent light bulb converts to heat, not light. This guy's filament is already fractured, the gap between the ends made smaller by thermal expansion, the stubs held in place by the flowing current's electromagnetic field. I throw the switch, killing the power, killing the light. When I toggle the switch again, the bulb above Sam and Monique's heads stays dark, the room now perfectly silent.

Sam says, "There's a lot that's not right about you."

I love you too, Sam.

Sam looks at his watch and grunts. "You need to get changed for dinner." He does too, and I'm about to tell him that, but he's charging toward me, pulling a length of dark green cord from his pocket. He loops the cord around Monique's doorknob as he shoves me out of the room and shuts the door. For the second time this afternoon I'm not quite having a conversation with Sam through a closed door. As I walk away, I hear him say to Monique, "Let me show you how to tie this so Uncle Kenny can't pop the chair."

## CHAPTER 2: PRESSING BUTTONS

As my hallway bounding rattles more useless crap on pointless display, I check my watch. Asshole convention in eleven minutes. About two minutes of travel time leaves me nine minutes to change. No problem. As long as I don't look at any of my computer screens, I'm good. Get in, get out. I stay focused, get changed, and I'm back down on the second floor just in time for this evening's catastrophe not to be me.

"It's an ambush," Monique says, catching me outside the dining room before I go in, and driving me back down the hall, back-pedaling with her palm on my chest.

"Press?"

"Print mags. Two. Sharing a getter." She pulls a necktie out of her suit pocket. When the getter gets to getting pictures, the solid color will look better than the non-power paisley thing I chose for myself (because the paisley swirls remind me of fractals). I yank my tie loose and pull the loop over my head. I jam it in my jacket pocket as Monique slips the new tie under my collar and makes like a sailor, tying knots and swearing.

"Goddammit," she says. "I can't wait to fuck those fuckers."

The wide end of the tie propellers past my face as fury builds in Monique's. Eyes fierce, the muscle at the corner of her jaw clenches and stays clenched. She breathes in hard through her nose, breathes out hard. But her hands remain precise and gentle, executing the knot with aplomb and snugging it up to my brand new Adam's apple with none of the roughness of her mood. Tweak tweak collar, lift smooth jacket. Done.

"Fucking fuckery fuckers," I say. I don't know who she's fighting, but against anybody, I'm on her side. Monique's eyes de-squint as she exhales one quick laugh. She drops her hands onto my shoulders. Relaxed for a split second, she smiles.

"You're a good kid, you son of a bitch."

I'd tell her she's a good kid, too, but there's no equivalent daughter-of-a-bitch phrase, so I stall out on that void and just smile back at her, watch her eyes dart as her gaze tracks around my face: right eye, left eye, my grin, and back to bouncing eye to eye.

"Ah, that's why," I say. "Mom took my dog out of the equation because I called Terry a bitch in front of press." Monique nods. It's accurate. Terry's a girl dog. To be fair, I said it a lot. I was kind of an ass.

"You're a *good* kid," I say.

"You're a good *kid*," she says, picking up our occasional game.

"*You're* a good kid."

"You're *a* good kid," Monique says, then asks, "Ready?"

"What's the worst that could happen?"

Monique rolls her eyes and we head for the door.

These go a few different ways. Birthdays usually get the Strafing Run. Senator Family Man blows in, holds up a slice of cake while he looks at every camera for three seconds, grinning and unblinking, then he glad-hands any dignitaries Mama Planning Committee wrangled, shakes a baby, and he's gone. He likes it if you look at him while he looks at the camera. But there is upside. The cameras and the scrutiny leave with him and I get to eat his slice of cake.

For a Campaign Event, it's the School Play. We get lines. If they ask you this, you say this. Say it. Say it again. Say it again. Once more, with feeling. The time our father spends away from the family makes our time together that much more special. The sacrifice we make to support his work sacking and pillaging for his own gain. Honored to serve and monkeys and platypus. Blah blah, vote Stockton. There's no upside. Hours under the lights, crap food, and a horde of self-important douchebags telling lies to people they don't care about. Be attentive through the speech and don't pick your nose on camera. We're live in four, three, two . . .

Worst though, is Dinner at Home. The coverage is always some limp fluff piece. No debate, no traps, no hard questions. We get lobbed softballs and we're supposed to point to the stands and hit a home run. Smaller horde of douchebags, but it's maximum interaction for maximum downside. No speeches— well, no formal speeches. Just hang out, look perfect, act nice. The Stocktons aren't good at nice. And if they purposefully haven't prepped us, there's no telling what's going to happen now.

Mom checks her watch when Monique and I step in, but we're not late, so we're not in trouble, so she doesn't bother to address us. If you don't have anything mean to say . . . She crosses her arms and turns her attention away from us props and back to the star attraction.

Flash. The camera motor advances the film automatically, bwsshhhhh. I like that sound.

At the far end of the room, Dad and Sam—all creases and sparkle now in his dress uniform—are posed against the big picture window that frames Mount Rainier. As a backdrop, it's unbeatable. Fourteen thousand feet of glacier-topped volcano awash in sunlight. Like the last guy here, the cameraman is angled so that his flash won't reflect off the glass. Dad is slightly taller than Sam, and the height the camera guy has his rig will make them both slightly taller than the mountain. Dad won't stand next to me with cameras around. I loom. We'll sit down before they take pictures with me.

Yep. The stage is all set for that. Ten of the table leaves are out. Usually Mom and Dad would sit about a quarter mile apart at the ends, Sam snuggled up on Dad's right, Monique and I next to each other on the opposite side from Sam, but in the middle of the table as far from everyone else as we can get.

Flash, bwsshhhhh.

"Great, gentlemen. I think we have those," the camera guy says and looks back and forth from Mom to the two reporters beside her to Monique and me standing just inside the door. Too much time goes by with no one saying anything, like when I get picked last for kickball. They'd love to use Monique, but she'll have her eyes closed in every shot and Mom won't give her the satisfaction. No one wants pictures of me.

Thankfully, the grandfather clock in the corner bings 6:00 and right on cue there's a light knock on the door, followed by Mom's chauffeur stepping in cautiously with a dog. Not my dog. Terry's a terrier. (I know. I was eight.) He's got a Golden Retriever at his heel, heeling perfectly. It sits when he stops. He looks at Mom, bends to unclip the leash. The dog doesn't move.

"And here's the baby of the family," Mom says. "This is Paul's dog, Terry."

Zat is not my dog. I catch the chauffeur's eye. He mouths something to me and nods, but he may as well be having a seizure for how much information I can read from his face. Your dog is okay, don't worry; or, Sorry, kid, stiff upper lip and all that. Pip, pip. Cheerio.

Dad declares, "It's good for a boy to learn responsibility."

"And what a precious face," Mom says. "Isn't that face precious, Andrew?"

One of the press guys says, "That's a handsome animal, Mrs. Stockton." He looks at the cameraman and—god, it's all so predictable. We should get some pictures with the dog. Sure enough. Press Guy Number One says, "What do you think about including Terry in some of the pictures of the family?"

"Andrew, that's a terrific idea." I'm sure she liked it from the second she thought of it, long enough ago to have lead time to rent this more photogenic dog. I'm surprised she didn't hire a movie star to do voice over. If I can't get myself out of here, maybe I can hire a stunt double for my more challenging scenes.

"Bring him over here, Paul," Dad says. Him. Yeah, it was the bitch thing. It's just a word. It only means something bad if you make it bad. Half the staff curses my mother to her face, but she'd never know because god forbid she learn more than "do it again" and "you're fired" in a language other than English.

"Today, Paul," Dad says.

I head for the windows and say, "Come," to the dog as I walk past him. Nothing. I get situated next to Dad and try again. "Terry, come." Nothing.

"Handle your dog, Paul," my dad says. I get out one questioning "Uhhh" that fades to nothing as it trails off to parts unknown—following, maybe, after my actual dog. When my "Uhhh" dies off, Dad just says it again. "Handle your dog."

I look at the dog. "Terry?" I look at the press guys. "She's just not herself today. This morning she—"

Shutting me down or showing me up or both, Sam snaps his fingers once, points to a spot on the floor, and says, "Here." The dog bounds over and sits on the spot where Sam pointed.

"Why don't you kneel down behind him, Paul?" Mom says, in the same zero-question tone that Sam's questions have. Fine. I kneel behind the replacement dog. He smells like baby shampoo.

The second I look up, flash, bwsshhhh. Green dot. Flash, bwsshhhh. Another green dot burned onto my retina. Flash, bwsshhh. No green dot, so I must have blinked on that one. I'm starting not to like that noise so much. Flash, bwsshhh, flash, bwsshhh, flash, bwsshhh. I'm blind and disoriented. Footsteps and Mom's voice behind me saying, "Abigail." Flash, bwsshhh, flash, bwsshhh, flash, bwsshhh.

I keep smiling and stare blindly in the direction of the camera sounds as Monique's voice gets closer. "Andrew, is it? I'm Monique. My friends call me Monique."

Coward or diplomat, Andrew omits both Monique and Abigail. "Pleased to meet you."

(I don't hear Monique's footsteps, but remember she's wearing heels so she'll be as tall as Dad.) More savage camera flashes. I have to work not to squint, but I've given up on getting a good look at the soup course. I don't hear Uncle Kenny's footsteps either, but that sneaky bastard was tucked away somewhere. Behind me, Monique says, "Uncle Kenny, you're going to lose that hand if you don't take it off my ass."

Immediately—*immeeeed*iatley—Mom says, "Don't be crass, Abigail."

And Dad adds nothing. He doesn't say a word.

Uncle Kenny says, "Umph," probably in response to an elbow.

I wait for the click of Monique's stiletto, but it doesn't come, just more shutter clicks and more, flash, bwsshhh, flash, bwsshhh, flash, bwsshhh. The cameraman gives innocuous directions for Sam to turn toward our father, for our mother to move closer to "her daughter," for everyone standing to squeeze in just a touch. On the last one I expect some violent reaction to Uncle Kenny misinterpreting touch or squeeze, but that doesn't come either. The dog and I receive no instructions and I wonder if we're even in the shot anymore. It'd be easy to crop in above our heads. I'm blind and starting to get dizzy and slightly nauseated.

The upside of migraines? The geometric patterns are kind of interesting.

Slightly nauseated? Not so slightly. I keep one hand gripped on the shoulder fur of this surprisingly robust dog and press the other hand to my stomach as I exhale. That does nothing to settle my stomach or clear my head, but my hand presses on a lump in my jacket pocket, my paisley tie, still tied. English is such a wonderful language, commandeering words from around the globe. From France: improvise, sabotage, derail. If I can get this ridiculous tie around the dog's neck, there's no way that's not the picture they'll run in their crappy magazines.

I'm working blind, but I make sure my legs are supporting me, let go of the dog and put my hands together on the loop of cloth. In one smooth motion, I find the back of the dog, slide up the back of his head and slip the tie over his head.

"Ah," says Andrew the camera guy. "Wonderful." I point my face at his voice, smile my most winning smile and force my eyes open to take all of that flash on the inside of my skull.

Flash, bwsshhh, flash, bwsshhh, flash, bwsshhh.

Three bright green spots against the black background of the nothing else I can see. I didn't plan to throw up; it's just a bonus. I miss the dog, hit the floor, and this photo shoot is *fini*. The greater victory is the 'rents losing their minds in front of the press. Mom's first with, "You little shit," but Dad's already talking over her with, "God damn it, Paul," before he can stop himself. Monique wouldn't laugh at me feeling ill, but neither of us can help it when the dog starts licking barf off my chin.

"Oh, who's a good boy? Who's a good boy? You're a good

boy." Until he gets his tongue in my mouth. "Eew. Gahhh. That is not a good boy. Euuch. Someone needs some tooth brushing."

"No pictures," Dad says, then stomps all over the camera guy's, "Yes, sir," with a direct order to Mom. "Three minutes." The 'handle your child' part is understood, I suppose, as is the pouring on of blame from on high. That'll trickle on down to me soon enough. That I can see coming. But out there in the green-splotched darkness, I can't see much else. Sam's turned on his cloaking device. No idea where he is. I assume the scuffling is the press pressing themselves against the walls, trying to disappear back into the woodwork. Monique lays her hand on my shoulder and I realize I'm receiving a literal pat on the back for wrecking the photo shoot.

"I," Sam says behind me, "will deal with *this*," meaning me, meaning maybe payback just might come tout de suite—right now, sudden and violent and sanctioned, oh my. His hand clamps down on my free shoulder, squeezing so hard it's like he's trying to rub my shoulder blade and collarbone together. Maybe he's trying to start a fire. His other hand seizes my upper arm and Sam lifts me off the floor, taking two steps with my feet dangling before he lets my shoes touch down again. Here we go.

Not so fast.

Somewhere near the door, Mom's talons sink into my forearm. I should have worn falconer's gauntlets. She yanks me down to her level and shoves her beak deep into my inner ear.

## CHAPTER 3: TONIGHT'S BOUT, SCHEDULED FOR INFINITE THREE-MINUTE ROUNDS . . .

Through gritted teeth an inch from my ear, Mom says, "Do *not* think that this gets you out of your duties on Independence Day, Paul. You will be ready on time. You will be presentable. You will not pull another stunt like this."

"I—" I don't know if I was going to say I wasn't late, or I'm sorry, or I think we should see other families, but Mom cuts me off.

"You will be cordial. You will be impressive. You will do what you're told," she says, tightening her grip with each word of Do What You're Told so the tips of her claws start digging pits into the bones of my arm. "And you will regret this. I promise you."

The talons retract. Sam's manhandling recommences. He lets go of my shoulder and switches hands so he's holding my left upper arm with his right hand. Lifting slightly, he's got me off balance and it's surprising how little control I have over our direction or speed, which might be good because I still can't really see very well. But might be, well . . . One of the press guys grunts as he has to take a quick step back to avoid having me dragged over him.

"Excuse me," Sam says. "I apologize for my brother."

I know I couldn't prove it in court, but as Sam knocks my shoulder against the dining room door on our way out, I'm pretty sure Mom says, "If only I'd miscarried."

A woman can dream.

In the hallway Sam and I diverge from the uneven footsteps of limping Uncle Kenny and fabric whish of our father's long strides.

"I think she's angry," I say to Sam.

"Anybody as angry as she is as often as she is likes being angry."

Sam's careful not to run me into anything that would break or rattle or clang, but he crashes me into the arched passageway into the what-the-hell-is-this-for room, bounces me off the arched passageway leaving it, and just as my vision starts to brighten to being merely sparkly, I see the bathroom door hurtling at me. I get a hand up in time to avoid taking the head-to-toe, full body whack. Dad said three minutes, so Sam will have me back in the dining room in exactly three minutes. Enough time to stop a nose bleed? Maybe. Pictures with me with toilet paper sticking out of my nose? Probably not. I'll be back in the dining room, not bleeding, de-pukified, within three minutes. We'll probably still have to wait for Dad. Around here, three minutes is whatever Dad decides it is. Sam deposits me on the commode.

Among the swirls of light, one swishy sparkle turns out to be Sam ripping a white hand towel off its ring and snapping my leg with the end before he tosses it in the sink. The towel ring swings back and forth as Sam runs cold water into the basin, his back to me.

"Done throwing up?" Sam asks.

"Yeah."

"You sure? Anything else you need to get out? I could put my fingers down your throat."

"No, I'll be— I'm OK."

Sam turns off the faucet. Water sluices down the drain in two splashes when he rings out the towel. As he squeezes, I picture his white knuckles squeezing his bedroom door a few minutes ago, only now he's crushing through the wood and coming free with a jagged wooden stake to plunge into my heart. But it's just the towel when he turns around.

"What are you doing, Paul?"

"Sitting?"

"You know what I mean." I don't say anything. Sam motions

for me to raise my head. I do. He wipes my mouth a couple of times, hard, but not violently so. "It's a bad play. You're pissing away advantage without gaining anything."

Advantage. Privilege. Power. The birthright of the American ruling class. Stockton family reporting for oligarchia.

Pass.

"Sam?"

"Paul?"

"Can I ask you something?"

"No." Sam rinses the towel—rinse, squeeze, rinse, squeeze—until it's clean again, then lays it over the edge of the sink. "See?" he asks as he dries his hands on a second towel from beneath the sink. "What are you going to do now? Don't ask permission. Don't give people the opportunity to say No to you. Don't give away your power." Sam opens the medicine cabinet and shakes some pills out of a bottle.

"Take these." Sam holds his fist out, and when I put my hand under his, Sam drops four round, white tablets into my palm. He keeps the bottle concealed in his other fist.

"What are they?"

"Just take them."

"What are they?"

He shakes his head, but tosses me the bottle in an arc high enough that I'm able to track the bottle and catch it, though I drop some of the pills already in my hand.

"Midol? That's for . . . lady problems."

"Lady problems. You're an idiot." Sam sits on the edge of the vanity and crosses his arms, the bars on his uniform sleeves playing havoc with my eyes. "Excedrin has pain reliever and caffeine. Excedrin Migraine has pain reliever and caffeine, in the exact same formula. What you want is caffeine, a vaso-constrictor. Midol has?"

Sam looks at the bottle in my hand and I read it. "Pain reliever and caffeine."

"And caffeine," Sam says with me. I stare at him. Sam doesn't do exasperated, but he takes the bottle out of my hand, shakes four pills into his palm, slaps them into his mouth, bends to the spigot for a drink, then straightens up, holding his mouth open. "Ahhh." He hands me the bottle.

"It says take two."

"Lawyers. Someone your size can safely quadruple whatever an over-the-counter says."

I look in my hand but only find two of the four pills he gave me.

"They're by the toilet." I look. They are. I'm not going to scarf pills off the bathroom floor, but maybe I should clean them up so— "Your dog won't eat them," Sam says. He always seems to know what I'm thinking. I don't like it.

"Eight?" I ask as I take off the cap.

"Start with four," Sam says and turns on the tap. He makes room for me at the sink. I scoop some water in my hand and take four pills at a go. I wipe my wet hand on my slacks before Sam can hand me the dry towel, so instead he loops it through the towel ring. When I start to put the bottle in my pocket, Sam says, "Mom won't know how many are in there, but she'll notice if you take her bottle." I pour out four more and put those in my pocket loose. Sam runs more cold water over the wet towel, wrings it less vigorously and hands it to me. It's ice cold.

"Don't get your hair or your clothes wet, but hold that to your temples and your throat. The twinkling that you're seeing is from pressure behind your eyes. Swelling." He rotates around me to look at me in the mirror from behind. I drape one end of the towel over my hand and hold it against my neck. The chill feels great. Is Sam being nice to me?

"Up high," Sam says, "on the artery and vein." Like you'd check a kid for swollen glands, he puts his thumb on one side of—thankfully, his own—neck, his first two fingers on the other side. When I make that adjustment, he sweeps his hand up his face and bridges his forehead to put his thumb and fingertips on his temples. I scoop up the other end of the towel with my other hand, sweep it over my face, and press the cold cloth to my temples. It feels divine.

I think Sam is being nice to me.

"I know Mom won't let us have ice," Sam says. It's true. She doesn't like it. The tinkling in the glasses gets on her nerves. (If she didn't put the W in WASP, she'd say it worked her last nerve, but let's face it: she puts the WASP in WASP. We'll get no ice and like it.) "But if you ask Antonia," Sam says, "she'll bring you super-chilled water through dinner and keep it topped off and cold."

Sam is being nice to me.

"Thanks, Sam."

I lower the towel from in front of my face so I can look at him in the mirror. But as the white cloth vanishes from the front of my head, the heavy, white lid to the toilet tank flashes into position behind my head, Sam swinging it in fast and hard, checking the swing at the last possible nanosecond to stop it a millimeter from the back of my skull. I can feel it touch my hair. There wasn't time to flinch.

"Didn't see that coming, did you?"

Nope. "I heard the porcelain scrape."

"But you didn't know what it was," he says. He's right. Of course. Sam says, "Know what will give you away," as he replaces the lid on the tank, then, "I'll give you credit for not flinching," as he turns back to me. "Head feel better?"

"Yeah." I omit the thank you.

"Outstanding," he says, taking the towel from my hand. "Now come on. The dinner that will never end can't start without us." He tosses the towel into the sink and steps out of the bathroom. I follow, stepping gingerly, noticing that I'm touching doorjambs and walls and bookshelves and stuff more than I probably really need to.

"Wait," I say, and the tone of command surprises both of us. Sam spins on his heel, makes a quick but elaborate display of saluting, then standing at attention, then easing into what's still a rather rigid "at ease" pose. He holds that for a robot second before breaking.

"There you go. What do you want?"

"I want you to help me get a fake ID."

I know he has at least two, but finding them in his room doesn't tell me how they got there. The way Sam's always in my head, I'm a little in his now. He skips denying he knows how, chooses to let me slide on how I must have found out, chooses to revel a bit and enjoy that he does—no smile, but a sparkle appears in his eyes that isn't from my migraine. I think I've actually interested him. Sam moves right to practicalities.

"You can't pass for twenty-one."

"I only need to be eighteen." My atypical height makes that at least semi-plausible.

"Sixteen for a job. You want to move out."

I nod. He'll want something. I have nothing to offer.

"Yeah, you do," he says. I hate it when he does that. "How much banking is done on computers now?"

"It's 1990, Sam. Tons."

Sam nods, stops, nods again.

"Tomorrow after school," he says before turning to march forward again. I guess we have a deal, though at this point only Sam knows all the terms we've agreed to.

Hurrying to not be left behind, I say, "Monique picks me up by the—"

"I know where you'll be."

In the what's-it-for room, I slap my palm down on the giant globe I'm not supposed to touch, obscuring what's rotten in Denmark, then jerk that sucker into a spin that would hurl us all off the face of the earth. Huh. What would the cold vacuum of space do for my headaches?

But, back to reality. Three minutes are up, so it's back to the dinner that will never end. Sam's words. So, Sam hates this stuff too. But he's playing along, biding his time, making some kind of investment. I wonder what return he's expecting, and what he'll extract from me in exchange for his help. But I suspect my nausea will return if I think too much about either of those. He says nothing more as we make our way back to the formal dining room, but out in the hall, and hitting the bull's eye without breaking stride, Sam spits four round, white pills into a vase machinegun style, tink, tink, tink, tink.

## Chapter 4: (b)READ / (d)RINK

When Sam and I walk in, the reporters have their little notepads out and Monique's telling them about starting at the University of Washington in the fall.

"No, not Poli-Sci," she says. "Probably business."

"Then law school like your—"

"No."

Dad's not back yet to be offended, but this reporter guy still jerks his head to the side like somebody just pulled the pin on a grenade and dropped it at his feet. They're never the same guys. Year after year, it's always new guys who get the shit job of coming out to the Stockton place to run the gauntlet. I bet they draw straws. Nobody ever comes here twice. And even the dog had the sense to leave while I was in the bathroom.

What are you going to be when you grow up, Paul?

Far, far away.

"Paul's taking math classes at U-dub, too," Sam says, then times it perfectly so they're both looking me in the face when he says, "The age difference makes it hard for him to make friends."

I say, "And computers," to try to cover my reaction to their pity. I go for cheery, up beat, isn't it fun? But Sam's painted the picture, defined the terms, and they know the whiz kid eats lunch by himself. "I like it." At least at college nobody takes my cookies.

"You're thirteen? Are you the youngest ever to—"

"I think some twelve year olds—"

"He'll be the youngest to graduate," Mom says, ignoring anything unexceptional. "Tell them your G.P.A."

"Four point," and most of the "oh" is out of my mouth before she fires the next command.

"Tell them how many units you're taking."

"Full load this summer." Anything that gets me out of the house. "I wanted to take swimming lessons, but—"

"Tell them—" How crazy my mother is? "—about basketball camp."

"Camp happens. It hurts my knees and I don't like—"

"Tell them—" That I can't have two of my own thoughts in a row while you're around. "—about the scholarship."

"That we turned down," I say and then Mom finishes my sentence with me. "Because we're so fortunate to have so much." She doesn't join in on, "So, we gave away my scholarship."

"Tell them—" That I'd quit this job if that were possible. "—about your—" but then shuts her pie hole when the door swings open. I didn't think it was possible, but I'm actually happy to see Uncle Kenny walk in. He and Dad march in all smiles like they're seeing old friends for the first time in years, like none of the puking or yelling happened, like, Hey, isn't it great to be here? What a treat for you to see me.

I say, "So that's why we had to stop training alligators to open the mail," and the look on the reporter's face tells me that that makes as much sense to him as any of this retarded puppet show has. I say, "Zoning. What are you going to do?"

Dad can't hear a voice not his own, so he ignores me and announces, "Time to break bread."

Everyone with a chair—not the press guys, who we're not feeding, and whose scholarships Mom would happily give away—everyone with a chair makes his or her way to the table. I grab my chair to pull it out and it doesn't budge. With the table all shrunk down, it's not where it usually is, so is the leg caught on the edge of some area rug? No. It's bolted in place. Screwed to the chair leg, there's a metal L-bracket, which in turn is screwed to the floor. I'd suspect Sam, but even he wouldn't put a hole in the parquet without the 'rents consents. What I don't notice until I crabwalk in sideways to sit down is that two or three inches have been sawed off the legs. To make me shorter in the pictures at the table. Awesome.

Did I say everyone takes their seats? Not Uncle Kenny. He's

sauntered over to stand between Monique and me. Because he's also slightly behind us, I can still see Monique when Uncle Kenny leans in to ask, "Feeling better, Paul?"

The words are all for me—or more accurately, all for the press—but ye olde hand-on-the-shoulder routine is all for Uncle Kenny. Unlike Sam's iron grip, his left hand is dead weight on my shoulder. But he's got his other hand high up on Monique's shoulder and he's slowly caressing the back of her neck with his index finger. The press guys probably can't see it. Dad can't from where he's seated. Mom could if she'd look. Sam's angle is wrong too, but he's otherwise occupied. He's hovering his hand and arm over his butter knife, but gripping the end of the blade with his fingertips. He leverages the handle off the table and flicks the knife up his sleeve. When I look at his face, he's already staring at me. I look to his hand again as he raises his elbow just enough to slide the blade back out into his fingertip grip. He lowers the knife into its original position on the table with no one else noticing.

A photo flash stabs me in the eyes just as Mom jabs me with, "Paul, your uncle asked you a question."

I have no idea what the question was. I'd say, 'Beg your pardon,' but I'm not handing him the opportunity to rehash his stupid joke about his daddy being governor, so I'd have to ask him for a pardon, har, har, har, har, ask my daddy, har, har, har, har, barf. Fuck you.

"Answer him," my mother says.

"Can you rephrase the question?"

Uncle Kenny laughs.

"That's Paul," he says. "Always joking. Always making things up. He and Abigail."

Monique says, "Monique," at a civilized volume but they all ignore her.

"Such vivid imaginations," Uncle Kenny says. "I love these kids." He bends and kisses me on the top of the head, then—no, he's not going to. No, he *is* going to—he turns and kisses Monique on the top of the head. I expect to see arterial spray, but the only splash is the explosion of light from the camera flash.

And by the time I've blinked that green dot out of my vision, Uncle Kenny's dead fish hand is off my shoulder and he's in his chair across the table from Monique.

The classic meal courses run soup to nuts, but we Stocktons seem to start with nuts and get weirder from there. Get it together, Paul. While Mom tells the camera guy where to stand next, I grab my glass of water and chug. Except that I reach left instead of right and it's not my water, it's Mom's. And it's not water, it's jet fuel. I've just downed about half a glass of high-octane, clear liquor. Holy mother of god. My mouth is on fire.

## Chapter 5: God's Filibuster

*or*  Breaking Bread

*or*  A Boy Adrift

*or*  `brain:~ paul$ mkfs.ext3 /dev/drunk1`

I manage not to scream when the liquor—maybe gin maybe vodka maybe napalm—scorches through my mouth and down my throat. Even the vapors burn through my sinuses as I struggle to keep cool and not take giant gasps of air. I set down Mom's glass of firewater, pick up my own glass of regular water and down half of it. That helps some. Chaser. That's what they call it. Water back? Ah! It still hurts. Why do people do this to themselves?

Then I find out.

Warmth radiates through my body, starting at my center and seeping out toward my gangly, awkward extremities. The heat spreads through my shoulders and up my neck and with it comes the kind of relaxation you feel when you didn't know how tense you were. The clench of tight muscles in my shoulders releases like somebody squirted grease into the joints. The muscle pinch between my shoulder blades? Gone. And the piercing reflections off the windows and silverware and glasses are suddenly not so sharp and assaulting. It's like somebody dimmed the lights, turned down the master volume and hit the slow-motion button. A warm, easy relaxation washes over me.

Mom's directing the camera guy and nobody noticed me drink from the wrong glass. I pick it up again and take another big swig. I'm ready for the scald this time, but this one doesn't burn nearly as much. Hardly at all. I set down the glass, take in a deep, calm breath and let it out slowly as I resurvey my surroundings.

Oh, you people. You fucking people.

Mom has the camera guy where she wants him for the family pictures of the family at the family table. Sam will look good turned in his chair to look at the camera, his back straight, uniform, etc. The angle makes Mom—by her design, I'm sure— the angle makes Mom turn in her chair too, twisted so it's a side shot that will show off her boobs without her looking like she's trying to show off her boobs. I don't know if she's intentionally obscuring Monique, but that's going on too. My chair is literally screwed to the floor, so I guess I'm where I'm supposed to be.

Smile, flash, smile, flash. Whatever.

Even without the aid of alcohol, I've spent a good bit of time riding around turtled inside my Paul shell anyway, my mind's eye pulled back deeper into my head, my sense of my self drawn in from the outside edges of my body, the foreign surface that interfaces imperfectly with the frequently hostile world around me. Now, with the alcohol soaking into every nook and cranny, I feel like I—me, my conscious self—like I'm floating in a tiny rowboat on a calm sea inside my head. The camera flashes seem far away, like a lighthouse on the horizon blinking on and off with its own rotation, or maybe even dipping beneath the horizon as I rise and fall on imperceptible swells. The camera guy, the reporters, Mom, Sam, Dad, Uncle Kenny, they're all ships passing in the night, motors silent at a distance, only running lights dimly visible through the darkening grey fog.

Monique alone stays in focus, her black hair falling smooth and graceful around her face, the blue of her eyes like the filtered light through the roof of an ice cave in a glacier, the corners of her eyes crinkled slightly even with her face slack, already the start of crow's feet from her usual Get Back stare. I paddle forward to the back of my own eyes, make an effort not to blink while I clamber out of the rowboat, out over my bottom lid and eyelash to stand on my cheek between my nose and the weird pink dot at the corner of my eye. I just get to my feet when the S.S. Mom hisses a call with her steam whistle.

"Look at the camera, you two, and smile."

Monique smiles a real smile at me, then plastics it up before we turn toward the camera guy.

"Sorry, Mom," I say, and a call goes down to the engine room, lies, full speed ahead. Aye-aye, Cap'n. Some weird lie engine whistles and steams, cranks over, belly fully of fire and belches out, "it's just nice to have everyone together."

Mom doesn't say anything, but the reporters scribble, scribble, scribble, and the camera guy flashy flashes a few more times until he says he needs to change film. Antonia takes this opportunity to make the voyage from some distant continent and sail in to refill our water glasses. She's got two pitchers like she usually does, but it's only now that I notice that I haven't noticed before how weird that is. One's for Mom, the other one is for everyone else. Antonia stands to my left at the corner of the table and deftly pours with both pitchers at the same time. She's correctly pouring Mom's "water" from the right, so she's not going to get chewed out for breaking decorum. Serving me doesn't count.

I remember Sam's atypically kind advice and whisper to her, "Antonia, can I have some water that's extra cold?" She knows we can't have ice. "I have kind of a headache."

"Yes, Mr. Paul. Of course."

She's done pouring, but I have time to say thanks before she speedboats out of there like a rum runner. No, rum's dark. And gin definitely has a smell. When that weird, fat Senator from the south visited last summer and they had sips of mint juleps or some such shit between dabs to the corner of his mouth with a folded, white hanky, that was gin and I don't smell that now. I think Mom's pitcher must be full of vodka. The camera flashes start up again like a thunderstorm on the horizon. My brain says to my brain, Pitcher, picture, pitcher, pick-a-chure, pit-chure, then it gets bored and stops. I smile and stare into the storm.

My fingers start tapping on the table. I want to reach over and grab Mom's glass again, but I know I can't get away with it. This proximity is usually not an issue when all the leaves are in the table and she's way out of reach at the end of the table with her newspapers and her telephone. Crammed together like real people, I'm too close to Mom's glass. I'm talking out loud before I realize it.

"When I was a kid, I couldn't remember which water glass was mine," I say. I start the M for Monique, but that weird lie engine kicks in, dodges the whole name change thing, and Monique's M stretches into, "Mmmy sister showed me a trick." I touch my index fingers to my thumbs to make two "OK" signs with my hands and hold them above my plate, palms facing each other. Still in "OK" mode, with my right hand I trace the 'b' shape my left hand makes. "B for bread." I switch hands and trace the 'd' on the right side. "D for drink." I hold my 'b' hand over my bread plate to the left, and my 'd' hand over my water glass to my right. I hold my hands there and mug for the camera. Flashy, flashy.

"That's very clever," Dad says, and replicates my hand position. Flashy, flashy.

Monique asks, "Then why are you always eating my bread?"

Mom and the reporters laugh too much, but the camera guy gets at least one shot of Monique genuinely smiling. I'm not sure if I'm fast enough, but I hope I've got my left hand into the 'Peace' sign in time for Monique's smile picture. 'V' for 'Vodka.' If I was in time, and if it comes out, and if they print that one, and if I see that magazine, then I'll cut out that picture and tell Monique about it.

That is so never going to happen.

There's a weird shift in the energy of the room.

I'm saying weird a lot.

Weird, weird, weird, weird, weird.

Weird is a weird word.

Anyway.

Maybe Mom and the photographer have talked about the sequence of shots because the camera guy is obviously waiting now that the turned-for-boobies-at-the-table pictures are all in the can, the oh-I-didn't-see-you-there-but-how-fake-great-it-is-to-see-you-please-notice-how-normal-we-always-are-this-isn't-staged-at-all photographs. There's a lull while all the ships ease into the harbor, slow, making no wake now, and nestle gently into their docks. The reporters and the photographer follow

Mom's shift of attention to Dad, who shifts his attention to me.

"Paul," Dad says, "I believe it's your turn to say grace."

Ah, I have made a tactical error by talking to people. Never talk to people. Never, ever. I should have stayed on the tiny little rowboat. Should have stayed off the radar. I doubt this is an opportunity. I think that Dad thinks that I should think it is, but I know it's going to go badly and I have only one chance to get out of— "Uh, Uncle Kenny is our guest."

"I'd like you to say grace, Paul," Dad says, meaning I'm going to say grace. For a split second I think of just saying the one word out loud—"grace"—but if I pulled that crap, it might be the last word I ever said.

Dad stares at me, his face neutral, his eyes unblinking. He looks like he's carved in stone, up on Mt. Rushmore, hard, cold, timeless, his expression decided by dynamite blasts, his visage immune to lightning or hurricane or the rising of the tides.

Dad rests his forearms on the tablecloth on either side of his place setting. Dad's cuffs, his cufflinks. Dad's cuffs are crisp within the double barrels of his sleeves, the fabric at once rich and supple but rigid. No grubby sweat stains at the wrist like my shirts. Dad's cuffs are as white as country music, white as the porcelain toilet tank lid Sam chose not to imbed in my skull.

Dad's hands are still, fingers in a relaxed curl like a Rodin study in bronze, the cuticles clean, neat, each nail precisely trimmed, each light band of nail beyond the nail bed a perfect arch three thirty-seconds of an inch wide.

Dad rotates his wrists, exposes both palms and wills Uncle Kenny and Monique to place their hands in his, joining hands for the grace I will unquestionably begin as soon as my heart drops out of my throat and goes back to clanging around in my ribcage.

Dad, Dad, Dad, Dad.

Our father, who art in Congress.

Away from home fifty-three weeks a year.

Uncle Kenny slides a hand into Dad's hand. Monique slides a hand into Dad's hand. Sam joins hands with Mom and Uncle Kenny. Mom and Monique grab mine and there's no getting out of it now, there's no getting away. But if you can't get away . . .

In a house full of rules, there's one rule that I actually kind of like: no one can interrupt grace. *No one.* We've joined hands, we're bowing our heads, and now—to the sound of a photographer activating chemicals with photons for the cover photo of the next issue of Ostensibly Wholesome Family Quarterly—I begin to say grace, or because of the no interrupting rule, what I like to think of as God's Filibuster.

"Dear Lord, we thank you for your many blessings. Thank you for making us Americans, citizens of the best country on the one planet out of trillions you chose to put people on. Thanks for putting us at the top of the food chain. For making us rich and white and born into the one and only absolutely true and correct religion. Thanks for choosing us, despite the claims of our Jewish brothers and sisters, for your exclusive salvation.

"And we ask your overall general forgiveness for those you chose to erroneously be born Muslim or Buddhist or Hindu or Rastafarian or Mormon or Scientologist. But especially today, star date July 2nd, in the year of you, 1990, may you lay a heavy hand of mercy upon the souls of the 1,426 people you killed this morning in Mecca by collapsing a tunnel on them while they went to praise their version of you by throwing stones at a pillar. May you place your mighty, human-shaped hands together and hijack their trip to their heaven, maybe somewhere between the thermosphere and exosphere, or out beyond the ionosphere, but, you know, wherever is convenient for you to redirect them to your glory, if that's past the moon or maybe in a Lagrange orbit, balanced gravitationally between the moon and the earth, or however you have Heaven located in your divine, massive, ever expanding cosmos—at least for the last thirteen point seven billion years since the Big Bang. Thanks for Pythagoras and Archimedes and Ptolemy and Newton and Leibniz. And thanks for evolving our brains to be able to understand Red Shift and the preponderance of evidence supporting evolution—possibly your best invention, except that black hole evaporation is pretty funny."

At this point, Monique is gripping my hand in quick

successions of squeezes like peels of laughter punctuating my rambling outburst. Meanwhile, Mom's clamped down and trying to sausage grind my metacarpals into jelly. Then Monique's grip shifts a bit and she pulls my hand under the table as she scooches her body off the front of her chair to slip under the table. She jerks a bit and Uncle Kenny grunts at what must have been a kick to the bad knee he picked up when he visited around Monique's 14th birthday.

"Thank you for having the foresight to have a bunch of guys write down your thoughts after only five or six generations so the stories wouldn't get all messed up and jumbly. Thank you for giving us the pleasure of finding out on our own things like germs and bacteria, medicine, the spherical nature of the earth and that not only aren't we the center of the solar system, but that our sun is kind of puny as stars go, at least among the two-hundred-billion stars in the Milky Way, never mind that we're way out in the boonies on an inferior sub-arm off one of six major arms of a medium-sized spiral galaxy that's one of a hundred billion galaxies that you made just so our sky would be all twinkly."

Mom clamps down harder than I would have thought possible without an elaborate system of levers and pulleys.

"And thank you for the strength of our parents." I wouldn't wish the hand crushing on anybody, but I wish I were clever enough to communicate to Monique what Mom's doing to try to reel me in. "Thank You for their constant guidance and all that they do for us for our own good. And for these many blessings, may the Lord make us truly thankful, or die trying. I yield the balance of my time. Amen."

Everyone but Mom murmurs their Amens with measured neutrality. Mom says, "Thank you so much, gentlemen," as she rises to shake hands slash drag the press guys to the door, which they're so eager to have happen that they start squirming when they have to stop there to hear the rest of Mom's filibuster. "It was our pleasure to welcome you into our home. We do so enjoy your periodicals and look forward to reading your articles in the upcoming issues." They also say words like Pleasure and

Honored, but their faces say Please let us please go please. When Mom says, "Antonia will see you out," they leave faster than if we'd shot them out of a cannon.

And now it's just Mom and Dad, Sam and Uncle Kenny, and Monique and me. Alone. Nobody to act normal for, nobody to serve as distraction or reality check, no witnesses to the crimes against humanity that will undoubtedly ensue.

I stretch my left hand, then squeeze it into a fist to keep it from reaching out on its own for Mom's drink.

## CHAPTER 6: THIRTEEN WAYS OF KILLING ALL THE BLACKBIRDS

"Carlson wants to kill SB-135," Uncle Kenny says to Dad as soon as the press is gone and they're alone with only us people who don't matter. He doesn't even wait for Mom to sit down. I don't know who Carlson is or what Senate Bill 135 is about. I know 135 is 5 times 3 times 3 times 3. And ultimately, the content of the bill—who it would help or how or why—doesn't matter, only what Dad and Uncle Kenny can get for themselves by killing it or jamming it through. That's the math they're good at.

Antonia has clearly delegated showing the press out, or they've run off on their own, because she steps in with a bowl of soup for Uncle Kenny and an ashtray for Mom before Mom's even seated. Mom produces a cigarette and lighter from her seat cushion and doesn't bother to pull her chair to the table. Our guest is served first. The instant Uncle Kenny's bowl donks on the table, Mom exhales, "Please begin," and sparks up a smoke on the inhale. She pushes her chair back even farther—it's not bolted to the floor—leans an elbow into the tapestry-covered armrest and crosses her legs as she blows smoke out of the left side of her mouth toward Antonia.

Mom checks out, or seems to. Antonia pops out into the hall, pops back in with two more bowls of soup. We could all get our soup at once. We have more servants. But Mom doesn't want to see those people. She says nothing when Antonia places her bowl in front of her. She could say thank you, or at least hold the cigarette away from Antonia. Instead, Mom puts the hot little burning cone end as close to Antonia's face as she can. Index and middle finger raised, she uses the pinky and ring fingers of her smoking hand to pinch the hem of her skirt and tug the fabric farther over her crossed knees as Antonia leans in to set Mom's bowl down.

Dad and Sam are served next. Without losing any momentum in his discussion with Uncle Kenny, the politician in Dad inserts a lightning thank you practically in the middle of a word. Sam makes eye contact and uses her name when he thanks Antonia. Since Monique's 18th birthday isn't until Friday, she's technically still a child and we're served last. We both say, "Obrigada, Antonia." Monique adds something that sounds like 'Chernobyl' and it takes me a second to remember that 'chera boa' means 'smells great.'

Uncle Kenny waits to try the soup until everyone else is served, so I guess he's not *wholly* without decency.

"You're going to like this soup," Dad says. Uncle Kenny scoops up some soup, doesn't drip, doesn't slurp. Dad says, "Your grandmother's recipe, I believe." The grandmother is Uncle Kenny's, but Dad looks to Antonia for confirmation.

"Yes, sir," she says.

Uncle Kenny nods his profoundly mild approval at Antonia. That done, the rest of us cease to exist, even as audience. Uncle Kenny and my father speak as two men used to not being questioned, used to being deferred to, to being listened to, used to being right even when they're wrong. They don't converse, they proclaim. Whatever they said would be so, would be so. I feel like I should have a hammer and chisel and a granite tablet in front of me to take dictation. Frankly, I'm happier with my soup.

But they're not even paying attention to whether or not I'm paying attention or not, none of the kids, not even Mom. Sam dips his spoon into his soup at the front edge of the bowl and scoops away from himself as manners dictate. He doesn't look at all dainty, or stiff. Precise. Sam looks precise. He occasionally points his face at our father or Uncle Kenny. Dad and Uncle Kenny only look at Dad and Uncle Kenny, each probably listening more to himself than to the other guy. They drone. I try not to slurp my soup. Monique succeeds. Same with Sam.

Antonia swaps out my water glass for another glass, opaque with condensation. The smoky film is broken by only a few tiny beads of condensation on the outside, confirming both that it's filled with ice-cold-without-ice water and that somebody ran it up seconds ago. It's crisp and frigid and Sam was right that it feels good for my head. The Midol is kicking in too, getting a jumpstart because of my empty stomach and probably interacting with the alcohol in some semi-beneficial, semi-dangerous way. I start to feel really good, warm and relaxed by the liquor, cooled and softened by the water and drugs. And the food is amazing.

Condor egg quiche. Wild brown rice, each grain individually wrapped in baby bean sprout leaves and drizzled with bee tears. Copper River salmon, vivid pinkish, reddish, salmonish, its flesh fat-infused in preparation for the icy, pre-death suffering the fish wasn't lucky enough to swim up to.

We skip the sorbet because flavored ice is too much like regular ice, so Momma be agin' it. She's kind of agin' everything. As the courses roll on and on and on, Mom smokes while full plates and bowls arrive in front of her, sit untouched, and are cleared.

Polar bear flank steaks, roast penguin. Regular old honey glazed carrots. Flash-seared, chilled dolphin with a snowy owl reduction. Little cookies with creamy filling that I called macaroni when I was a kid but are just as sweet no matter how French you say 'macaron.' My plate arrives with one more than anybody else's, he-he! Monique eats one of hers and swaps me for my empty plate.

For savoureaux after sweet: imported-then-exported-then-re-imported smoked baby alligator compote on a toasted artisanal roll inside another larger, non-toasted artisan roll. Then truffle-infused panda-milk cheese. Then before it's coffee time, we finish off with blueberries over cashew ice cream.

That shit is good. Subtle. Nuanced. The lightest of evaporated flavors float in my mouth like a magnet bouncing around on a super-chilled superconductor boiling off liquid nitrogen.

All this takes a week and a half. There's a near-constant

rotation of plates and new silverware and scraping of crumbs, but it still takes nearly a full pack of cigarettes. Antonia has kept my water glass topped off with frigid refreshment, and Mom's water glass filled with liquid fire. Despite my strong desire, and enough distractions to create opportunity—Sam says that people are usually too wrapped up in themselves to notice much that other people are doing—I haven't tried to sneak any more of Mom's liquor, and I am now, sadly, disappointingly, sober.

And the Dad and Uncle Kenny Show, proceeding unabated, has circled back to Senate Bill 135. There's one last little shaky uptick of intoxication that peaks just before dropping me onto hard clarity. With it comes the sickening idea that we actually are circling back in time and dinner is once again only starting. If it is, I'm going for Mom's glass. But my déjà ew gets headed off at the pass.

Sam stops, mid spoon raise, one perfect round blueberry absolutely *not* shaking in his spoon, turns to Dad and says, "Winfield."

The bubble around Dad and Uncle Kenny shatters and they both rotate their toothy skulls toward Sam. I expect the sounds of German Shepherds to start barking out of their lie holes, but they just stare at Sam for a beat and a half, before Sam says, "Winfield has too much corn and needs an Air Force base."

I don't know who Winfield is or where he's growing too much corn or why he needs an Air Force base there, but it's clearly some other senator who factors into some deal that Dad and Uncle Kenny previously made sound like, "Rhubarb, rhubarb, rhubarb." Air bases need airplanes and that's good for Boeing— thousands of union machinist jobs—which is good for Seattle and thereby, good for the illustrious Senator from the fine state of Washington. What's the opposite of Not In My Back Yard? Anyway, Sam's been quietly paying attention, chose his moment, and dropped the right bomb on the right target at the right time. Bull's-eye, like four Midol in a Ming vase.

Uncle Kenny turns back to my father, says, "Taylor comes with Winfield."

"And Morgan," Dad says. He looks to Uncle Kenny then back

to Sam. Dad dips his head in the tiniest nod. Sam nods back and I realize Sam has made a leap. There's a new line drawn dividing who matters and who doesn't. Instead of just the one corner of the table with Uncle Kenny and Dad, there's now a clear diagonal cut from corner to corner like a kid's sandwich. Sam's on the power side now. I'm on the side with people who use school lunch items as metaphors. Sigh.

"Thank you, Antonia," Dad says as he pushes away from the table and stands. "We'll take our coffee in my study." As Uncle Kenny rises too, he and my father trade more glances and nods, these exchanges unreadable until they're revealed as deliberation and confirmation when Dad says, "Sam, why don't you join us."

"Thank you, sir." That's all he says. Neutral as can be.

Antonia holds the door for the gentlemen as they leave the dining room, follows them out. When you're swimming in a pool full of Great Whites, you don't worry so much about the Barracuda. But suddenly Monique and I are alone with Mom and we're fresh out of sharks.

Monique gets up from the table as soon as the door closes behind Dad, Uncle Kenny and Sam. Mom stops her at the corner of the table just to my left before Monique takes two steps.

"Really," Mom says, looking my sister up and down, frowning and shaking her head at Monique's shoes, slacks, blouse, jacket, belt—maybe? I forget if she's wearing a belt, but there's a lot of head shaking happening as Mom disapproves of each sartorial choice in turn. "When attending a formal function, a lady wears a skirt."

"Then why are you wearing one?"

Oh, I got a *dys*function joke half-cocked, but Monique beat me to the opening. I snort, but keep myself from laughing outright. I could probably get away with it now though, as Mom's grind is focused full bore on Monique. Mom, as a rule, is kind of passive-aggressive. Monique, more and more, is decidedly aggressive-aggressive.

Mom carefully wipes the corners of her mouth with her napkin, which is pointless because I don't think she ate anything the whole meal. She folds the napkin once, twice, and places it on the table before rising.

"I see that your finishing school tuition was money wasted."

She actually said "finishing school." You'd think they'd have a less oldey-timey word, but I guess not. Monique and I called my manners lessons "good boy school" until I got wise that it was just more stuff to have to get perfect all the time. Then we called it punishment avoidance class. The more you go, the more you learn you shouldn't do. Monique has her right hand in her pocket, which is so fucking rude I can't believe the stormtroopers haven't stormed in.

"Save your charm school bullshit for somebody who cares," Monique says. "I'd rather be human. And if you're looking for refunds, check with your alma mater." Monique breaks etiquette into smaller pieces by pointing an index finger at Mom and waving it around. "They have certainly failed to deliver."

"Abigail, you're—"

"Monique."

"—going to have to—" Mom stops herself mid-sentence, amazed to have been corrected or interrupted or both. Her chin darts an inch up and to the side. "Abigail."

"Monique."

"Abigail! I named you Abigail, our friends know you as Abigail—"

"Your friends."

"—And this Spring when your father and I present you to society at your debutante ball, our daughter will be Abigail."

"Your daughter will be absent. Talk about wasted money. I hope you didn't put down a big deposit on the hall."

"You have an obligation."

"Hire an actress. Hell, hire a dog for your dog and pony show."

"You will be there and you will represent this family in a manner becoming—"

"Not going to happen."

"You'll do as you're told."

"The fuck I will."

Mom's eyebrows shoot into her hair, then bounce down to shove her eyes into a squint. She reels back an open, right hand and then this huge, wide, roundhouse slap is sweeping around towards Monique's cheek. Leaning back ever so slightly to pull her face barely out of range, Monique dodges like Muhammad Ali. Actually, I guess it's a rotation, and Monique's body moves toward Mom's hand as Monique twists through, shifting her weight as she brings up her own right hand. She's already made a fist—a good fist like Sam showed us, with the thumb on the outside so it won't break on impact. When Mom's slap gets to where Monique's face was, Mom's bony hand instead meets the impact of Monique's punch.

And Monique's fingers, bare throughout dinner, are covered in rings.

Mom jerks her hand back, clutches it in her left and rubs the palm with her thumb. She's otherwise frozen, wide-eyed and speechless in the face of violence met with violence.

"Anything broken?" Monique asks. "Want to try it again?"

Monique slips back into her shoes, which I hadn't noticed she stepped out of. She strides past our mother toward the door, but stops, turns and waits for me. I squeeze out of my bolted-down chair and take the cowardly route around the empty end of the table to scramble after her, thump, thump, thump. As I pass Monique, she locks eyes with Mom, pops her middle finger out of her still-clenched fist to flip Mom the bird. The gesture's adorned with a gigantic, gnarly gold ring. If it's not Sam's class ring, it's at least as big. No dainty ornament. With her other hand, Monique points at it.

"Charm school."

CHAPTER 8: ASKING FOR DIRECTIONS

After I change out of my suit, I climb out my window, monkey down a floor to Monique's room and tap on the glass. Monique is as winter a girl as will ever be. She'll jack up the AC so she can put on a sweater. Now she's changed into black jeans and a summery black, long-sleeve T-shirt, the pantsuit she wore to dinner already semi-wadded with some other disposable suits on top of a big cardboard box labeled in Monique's neat script: Goodwill. She swings her window open, mooshing a space between piles of clothes on the window seat so I can step inside.

"Entre'," she says.

"If you're giving all this away, you're not going to have anything left."

"We need a lot less than we have."

And get a lot less than we need. "That was crazy, Monique. I thought Mom was going to shit herself when you punched her hand."

She pulls her sleeves up toward her elbows. All the rings are off her fingers. "I've been waiting a long time to do that."

"Why now?"

"Keep it on the juvenile record?"

"What do you think she'll do?"

"Probably take it out on you," Monique says, shrugging and clenching into a half-smile/half-grimace, eh-whatcha-gonna-do? sorry face, then dropping it. "Pass me that stack of shirts." From behind me on the bed, I retrieve the bundle of dressy shirts—all ones that Monique likes. She places them in a box on top of the silky aqua dress she wouldn't wear to dinner, the dress that the birthday earrings I got her will perfectly match. Oh.

"Are you getting rid of that? Those?" I don't want to ruin the birthday surprise, but if she's giving away the outfit . . .

"No," she says, folding the flaps closed and dropping the box next to two others by her bedroom door. "These are ready for tape." She holds out the dispenser thingy—tape gun—and doesn't have to ask me once. I love the sounds it makes, the tape peeling off *skrihk*, the *zft* of the cutter. One strip of tape would suffice. I use three on the first box.

Monique throws herself sideways across the bed, saying, "Errrrr," as she stretches out, hands and feet extended off the edges of the bed. "Errrrr-ah!" She rolls onto her back and props herself up on her elbows.

"Sam thought I should punch Mom in the face."

"You still could."

Monique taps the toes of her sneakers together. I finish my *skrihk* and *zft* routine on the second box and start the third.

"It'd show," she says.

"Know what will give you away?" I ask, quoting a Sam-ism from his Perfect Crimes lecture series.

"That's not bad advice." She looks out the window, looks around the room. "Though it's amazing what people won't see when they don't want to."

I fixate on the dozen or so boxes of stuff she's giving away. Dozen or so? It's five rows of three boxes high, plus two more. Seventeen. One point four one seven dozen. Plus five unconstructed boxes. The ratio of keepers to giver awayers is just south of eighteen percent, with a potential to drop below fourteen.

Paul?

Yes, Paul?

Stick to a dozen or so.

Good plan.

I wave the tape gun at the wall of cardboard boxes headed to the charity shop. "Close those up?"

"No, but you can make the rest." As I circle around behind her to unflatten and secure the bottoms for new boxes, Monique says, "One strip of tape per box is enough."

"K." Donation centers won't reject your offering because of an insufficiently excellent box. Your gift be damned! Away with you and your mediocre cardboard containers.

Stay in the room, Paul. Be here.

It'd be nice if I didn't have to invest so much energy in self-management.

Or if there were a better return on investment.

Anyway. Here. Not away.

Damn.

Giving away . . .

"Monique . . ."

When I don't continue, Monique drops flat on her back and lets her head hang over the edge of the bed to look at me upside down.

"Yeah."

"When you drive me to school tomorrow . . ."

"Yeah." She rolls onto her stomach and re-props her elbows beneath her. "What?" After a couple of seconds she rolls onto her back again to dig into the pocket of her jeans. Her hand emerges full of the rings she was wearing when she brass-knuckled Mom. Now as Monique rolls back onto her stomach, she strews the rings onto the bedspread beside her, the ornaments clinking together and catching light from the overhead cans as they roll. She hoinks herself up on her elbows one more time, and repeats, "What? When I drive you to school tomorrow, what?"

"Can we swing by Woodinville on the way?"

"Woodinville's not really on the way," she says, and she's right. If you drew a triangle with home, school and Woodinville at the points, the home-to-school leg is the only short leg, by a lot. But she's not saying no. In fact, she says, "Yes," agreeing to my request before she even knows the reason. "But what's going on, Paul?"

"There's a no-kill shelter there. I want to take Terry."

I place the tape gun on top of the stack of cardboard boxes full of other items destined for places away. Thoughts twitch across Monique's face as she stares at me, but she doesn't say anything. I feel compelled to fill the silence, to explain why I need to give away my dog, but I know that Monique will do a better job of convincing Monique than I would. Mom hijacked Terry, not Sam. True. Sam didn't kill my dog. But he's killed my ability to have a dog.

"Shit," she says, everything finalized, accepted and all but executed. We live in a house of inevitabilities. Monique sighs. "I'm glad we got some pictures today to remember her by."

"We'll always have the dining room."

"Well," Monique starts, then trails off. She sits up, turning and dropping her feet over the foot of the bed, which points her toward the nearer window. Even past nine o'clock the sun is still an hour from setting over Seattle in the distance. With the orientation of the house and the depth of the window seats, only a narrow beam of low-angled sunlight makes it into the room. And it's actually light from the far window that cuts across the room to fall on Monique's hands where she's cupping her kneecaps and pulling on the fabric of her jeans with her fingertips, a slow tug up, and release, a slow tug up, and release. Her head's tilted down a bit and I can't see her face behind her hair.

"Woodinville," she says, practically whispering. "Okay."

"I accidentally drank Mom's water at dinner," I say.

"Jesus." Monique's definitely not whispering now, and her head spins around so fast I expect to hear a whip crack. "Are you okay?"

"So you knew it was— What is it?"

"Vodka." Monique's on her feet and in my face, her hands actually on my face, turning my face side to side like she's looking for scorch marks. "Are you okay?" She pushes one of my eyebrows up with her thumb, tries to tug at my cheek, but—

"I was until you poked me in the eye."

"Sorry. How much did you drink?"

"About half a glass."

"Oh, Jesus."

"A little more, maybe."

Monique closes her eyes and lets go of my face to put her

hands over her own. It's not a move I've ever seen her do before. Face buried, she hums a long exhale. Eventually, she lifts her head and interlaces her fingers under her chin, squeezing hard enough that her knuckles whiten like Sam's did when he was gripping his door. Monique looks at me for a solid ten count before she asks, "Did you love it?"

"Felt pretty good."

"You need to be careful, Paul."

"Nobody saw. I didn't get caught."

"That's not what I mean. You're 13. Your brain isn't done cooking yet." Would bourbon be better for brand-new brains? Which cocktail goes best with Pop Tarts? "You need to stay away from that stuff."

"Yeah, I know."

"No, I mean it. Promise me."

"Promise you?"

She puts her hands on my shoulders like she did after tying my tie in the hallway.

"Promise me," she says, "even when things seem really, really bad, stay away from it."

"Alright, whatever." It didn't seem like that big a deal. Monique keeps her grip on my shoulders and stares up into my eyes until—what never happens with Monique—until I get uncomfortable and say, "Okay," just to say something. She relaxes a bit. I ask, "You want to poke my other eye?" Monique laughs harder than warranted. "Just to even them out?" Instead she pokes an index finger into one of my nostrils. When I'm done jerking my head back and shaking off the heebie jeebies, she's across the room standing at her desk. "The health department advises that consumption of undercooked brains is bad for pregnant seafood."

"Let's see if this crab can get through the week without getting pregnant," Monique says, writing in her day planner. "Woodinville, tomorrow." She flips pages forward and back. "Sorry about your eye."

"De nada." In two steps forward one step back style, I watch Monique flip pages and can't help but track the days. Birthday

Thursday, Tuesday, Wednesday the 4th of July, Friday, birthday Thursday again, tomorrow, dog-dumping Tuesday. "I did like that fake dog."

"He smelled good."

"Until I barfed on him."

"He didn't seem to mind." Monique writes something on Thursday and erases something on Tuesday.

"Am I screwing you up?"

"Nope. Not with Sam picking you up tomorrow."

I'm about to ask how she knows that when I figure maybe we talked about it at dinner and maybe I shouldn't ask about that now if I don't want to have our second Vodka talk right away (or our ten thousandth talk about paying attention to humans.)

Unlike Sam's impersonation of my own clanging approach down the hall earlier, now the first hint we have that he's outside Monique's door is a light knock followed by, "It's Sam."

Monique says, "Come in," and the knob doesn't jiggle before she speaks, Sam respecting her door. Oh, that and Monique is fucking with Sam. Her desk chair is jammed under the doorknob, loops of Sam's nylon cord securing it in place. Sam trusts Sam's system, and doesn't fall for trying to open the door. Monique pulls an end of cord and one knot dissolves. She undoes the winding around the knob and kicks out the chair. Only after that screech does Sam try the door.

Sam's changed clothes too, so he must have been dismissed from post-dinner diabolicalness pretty quickly. He's back in his other uniform, a T-shirt and cargo pants, the myriad compartments bulging in odd lumps and contours. They don't rattle or clang or jingle, though, and I think I'd rather not know what he keeps in all those pockets.

"How's your hand?" Sam asks Monique.

"Oh, my god, it hurt like hell."

"Pain is never a one way street," he says, holding out a Zip-lock bag half-full of crushed ice.

After a quick comparison of knuckles side-by-side, she says, "No thanks," and waves off the ice. "I think all my knuckles cracked."

"Face or—" Sam asks, then immediately predicts her answer. "Hand." He replies to Monique's nod with, "That'll be fun on Wednesday when she's shaking hands all day." He looks at me and repeats, "All day," with a broad smile. And by broad I mean wild-eyed and scary and holy shit. Sam lobs the bag of ice into Monique's bathroom, where it lands in the bathtub with a crash. He says to Monique, "Show me the knot?"

Monique rams the chair under the doorknob in one smooth motion like she's done it a thousand times. Because she's done it a thousand times. I don't know how much they practiced the knot she just undid to let Sam in, but without a word she yanks taut the cord's loose end, whirls it around the doorknob like the calf-roping cowboys on TV, and ties it off to the chair arm well within the eight second time limit. I'd guess that I'm screwing up the rodeo details, but I have no doubt that Monique's knot will hold.

Sam says, "Perfect," then turns to me. "You. I need you to get to work. Their money guy is Shaw." Sam steps over to pluck pieces of assault jewelry from Monique's bedspread while he fires instructions to me. "Find him. Anywhere he touches your little nerd-iverse. Find any and every account he's opened, closed, touched or looked at, every deposit, withdrawal, transfer, everything. He's spider number three. I want to know where his web crosses Dad's web crosses Uncle Kenny's web. But don't *do* anything. Just recon."

Sam pockets the handful of rings, which somehow make zero noise going into his pocket.

"Do you know what recon is?"

I don't know if it's reconnoiter or reconnaissance, or if those two are the same thing, so I say, "Snooping."

"Full report tomorrow. Got it?" I nod. "Then why are you still here?" I guess I asked for this. This is me getting what I want. "Out, monkey boy."

As I head for the window, Sam unties the chair blocking the door. Monique nods when he asks, "Ready?" Sam steps into the hall, but when the door's about six inches from closed, Sam says, "Monique," and inserts just his face into the opening. I pause crouched on the windowsill, half in, half out of Monique's bedroom. The heavy copper drainpipe outside is almost too warm to hold on to. The stone cladding isn't any cooler. I can barely hear Sam.

"You sure you don't want a gun?"

"No."

"No, you're not sure, or no, you don't want a gun?"

"I don't know."

You kill with a gun, Sam says. You kill with a gun, or you threaten to kill with a gun. And don't threaten if you don't mean it because having that bluff called means you get your gun taken away and pointed back at you.

"I don't know," Monique repeats.

"Fair enough. Offer stands." Sam glances at me, but doesn't nod or say anything, just retracts his face.

Monique eases the door closed, replaces the chair, and ties it in place. She turns and looks around the room, at the empty bed, at the boxes of clothes and stuff to donate, at her even-cleaner-than-usual desk. She runs both hands up into her hair, tilting her head back and shaking out her long, black hair with her fingertips, simultaneously rubbing the back of her head. She interlaces her fingers and pulls her head down, stretching her neck forward. When she lifts her head again, bringing her hands around to the sides of her neck and squeezing her elbows together in front of her chest, she gazes out the other window at Seattle darkening behind me. She stares and stares, and it's a while before I realize that she doesn't know I'm still here, that maybe I shouldn't be watching her, that I should leave or say something or make some sound to announce myself. But she's not alarmed when she spots me.

"Go on up," she says, her voice flat, unreadable. "I'll be okay."

## CHAPTER 9: MINIONS
*or* `whoami`
*or* LOST AND FOUND AND LOST AND FOUND AND LOST
*or* BYE

All the pretty colors are out of the sky by the time Monique climbs through my window, moving out of the eerie gray light of the three-quarter moon outside into the green-but-unnatural glow of my computer screen. I got Windows 3.0 the day it came out a few weeks ago, and I love all my Apples, but I always seem to cycle back to these monochrome command lines. Just me and a machine. Or a bunch of machines.

"You're going to wreck your eyes," Monique says, closing the window behind her.

My little desk lamp is cranked 180 degrees up and away from the desktop. I pop that on, bouncing 40 whole watts off the ceiling to even out the lighting. Candlelight is really nice on migraine days, soft, serene, but my inattention keeps dripping wax into peripherals and melting the computer disks I use as coasters. So, you know, the relative safety of 15 lethal amps of 110 wall current.

Monique asks, "Mind if I bunk with you?"

I shake my head. I still fit on my couch if I need to rest. But I also find that I'm not sleeping as much as I used to, and less and less predictably with regard to schedule. In my head I just said "shed-ew-ool," like the Brits—more evidence that right now I'm pretty worked up, and that tired would seem like a foreign concept if there weren't so much fatigue evident on Monique's face. She kicks off her sneakers and slides under the covers.

"Thanks."

A soft tone tells me one of my minions has completed something important.

"I'll turn that off," I tell Monique.

"Mmm," she says. She draws the covers under her chin as she rolls on her side to face me. But she keeps her eyes closed when she asks, "What are you doing?"

"I'm a bank."

"Mmm."

The computer I'm on isn't one of the dozen or so here in my room—and, yes, I'm going to stick with "a dozen or so" because half of them are in pieces and could be reconfigured in any number of permutations. So. I have a bunch of computers in my bedroom. But at the moment I'm connected semi-legitimately to a mainframe at U-dub, and quietly branching out from there. My keyboard and monitor here in my bedroom have become what we call a dumb terminal. But, because you can have many sessions active at once, and be logged on as many users at once—even before you leave that first server—the dumb is sometimes how I feel, not remembering which is which or who is who. Typing in the simple command

> whoami

tells me, and I'm back in business. I redirect my digital henchman to carry on carrying on, doing my handiwork. I press Enter, fake-screaming at the screen, "You'll do as you're told."

Monique smiles, "Hmmm."

"I found Shaw."

My minions found Shaw. I've got a bunch of little utility programs bouncing around in computer systems in the U.S. and Europe, but—once we left the mainland—mostly throughout the Caribbean, hopping from physical island to physical island, former European colonies just like little ol' us, hopping from metaphorical island to metaphorical island, machine to machine, network to network, accounts within banks within corporations within holding companies (within holding companies)$^{\wedge n}$.

"Beyond a certain sample size," I explain, "there's a predictable pattern to the leading digits in a group of organically generated numbers. Especially in banking. Your balance is *six* times more likely to start with a one than with an eight. When you start cooking the books, that pattern gets messed up, and it's not that hard to find the deviation. It's so cool. It's called Benford's law and it's . . ."

I trail off because Monique doesn't give a crap about any of this.

"Sorry," Monique says. She still hasn't opened her eyes. She tugs the comforter, gathering more comfort under her chin. "Just tired."

"I can tell you about it tomorrow." I turn off my desk lamp.

"Mmm. Tomorrow."

I create and corral and cajole some more minions to creep into every corner, but more importantly now to clean up after myself and make sure I'm getting everything. I don't know what I expected—I guess I didn't really think about it—but Dad and Uncle Kenny's crimes are not all nouveau fleece. The pillaging goes back a long time. Luckily, that gives me enough good data to squeeze Benford's law for a high degree of statistical certainty about having actually tracked it all down.

By midnight I've got all dozen or so million bucks accounted for. I make sure I can crack loose all the big hunks, transferring money out of accounts into brand new accounts and back into place in the old accounts, then erasing everything that would give away any little piece of that activity. I make sure the medium hunks are loose in their sockets too. For the smallest hunks, I actually burrow deeper into the system to create a class of account that I can batch select and apply . . .

I'll tell you about it tomorrow.

At 2:02 a.m. there's some knob rattling beneath us. Knob rattling sounds sleazy enough, but knowing the rattler at Monique's door is Uncle Kenny makes me mad.

By 2:10 that jackass doesn't have a penny to his name.

By 2:13 he does again because I put it all back.

One, Sam will kill me. Two, my steal won't stay stolen.

Somebody—some *body*—is going to have to walk into a brick and mortar bank branch and get some human to cut a cashier's check. No, I bet I can get a computer to print a check. Still need a body to hand a body a check. Show ID. Yes, I'm Mr. Jimblejamble, recipient of a not-at-all-unusual check for twelve million dollars.

Or.

Before 4:00 a.m. I've got a domino line of cascading digital minions set to grab everything, move/funnel/collect everything at a single bank in Seattle, queue printing of one cashier's check (automated!), override branch manager signoff-age (bumping *up* for district manager review, offsite), instruct that the check be sealed in a #10 business envelope (marked with code for internal audit at corporate V.P. level), instruct that the otherwise nondescript #10 be placed into a fully nondescript 9x12 manila, and get that 108 square inches of innocuous beige boredom set out for private courier pickup.

Hi. I'm nobody on a bike. You got uh envelope needs going someplace?

You could wear full-fingered bike gloves and not leave prints. Wig under a helmet. Wrap-around glasses.

At or about 3:47 a.m. Pacific Daylight Savings Time, I do manage to fuck up rather ferociously: I cycle a page through a printer in a bank in Turks and Caicos.

It's a single sheet of paper with absolutely nothing printed on it. But it's check paper and it's something weird that shouldn't have happened. I tickled the printer too hard. Hopefully the Turks will blame the Caicos and the Caicos will blame the Turks. It's too hot to fight, guys. Forget about it. Pass the hummus. Little sheet of paper? Forget about it. It's hurricane season. We're not even technically in the Caribbean. But we speak English and we use the U.S. dollar for currency, which is weird for what's still a British territory. What were we talking about?

When my little psychotic break is over, I decide that on that distant island paradise it's quarter to seven in the morning and no one in that office is going to be anywhere near as uptight as me.

Before 4:00 a.m. I've got everything cleaned up except that piece of paper.

After 4:00 a.m. it's anybody's guess what happens there or here or anywhere because the next thing I know—

"Who am I?" I yell, jerking awake, quickly registering that the room's filled with daylight and that some Caribbean Sea creature is attaching itself to my face. "Ah!" Recoiling, I manage only to start falling backward in my chair before I realize it's Terry—Terry!—standing on my desk and licking my face. I kick my feet under my desktop to catch my fall, Terry already stepping off my desk onto my lap and chest, intent that her tongue-bath miss no part of my face. Slurp, slurp, slurp. It's awesome and awful at the same time. I pet her sides with both hands and rub my face against her chest and neck. "Oh, Terry."

"She does not smell like baby shampoo," Monique says.

"No, she smells like cookies," I squeal. Yeah, squeal. Sorry. That's less embarrassing than me pretending to eat my dog, but I do that anyway because it delights my dog.

My dog. Not my dog in T-minus— "Shit! We gotta go." The sun's been up for hours. Monique, wearing different jeans and black T-shirt, deposits a plate of eggs and toast and apple/chicken sausage on my desk before she relocates Terry to the floor.

"Eat."

Monique lays out some fresh clothes for me while I scarf breakfast. No time for a shower, but I swab the pits, don the duds and bring the toast for the car ride. I know my dog loves me, but my dog is only aware of me where I come in contact with the toast. I give her the last bite.

"All gone," I say, then groan.

"Wish you hadn't said that?" Monique asks. "Doggone it, Paul."

Sigh.

Terry spins three circuits around my lap before plopping down, curling up and falling asleep. We drive in silence, one hand cradling Terry's hip, the other her apple-sized head. She licks my wrist once when I stroke her haunch with my thumb.

It's a long drive to Woodinville, but not long enough that we never arrive.

Hooterville Pet SafeHaus.

Hooterville is not a real place as far as I know, but Safe sounds good.

Terry lifts her head when Monique cuts the engine, has her front paws on the side window before Monique stomps down on the emergency brake pedal. I collect Terry in my arms as I climb out. Monique closes the car door, opens the shelter door. The lady in the lobby puts a binder away under the counter, says, "Good morning." She seems nice. She smiles. "What a cutie." There's a lot of barking behind a second door leading off to what must be a room full of other dogs waiting to be paroled. There are cats here too, but they're not making any noise. Terry gets squirmy. Can I go play? New friends! Can I go play?

I'm very sorry, but I need to surrender my dog.

I'm terribly sorry, but unfortunate circumstances at home force me to surrender my dog.

I'm sorry, but I have to surrender my dog because she's not safe.

I practiced in my head in the car, but in my real life in the world all I can manage before the lady blurs out from my eyes welling up is, "I surrender."

Monique whispers, "Can you find the car?" as she eases Terry out of my arms.

I nod, dig into my pocket for the $782$^{00}$ I had left over from Monique's present, throw the cash on the counter and throw myself at the exit, shoulders shaking, throat closing. Before the door closes behind me, I say—to Terry, to Monique, to the nice lady—"I'm sorry."

I sit in the car like an asshole, like a coward. I sit for five or so minutes before I work up the courage to go back in to say a proper goodbye. But when I open the shelter door, what Monique's holding is a clipboard. Terry's gone.

Monique and the nice lady both turn to look at me, stopped in the doorway.

Nobody says anything. Nobody moves.

The lady stares at me. Monique stares at me. I stare at them.

I step back.

Close the door.

Go lay my self across the back seat of the car to wait for death.

Instead, the world keeps turning imperceptibly. I lie on my back and stare at the fabric headliner inside the roof. At one point a cloud passes between me and the sun, casting a faint shadow over the car. I count nineteen seconds before it clears. Could be a small cloud moving slowly or a big cloud moving fast. If I knew its altitude and speed, I could figure out its length. Or if I knew its length and speed, I could calculate its altitude.

But I don't know anything.

A car arrives and parks nearby. One car door, one set of footsteps, one shelter door.

A seventeen second cloud floats by.

One shelter door, no discernable footsteps, Monique's driver door. She doesn't start the car.

I crawl out of the back, drop into the front passenger seat. She doesn't start the car.

"Paul, I want to say the perfect thing to you right now, but I don't know what to say."

"You always— That's the perfect thing."

"She'll be okay."

When it's clear I'm unable or unwilling to respond, Monique starts the car and we say nothing else to each other, perfect or imperfect, while completing the second long leg of the Home/Shelter/College triangle. From the Woodinville vertex, she takes the scenic route around the top of Lake Washington, 522 to 5 to 45th to 15th. Random people around us venture from their various Point A's to their various Point B's, charting their own triangles and quadrangles and pentangles and so forth, A to B to C to $X_n$ and back to A. Always back to A.

A Sweet A. There's No Place Like A. A Is Where the Heart Is.

But not my dog.

Monique also likes to walk, so we always park far away from both our classes. Cons: none in good summer weather. Pros: more exercise; less chance of getting stuck waiting behind idiots waiting for other idiots to pull out of spaces in more crowded lots; stretching out the time that I get to walk around with an actual destination to give me a sense of purpose; stretching out the time when it's possible to trick myself into feeling like I'm just one of the students in the body student, before I get to class and I'm so obviously Other.

Monique just likes to walk.

Before we head our separate ways, she looks at me over the roof of the car.

"You found Shaw?"

"I own Shaw," I say, immediately feeling a little overconfident, though it is—at least electronically—true. I manage to avoid unfortunate phrases like, I'm so far up his ass, or I've got my hand in his pocket, but I'm not wild about how Sam-ish I sound with what does make it through the filter: "He's ours to destroy." Monique nods somberly, and starts for the break where a giant hedge parts for the path. But she turns and smiles when I say, "Play nice with the other kids."

When I was little—seems impossible that I was ever little—when I was younger, most days before school Monique would tell me to play nice with the other kids. Mom's repertoire, when she was engaged, was usually more along the lines of "Stay away from the stupid kids." No. Children. Stupid children. Because kids would be too humanizing? Fix your tie, sit up straight, stay away from the stupid children. Unsophisticated children. Blue-collar children, she'd say if there ever were any at my private schools. Not like it mattered. Pick a clique; nobody was lining up to be my pal.

Monique pulls the strap of her book bag over her head, says, "See you tonight," and disappears through the hedge. I put my backpack over both shoulders and stand still next to the car, missing my dog, missing my sister.

A slight breeze occasionally rustles the leaves in the trees looming over me. The rich spice of Cypress wafts in from across campus, smelling so much like an old boat that I can practically hear the creak of joints and feel the hull rolling under my feet. I close my eyes and take a deep breath, pulling in the taste of eucalyptus from the two giant trees next to Bloedel Hall, survivors of the blizzards of '83 and '85, but beat to crap by '88 and probably not long for this world. I open my eyes and gaze skyward. No clouds. No cloud shadows. Every April, at the turn of season, the fluffy pink flowers of the Cherry Blossoms in the Quad look like the trees' limbs have snagged tufts of cloud at sunset, the dream-like softness of light soaking the courtyard at magic hour, the gentle clicks of camera shutters, everyone whispering to not break the spell, breathing in the round-edged, fragile scent, releasing only the tiniest murmurs of wonder and awe at being party to this ephemeral perfection, everything soft and quiet and peaceful, the opposite of every loud and jagged thing at my Point A in April, May, June—

"You leaving?"

I hope so.

It takes me a second to realize that those were actual words out in the air. I shake the trees and calendar out of my head. The parking lot's filled up while I've stood here. A guy sits idling in a newish compact in the lane a car length behind me.

"Sorry," I tell the guy. "Just parked. Sorry."

Weaving through the lanes, I end up causing a few other cars to slow, their drivers thinking I'm headed for one of the parked vehicles I'm darting between. Nope. Sorry. I wave and shrug and shake my head and apologize to anyone and everyone for taking up space on the planet. Monique is pathologically early, so I'd still have plenty of time to take the really long way from the parking lot to my building, but I'm rattled so I screw up and beeline it to class, arriving *almost* without incident, arriving having only accidentally bought a fistful of what I assume to be marijuana—Placing hand in pocket to act casual. What's this? A hundred I failed to give to the shelter. "Dude, be cool." A guy in a red-, yellow- and green-striped beanie stepping out of the bushes. "Don't wave the money around." Him plucking the bill from my hand while closing my fingers around a baggie, stepping back into the bushes. "Alright, man, get out of here." Walking, fast walking, running—arriving at class, out of breath, 4th out of 19 possible attendees on the eve of a national holiday to take my unassigned seat at the very, very back of the room.

Fuck.

Settle.

Xiao, the Chinese guy up front who hates me for also acing all the tests ignores me like he always does. There's a girl, a woman, Cassandra, shaped like a cardboard box, *shrihk*, *zft*, who's taken an interest in me as a novelty, who will twist around to talk at me until Sideburns, the guy she has a crush on, arrives and she flips like a switch to tawkward at him. But I get only a cursory, "Hi, Paul," from her today because thankfully he's made the mistake of showing up early in hopes of maximizing *his* time talking with the one *other* girl in Physics class, Runa, the pretty girl, the girl-shaped girl that *he* has a crush on, who looks good in running shorts and a tank top, who sits at the side of the room with one tanned leg crossed over her knee, dangling a flip-flop, bouncing it at 80 Hz and knowing all the answers when she's called on. But Runa isn't here yet, so Sideburns is taking the brunt of Cassandra, and I'm grateful to be left alone to wait, to calm myself before Professor Dave gets here and I can crack open my brain and pour in stuff that doesn't hurt.

My dog is going to be okay.

## Chapter 10: Birth, School, Work, Death. Not Necessarily in That Order

I don't want to be late to meet Sam after class, so I run across campus with my backpack bouncing side to side, knocking me off balance. I'm sure I look like a total spaz. Well, even more of a total spaz than usual. There's got to be some resonant frequency where my footsteps would work with instead of against the shifting weight, but I quickly figure out that it's a cadence I can't maintain, no matter how much Sam is going to kill me for being late. So I truck down the pathways and sidewalks, lurching side-to-side, being pulled wide around turns and overshooting any safety stops at blind corners where I'd usually look both ways.

Usually. I'm spending the afternoon with Sam and there'll be no usually about it. Sure enough, long before I get to what Sam would call the extraction point, a giant sedan, mid-70s American, diarrhea brown with rusted-out pocks around the fenders, pulls into the bike lane and stops at the curb. I've never seen this vehicle before, but I know it's Sam. I stop next to it, bending to look through the open passenger window.

"Want some candy, little girl?" Sam asks.

The corner of the door grinds on the sidewalk when I swing it open.

I say, "Sorry," but Sam doesn't seem to mind. He makes an "eh," sound, like it is what it is. I chuck my backpack in the back seat and start to climb in.

"Hold it," Sam says. "How'd your little Nancy Drew Mystery pan out? Did you find Shaw or are you walking home?"

"Shaw, Dad, Uncle Kenny. All their accounts. All twelve million."

"What else did you do?"

"You told me not to do anything."

"I know what I told you. What else did you do? "

I'm not quick to respond, but before I can, Sam flashes me a Halt palm. We wait while two coeds saunter by, paying no attention to me or the car or Sam. When they're out of earshot in front of us, Sam says, "You'll have automated something."

"If we pull the trigger tonight, we can get a check Thursday morning, first thing. Tomorrow's a bank holiday." Here. Not in Turks or Caicos.

"Good. What did you fuck up?"

"Nothing," is my immediate and automatic response, but Sam must read my face when I remember tickling the printer. "I cycled a blank sheet of check paper through a printer in Turks and Caicos. Blank."

Sam turns his head and looks up at the sun visor. "If it wasn't blank?" he asks.

"We could incriminate persons not ourselves."

"Get in."

Despite my height, I don't weigh that much. Still, my mass is enough to lower the car and now the door is stuck on top of the sidewalk. Leaned out over the gutter to pull with both hands, I can't yank the door closed. Sam frees it by stabbing the gas and angling into the traffic lane. I'm un-seat-belted, watching pavement whip by below me as I draw the door in. I manage not to fall out, and get the door latched just before we hit the campus speed limit of 20 miles per hour.

"You won't need to know that one," Sam says as we pass a sign.

"The speed limit?"

"Glove box." In the glove compartment I find no gloves, but there is a booklet from the Department of Licensing, a study guide for taking the written knowledge test for a drivers license. "Read." Sam drives. I read. There's a radio, but Sam leaves it quiet.

By the time I close the booklet and look up, we've traveled far enough that I don't know where we are. We're on a freeway between exits, tall trees flanking both sides. No signs, but there's info everywhere. Here it's the service markers on the side of the interstate, the white plastic stakes that are totally invisible unless you're looking for them. Everything is measured in miles north from the Oregon border. Within a tenth of a mile, I find a marker, read the number and know exactly how far north I am. Which, is clever and smart and neato, but honestly doesn't do me a whole crap lot of good. I still don't know where I am.

I drop the DMV booklet back in the glove compartment.

"The curb is painted white," Sam says. "How long can you park?"

"Loading or unloading only."

"Your turn signals don't work. Show me the hand sign for slowing down."

I lift my elbow to shoulder height and let my hand dangle down.

"Stopping?"

"Same."

"Right turn."

I lift my hand like I'm asking a question in class, but that's too lame a joke for Sam to make.

Sam grills me while he drives. We don't leave the freeway until we've passed the county line, by which point he's asked me dozens of questions, never about the exact situation we're in as we work our way through town, never about the exact situation we were just in or were about to be in. He's not following the structure of the DMV pamphlet either. I don't discern any pattern. Sam's good at random. And I'm good at the fancy book learnin'. My confidence ticks up a notch when I realize I've never once needed to fall back on the study guide.

"When can you turn left on red?" Sam asks.

"Turning onto a one way street, from a one way street." Sam doesn't shoot another question to me, so I add, "After coming to a full stop at the red."

"Good. You only need twenty out of twenty-five on the test. Those are the hard ones. You've got all the numbers." He doesn't ask me about any of the speed limits, because, indeed I do have all the numbers locked in my head. Some of the other gray areas don't make as much concrete sense to me, though.

"Sam, the twenty miles per hour in a school zone when children are present thing? How old is a children? And does one kid not count? And how far away is 'present'?"

"Unknowable," Sam says, slowing down and drifting the car over onto the wide, but soft-looking shoulder of the two-lane road we're on now. Or leaving now. Sam's parking, in the middle of nowhere. Tall trees again, but no roadside markers that I can see. Sam turns off the engine, and stares down the empty roadway. I hear birds. I know most of the local owls, the nighttime birds, but this afternoon is so sunny and bright that it's actually more terrifying to think that Sam is probably going to walk me into the woods and leave me. He takes the keys out of the ignition, resting his hand on the flat bench of seat between us and continuing to stare down the lonely strip of asphalt where later I'll be trying to hail a passing motorist.

"Children would be any minors," he says finally. "Just one to trigger the limit. The distance is probably officer discretion. Which means," Sam says, punctuating his sentence with a stomp on the sedan's emergency brake pedal before turning to look at me. "You should drive the twenty until you're driving with a real license."

Sam steps out with a curt, "come on," and crosses the road. By the time I get unbuckled and extricated and vertical, Sam's thirty feet ahead of me, marching through the woods. I hop the culvert and run to catch up with him.

"Where are we?"

"Mars."

There's no real path, so I stick to Sam's heels the best I can, stepping over fallen logs, ducking around giant ferns and scrabbly underbrush. After three or four minutes, we reach the edge of the woods. I stop where the trees stop. It's not a meadow. It's a cemetery.

Rows of weathered, mismatched headstones thrust out of the ground like the jumble of teeth in a shark's jaw. I hope Sam doesn't have a fresh hole dug for me.

He's ahead of me again, walking along the tree line,

perpendicular to the lines of graves. As he passes the end of each row, he bounces his fist off the top of the headstone there, like some weird game of duck, duck, goose. Sam turns down a row before I can even step onto the grass. Creeping along to the end of Sam's row, I find no urge to touch the stones.

I do encounter my irresistible habit of vacuuming up numbers, in this case dates. Date of birth, date of death—the math is automatic for ages. Seventy six. Eighty one. Sixty five. I look at names too, but they're gone before I finish reading them. Beloved, much loved, beloved, beloved, devoted. Except for the ages skewing old, no patterns here either. Random. Life and death are random.

I reach Sam and stand next to him before a small, white-marble headstone.

James Tenor Drinbell. He'd be eighteen if he'd made it to his first birthday.

I hear myself swallow. Sam keeps his gaze on the stone while he talks.

"What you need is a person who died before they got into any of the systems. Live birth, clean death, preferably out of state so there's no local death record attached to the birth certificate. States are computerizing records more and more; you probably know more about that than I do," Sam says, looking at me for a second before returning his gaze to the stone. "This won't work once they get everything connected and cross-checking. For now, though, you want somebody who existed on paper, but won't be around to catch you out. If they do already have a Social Security number, that doesn't always work against you."

Sam takes a piece of paper out of his pocket and holds it out to me. He doesn't release his grip when I grab it, so I just look and let go. It's a social security number.

"Got it?" Sam asks. When I nod, Sam puts the paper back in his pocket. "Eighteen, you'd have spent the last year applying for colleges and filling in your social security number over and over on applications. Even regular people would have it memorized, so don't try to hide that you know it. Think of the senior class at your high school. Use specifics about them if you have to, but only if you're asked. Oh, do you know Johnny Quarterback? He plays football, right? You know of him, but you're not friends. Never offer information about yourself."

"Know what will give you away."

"Exactly."

"To who?" Whom. To whom. I'm scrutinizing my lazy grammar. Sam turns to scrutinize my mode of being.

"Everyone. Always. Today, the Department of Licensing." I think of Thomas Jefferson's line about constant vigilance being the price of liberty, but catch myself before I interrupt Sam in the rare act of revealing his plans. "At eighteen you don't need a learner's permit. We'll take your birth certificate"—Still looking at me, Sam points at the headstone when he says 'your'—"and your social security card to the DOL. You take the written test, take the driving test, they take your picture and a thumbprint, you get a driver's license and are resurrected. James Tenor Drinbell."

Sam is sharing with me the upside of dead babies.

I do not like that.

I feel my mind start to dart around, looking for exits, trying to dodge the reality of this situation. Nimble is the mind's avoidance. I find distraction in logistics.

"The card and the birth certificate, how long will it take to get the paperwork?"

"I've got all that."

Charged by discomfort, I can't stop myself blurting, "Then why are we here?"

"Because you need to know what you're doing, Paul. What you're asking for and what you're taking." Sam briefly releases me from his stare to look at the headstone, then points at my feet and locks his gaze on my eyes. "Somebody stood right there and cried. For this child. And if they didn't cry it was only because they were so mad, so profoundly pissed off, at a doctor or at God, at somebody or everybody who couldn't save their baby."

I feel dirty and ugly and crass.

Because I am dirty and ugly and crass.

"Anger," Sam says. "Anger can get you through a lot."

I want to cry. My face burns with the need to cry. For this child. For myself. For this crime and my reasons for it. For my need to escape the family that created this monster that is my brother, this monster that is me. I could be angry. I wouldn't be wrong to be angry. But I'm sad. I'm hurt and disappointed and sad.

"But if you need to cry," Sam says, in my head again, but different now. He's actually gentle, possibly kind, more connected than conniving. "I won't give you shit about it." And I know it really isn't a trap. It's not an invitation to do something weak and pathetic so he can turn around and ridicule me. Maybe Sam does have a heart. A layer of Fear Of Sam peels off me, exposing a layer of Love Of Sam that I'm surprised to find. Through the love, I find empathy and—

Grief. A grief for Sam and what he must have lost to bring us together in this place.

I feel lightheaded. I put a hand on the headstone next to me and—more surprises—the stone is warm, having silently soaked up sun all day. Steadied, with the heat pushing into my hand, my mind stops bouncing around, slows, drifts, floats down, down, down like snowflakes in still air, the grief settling upon me, accumulating.

"Eleven months," Sam says, summing up the life of little Jimmy Drinbell. Eleven months of cooing and giggling and squirming ending with sudden, shocking catastrophe. Or was it eleven months of incremental decay, a slow, draining decline from a not-so-great height to begin with? Either way, eleven months.

"A few rows over," Sam says, turning his head to look down the hill, "there's a kid with the same date listed twice." I can't follow his gaze specifically, but I have the sense that he's looking at a particular marker, that Sam knows the stone. "Born. Died."

Beloved, beloved, much loved. Too soon.

"They named her. First, middle, last. Can you imagine doing that? Picking a name for the baby you'll never bring home but you'll carry for the rest of your life?"

"Naming your pain," I say.

"Yeah," Sam says quietly.

I want to ask him what the name of his pain is, but I don't. This . . . This what? This *opening* is so fragile, so tenuous. If I probe at all, if I ask Sam about Sam, I know all the gates will clang shut, all his defenses reinstated, all weapons armed and ready to fire. So, I embrace this moment of standing with Sam under a cloudless, baby-blue sky, the sun warm on my face, the heat of ancient granite against my palm, birds I can't identify making small sounds out of sight in the trees. The air is still and nothing moves in the meadow.

I don't really know where I am, but I'm okay here with Sam. Not quite comfortable, but quiet, still. Peaceful. This moment— our moment—suspended. Apart. The whole of my regular irregular life feels very far away. My ease with school and the never-changing rules of mathematics, my struggle with the ever-shifting, irrational world of life at home.

Zero days for almost-daughter First Middle Last. Eleven months for James Tenor Drinbell.

Math works its way up to the front again and—

"Wait. You already have the paperwork? Wouldn't this be too young for you? Why—"

"Monique."

Oh.

No, wait again. "She's a girl. James wouldn't work for—"

Oh.

Oh.

Monique asked for me.

And that's what makes me cry.

## Chapter 11: How Do You Get To Carnegie Hall?
### or   Real Drivers License=Real Driving Test=Learn Your Ass To Drive

Sam walks past me into the woods. I don't get super blubbery, maybe because I already cried this morning and I'm not really all that big a crier. I'm not.

I head after Sam, tracking him more by movement than actual path. He makes better time through the brush, quieter too, and he's vanished before I can see where the trees break for the road. Sam's behind the wheel with the car rumbling at idle when I step out of the woods. He doesn't ask me how I am, honoring his promise of not giving me shit for crying. Long ago, Sam must have removed "moral" from "moral code," or at least tacked on the "A" for "amoral," but he does keep his word.

"Hard part's done," he says, and eases us onto the empty road.

Judging by shadows, we head out of the boonies in generally the direction we came. Uninhabited areas of trees and open, grassy fields. Repetitive small towns with clusters of the same fast food places over and over. McDonalds and a Shell station. Dairy Queen and a Chevron. Burger King and Exxon. Grease and petroleum, grease and petroleum, grease and petroleum. Sam could be driving in circles for how much differentiation there is between these sad-sack little towns, each unique only in its particular permutation of run down, beat up, hopeless lack of opportunity.

Suddenly my Point A doesn't seem so—

Yes it does.

Though we're still a ways out, the population density increases as we get closer to Seattle, and with it, the repair and variation of businesses.

"See that hospital?" Sam says as we drive by. "See where you pull into the parking lot, there or there?" I nod. "See the doors for the E.R.?" I nod again. Sam says, "Nodding to a driver watching the road is not the most effective mode of communication, Paul."

I want to say, You saw me nod, Sam. I want to say, You're not watching the road, Sam. I want to say, Please don't send me to the E.R., Sam. But he is watching both me and the road, and we are driving past all the hospital entrances, so I just say, "Eyes on."

"Nice," Sam says.

I'm not sure that's strictly military jargon, but it has served its ingratiating purpose. I only say it once, though I've read that Sam's pals in the military use a lot of redundancy on the radio, repeating themselves in regular practice to cover breaks in communication from signal loss. Computers, even supercomputers do that, with as much as an eighth of the data dedicated to making sure the data you have are the data you're supposed to have. Not all the time, and rarely that inefficiently, but you always have to—

Never mind.

"Hospital's there," Sam says, then, "One light," as we pass through an intersection, "Two lights," when we go through another, then, "You'd go left out of here," as he makes a right turn, providing instruction for backtracking. He drives half a block and pulls into a giant parking lot behind what looks like an empty factory. So, now I know where the hospital is. I need to know that why?

"Don't worry," he says. "It won't be you." But before we roll to a complete stop, Sam reaches across the seat, says, "Probably," then simultaneously presses the button that unlatches my seatbelt and slams on the brakes. The seatbelt zips across my lap and I pitch forward, half-bouncing off the dash, half-crumpling under it in a wad in the foot well. We kids are off the hook for tonight's fund-draining dinner, so I am on the hook for anything that can heal or be covered up by morning.

Sam asks, "Have you learned a valuable lesson?"

I say, "I have learned a valuable lesson." And relearned another.

Sam shuts off the car and climbs out. I follow him to the back of the car, because . . . I don't know why. Whatever's happening now is what I'm trading—or part of what I'm trading—for Sam's help getting the fake identity. I'm hopeful, given that the cemetery was supposedly the hard part. Sam unlocks the trunk with a key. It's just one key, by itself, not on a ring. That seems weird, but I carry no keys and climb in my bedroom window, so I'm going to keep my mouth shut about weirdness.

Oh, god, please don't let there be a body in the trunk.

Phew. Just some traffic cones and a duffel bag, too small to contain a— Well, a whole—

So the parking lot.

The parking lot is a vast sea of asphalt, flat and barren except for a few straggly weeds popping out of small cracks here and there. The lines marking parking spaces are faded to mere suggestion. The only break in the factory or whatever's blank concrete wall is six giant, loading-dock-style doors standing five feet off the ground above black bumpers at one end of the building. The other three sides of the lot are flanked with established trees. And I guess the factory never needed lights out here at night because there aren't any lampposts breaking up the acres and acres of paved open space.

Sam starts to take off his T-shirt. When he lifts the hem, I see that Sam's been doing a lot of sit-ups. And by a lot, I mean Sam has been doing all the sit-ups. His stomach looks like eight dinner rolls in two neat columns. In the split second while he's got both arms over his head and his face is covered with fabric, I poke Sam's tummy.

"Hey," he says, doubling over, pulling his shirt down instead of off. "Hey," he says again, smiling, trying not to smile but smiling more, almost laughing.

Sam's ticklish. Who'd have guessed that Sam's ticklish? It's like Godzilla being ticklish.

"Don't do that." He lifts the hem of his shirt halfway, but brings it down again. "Hey."

"I didn't."

"I know, but don't." Sam quickly grabs the shirt, pulls one arm inside without lifting up the torso part, pulls in the other arm. From inside, he bunches the shirt around his neck with one hand, pauses with the other hand sticking out between us ready to grab whatever part of me advances if I make a move. "Hey," he says, adjusting his grip on the gathered fabric beneath his chin and pointing at me. Sam's having fun. Sam's in a good mood. He feints left, "Don't," right, "Hey." He whips the shirt over his head. "Haha! Hey."

Shirt off, Sam folds it quickly and lays it in the trunk. What comes out of the duffel bag is dark-blue coveralls like a mechanic wears. Sam pulls that on over his pants and running shoes. Tan leather gardening gloves. A helmet like the kids who can stay on a skateboard more than two seconds wear. It looks freshly spray-painted, the same bright orange as the safety cones.

"What's your birthday?" he asks.

I start to answer with my own date o' birth, but realize he's not talking to Paul David Stockton; he's talking to James Tenor Drinbell, R.I.P. I recite the date I read off the gravestone.

"Social?"

I rattle off James'es'es' Social Security Number.

"How old are you?"

"Eighteen in March."

"Which makes you?"

"Eighteen?"

Sam pulls the traffic cones out of the trunk. "Zodiac Sign."

"Pisces."

"Which is funny for a kid who can't swim. Watch your feet." Sam drops a traffic cone on the ground between us. He closes the trunk, pulls the one weird key out of the lock and hands it to me.

"Don't start it 'til I tell you."

I get in the car. Sam gets on the car.

He plants himself on the hood in front of the rear-view mirror, sitting cross-legged facing the windshield, his left hand clamped on the edge of the hood between the wipers. With his right, he points down, tapping his bulky gloved index finger in three spots along the hood, saying words I can't make out. Sam pulls the second safety cone off the roof of the car and uses it like a bullhorn.

"Roll. Down. Your."

I roll down my window and Sam returns the cone to the roof of the car. He taps on the hood again and now I understand he's pointing through to the pedals, from (my) right to left:

"Gas, brake, emergency brake. Stay off the emergency brake. Never use your left foot for anything except bracing yourself for hard turns." When I nod assent, he says, "Right foot brake. Fire it up." I turn the key and the engine under Sam's butt comes to life. "It's a V8," Sam says. I don't really know what that means. "Lots of torque." *That* we've studied in physics class. Power. Sam says, "No gas. Don't do it yet, but you're going to ease your foot off the brake, then ease it back on. Did you hear me say 'ease'?"

"Easy."

"Easy does it. Go ahead."

I slowly remove my foot from the brake, lifting, lifting, lifting . . . and nothing happens.

"You have achieved parking. Would you like to learn to drive?"

"Affirmative."

"Foot on the brake," Sam says. When I grab the stalk on the steering column, he adds, "Pull it toward you."

"Roger." I shift—clunk, clunk, clunk, clunk, clunk—all the way over to L1, which I suspect has nothing to do with a gravitationally neutral Lagrange orbit. Clunk, clunk, back up to Drive. I report, "Equipment operational and ready for deployment."

"Proceed in the prescribed manner."

I creep my foot back and the car starts rolling forward as I lessen my pressure on the brake. We reach about four and a half miles per hour and top out there. It's an analog gauge with infinite display increments. (Yeah, so shoot me for rounding up to infinity from the $6.1873559 \times 10^{32}$ or so Planck lengths along the 1-ish centimeter arc the tip of the needle draws from motionless to 4-ish point 5-ish miles per hour. Our eyes can't tell the difference anyway.) But however accurate the measure, your readings are always going to be vague. Monique's car has a big, ugly digital readout that's super easy to read, but dumb computing means it lags in reporting changes in velocity. Precise, but wrong.

"And eeeasy stop," Sam says. I manage that. "Good. Do it again, still just with the brake, and math it out."

I'm not sure what he means until I'm doing it and I realize the acceleration and deceleration follow exponential curves, which makes more sense to me than I can explain today or tomorrow or ever. "Cool." I bring us to a gentle stop.

"Now we'll try cooking with gas. Don't stomp on it. Don't stomp on the brake. Easy up, easy down. Bring it up to about ten miles per hour. And remember to move your foot to the brake pedal when you want to hit the brake pedal. Go."

I ease us up, smooth as the chauffeur, eight miles per hour, nine, nine and half, ten.

"Heads up, Paul," Sam says, tapping on the windshield. When I look up, we're almost in the trees. I stomp on the brake. Sam's legs slide out from under him, momentum shooting his body forward when the car lurches to a halt. But he's got a death-grip on the edge of the hood between the windshield wipers, so he just lengthens out into the air, whacks down flat on his stomach and outstretched legs, his feet dangling over the grill.

"Sorry." I smile, trying to show every single tooth I have, while I still have them.

Fuckity, fuckity, fuck, fuck, fuck.

Sam draws himself up. He retrieves the toppled safety cone from the hood (Did he catch it?) and places it back on the roof. He sits, cross-legged again in the same spot I just launched him from.

Unfazed, Sam says quietly, "Let's try backing up."

I clunk, clunk it into Reverse, look again to Sam to await instruction.

"Left hand at twelve o'clock. Turn in the seat and lay your right arm along the top of the back seat to look out the back window."

I get myself situated as directed. "There's going to be a stranger sitting next to you, Paul. Paul, if your examiner is a woman, do not touch her hair. If your examiner is a man?"

"Do not touch his hair."

Sam caught me braiding Monique's hair *one time* when I was eight. He thinks I have a hair thing. Actually, that may be why we got Terry. The timing would be right. Anyway.

"Always look out the back window when you're backing up. Points off if you don't."

"Gotcha."

"Slowly now," he says. I ease us backward without the gas, coasting toward the distant wall of trees on the other side of the lot. Fairly soon, Sam says, "Stop here," so I do, gently, not pitching Sam against the windshield. He takes the orange safety cone off the roof and leans out to drop it carefully onto the pavement next to the car.

"Okay, keep going. Keep your hand at twelve and try out the steering going backward." That makes sense pretty quickly: move the top of the wheel toward the way you want to go. "Now, head straight for the other cone." Again, that's not too hard, until I get close to it. "Slow up," Sam says. "Easy. Go until you can't see the top of it." When it disappears below my line of sight over the trunk, I stop. Sam's still gripping the edge of the hood, still sitting like he's in a Kindergarten circle. "Good. Put it in Park."

I do. Sam collects the orange cone and gets in the passenger seat with it across his lap. Instead of a seatbelt, he braces his feet against the dash.

"Forward gear." Check. "Aim for the cone." It's a tiny orange dot across the lot.

"Roger."

"Stab it."

The back wheels squeal and spin before they bite, the rear end actually moving sideways before the front end jerks up and we lunge forward. It might be my imagination, but I think I hear the wheels squeal again when the transmission shifts to second. It's like a roller coaster plunge, the acceleration shoving me back against the seat. No wheel squeal when we shift to third gear, but the tiny orange dot of the safety cone is suddenly growing larger against the backdrop of trees.

"Brakes!"

I pound on the brake pedal with both feet. The front end of the car dives down before we lose traction and skid, slowly drifting to thirty degrees off parallel from our direction of travel. The car rocks when the tires finally grip again and we jerk to a stop.

"Here's good," Sam says, stepping out with his cone. Kneeling in the tall grass off the edge of the parking lot, he pulls the other cone out from under the front of the car, tugging, then yanking once to free it. "Close enough for government work." He nests the cones and places them on the roof as he returns to his spot on the hood. "No gas," he says, pointing behind me at the loading dock doors. "Head for the wall."

I reverse a tidy arc, then cruise us forward across the parking lot at four and half miles an hour while Sam has me turn on the lights, turn off the lights, flash the hazards, use the left blinker, right blinker. He looks over his shoulder to gauge his time before he releases his grip on the hood to have me run the windshield wipers. We have time, I do that right, and I stop us with neither the car nor Sam's feet hitting the wall.

He puts the cones about a car-length and a half apart, each about six feet from the wall.

"Parallel parking is angles," he says, climbing back onto the hood. And parallel parking does turn out to be angles, so I quickly log three-for-three on parallel parking practice, performing perfectly, hitting no cones, hitting no walls, needing no more instruction from Sam than where to start the first cut-in to end up in the right place. When I put the car in Park after my third success, Sam even says, "Well done." I can hardly believe it.

"Thanks."

"Pop the trunk." Sam rolls off the hood to collect the cone in front of the car while I search for the knob or button or pulley or—

"Paul?"

He's behind the car now, having collected the other cone and waiting now for me to open the trunk. Shit.

"Remember where the hospital is?"

Shit, shit, shit, shit, shit.

In the side mirror, Sam tucking the cones under one arm to free a hand to kill me. He arrives at my door. Roll up the window? Too late. I click off my seatbelt because he's for sure going to drag me out through the—

"There's no latch inside the car," Sam says, grabbing instead the keys from the steering column, killing instead the engine.

There's no latch. You can't open the trunk from inside. Sam was fucking with me. Again. Of course. The trunk lid pops up and I try to collect myself while Sam changes into his regular clothes. But. Two buts. Sam slams the trunk right away. And he's doesn't change clothes. He ducks his helmeted head to sit in the passenger seat.

"Remember where the hospital is?"

"Yes."

Sam hands me the key.

"Okay. Remember where the cones were?" I look at the wall next to us, the rusty steel brackets at the bottoms of the loading doors even with the top of the car. "The other ones," he says. "You're going to do three laps. Straight, U-ey, straight, U-ey. Three times. Clockwise. Once at 10 miles per hour, once at 15, and I'll let you know about the last one. Let's go."

I start the car and drive us over to where the first cone isn't, using just a bit of gas and the right amount of brake, and looping around to get us pointed at where the second cone isn't either.

"If your examiner doesn't put her seatbelt on, ask her to before you move the car."

And don't touch her hair.

Sam isn't wearing his seatbelt. Somehow I know that Sam does not want me to ask him to put on his seatbelt. When I shift my gaze from his waist to the part of his face not obscured by the helmet, he's looking forward. He nods. I use a reasonable amount of gas to keep the back wheels from spinning, but bring us right up to 10 miles per hour.

About halfway across the lot, Sam opens his door and tumbles out.

I slam on the brakes, looking in the rearview mirror, Sam rolling and rolling and finally coming to a stop. He pops up onto his feet, shaking his giant orange head and waving go, go, go at me. He mimics driving, hands on the steering wheel making quick adjustments, then waves again. Go, go, go.

I head for the trees, slow, swing a not-too-wide right turn and start back toward the other conical vacancy. Sam, standing on the centerline between the imaginary lane I was in and the imaginary lane I'm in now, waves both gardening-gloved hands like the guys who line up jet planes approaching the gate. Straight. Stay straight.

Having driven a grand total of maybe half a mile in my entire life, I am now being asked to hurl the vehicle directly at Sam.

Remember where the hospital is?

Jesus Christ. Sam really is insane.

Sam starts running before I get to him, running the same direction I'm driving, looking back, looking back, pumping his arms, looking back, moving closer to my line of travel until the moment I'm upon him, orange head spinning around to face me. Sam grabs the door handle, jerks the door open and leaps into the passenger seat.

Panting, Sam leans over to make sure I'm still going 10 miles per hour. I was and am, but I slow for the turn to start lap two.

"Okay," Sam says. He rolls down his window to get more air. "Fifteen."

After the turn, I give the big V-8 more gas and Sam pitches himself out of the car at 15 miles per hour. I watch him spin and tumble in the rearview mirror.

It won't be you.

Math. I love math. Fifteen miles per hour and 60 minutes per hour means Sam's going to have to run at 4-minute mile pace. I know that's fast, world-class speed, which I wouldn't put past Sam, but still. Well, that is for a mile, and this will be a sprint, so I guess faster is possible. If I knew anything about sports, I'd know more about what to expect. Instead I get turned, point the car at Sam and spin the tires.

This time Sam doesn't try to open the door; he dives through the window he opened. When I slam on the brakes because I'm watching him and paying no attention to the approaching trees, he slides off the seat and ends up head down in the foot well, feet sticking out the window.

"Sorry," I say. "What speed would you like for lap three?"

"Practice some at 30," Sam says, pulling himself up. Perhaps he has hit his head. In fact, as I launch us up to 30, cruise, and crank us down to five for the next turn, Sam takes off his helmet. His hair is too short to be messed up. There's one scratch on the side of the helmet. Sam leans over and runs his thumbnail along the underside of the dashboard, retracting it with a few flakes of neon-orange paint. The scratch on the helmet did not come from contact with the pavement. Sam glances over at the speedometer as I bring us up to 30, looks at the ground moving alongside us. I slow for the turn.

"Let's do fifteen again," Sam says.

I judge the gas correctly to get us right up to 15 without squealing the tires.

Sam does not put his helmet back on.

Out he goes.

I don't look in the rearview this time. I can't. I slow the car before I hit the trees, but I turn no turns. The empty helmet, tossed off the passenger seat by deceleration, rocks absurdly in the foot well. Speed doesn't kill you; sudden changes in velocity kill you. I close my eyes. I remember where the hospital is. From the street, I'd turn left. I *would* or I *will*? Did Sam plan this? Was this Sam's way out? Taking me with him? How am I going to explain—

I open my eyes to—

Sam is lying motionless in the rearview, a lump on the pavement, limbs akimbo. "Akimbo," I say out loud. Akimbo I learned last year studying for the SAT. Is there a Prison Aptitude Test? Probably wouldn't ace that one. Would not or will not?

"Shit."

I rev the engine ineffectually because I guess at some point I put the car in Park. I shift. I turn. I just-brake-no-gas my way up to Sam's body. Shift into Park. Kill the—shut off the engine. I sit. I used to watch Terry breathe sometimes while she was sleeping. Sam does not appear to be breathing, not even foot-twitch dreams of chasing rabbits. I sit. I sit in the car in the middle of the giant parking lot, another vast meadow surrounded by trees, this one with much less grass and only one dead body. I step out and as I round the corner of the hood, I realize that I don't think I can lift Sam. Then—

Ah. I am, finally, at the ripe old age of 13, getting a tiny bit wise. I help myself to the passenger seat, bypassing the alleged meat pile.

"The most dangerous part of that was letting me drive up to your mangled corpse, Sam."

Sam pops up. He slaps both hands on his torso twice, says, "You could call that trust."

I could call that a lot of things. For now I'll just call that Sam Stockton.

"I think I could do twenty," he says, stretching out his shoulders and rolling his head around as he steps up to the window/alternate vehicle entry hatch. "But we are on a schedule," he says, forgoing another go 'round and instead taking off his gardening gloves and unzipping his now rather scuffed-up coveralls. "Key me." I do, also passing him the helmet. He peels off the coveralls as he heads for the poke-free zone behind the car. When he slams the trunk, again wearing his original, rumple-free shirt, Sam says, "Enough with the misdemeanors." He takes his place behind the steering wheel and starts the car before finishing his thought.

"You, my friend,"—poking me in the ribs—"have felonies to commit."

I'm not ticklish. I don't laugh.

Sam appears to, though he's inaudible over the engine roar and screaming tires, the car rotating now around its front tires, me drifting around in a circle following after Sam, shifting to occupy the point in space that Sam's shifting to vacate. The car floats fully sideways before the tires grab, slamming my head back against the headrest. Maybe I should have kept the helmet. But it's locked in the trunk and I'm glad that at least I'm not locked in there with it.

Sam rights the car in time to miss the corner of the building and we are off to commit crimes.

## Chapter 11.1: Just Did It

On the way to DMV to take my driving test, Sam and I stop in at a public library to jump on a public computer to pull the trigger on stealing the stolen money our shitty public father and our even shittier public uncle stole.

Takes three minutes.

If Sam hadn't made me split the money in half, I bet I could have done it in one.

Forty-five seconds. Could have done it in forty-five.

Easy.

## CHAPTER 12: VERY UNRESTRICTED LICENSE

"Right thumb," Sam says when he shuts off the car in a quiet corner of the parking lot at the Department of Licensing.

"What?" I ask. Sam doesn't answer. He pulls a razor blade out of one of his pockets, removes the protective cardboard wrapper from the sharp side. "Right thumb?" I ask. I heard him; it just didn't make sense.

"They're going to take your fingerprint. And I'm going to take off the end of your thumb if you don't hold still."

Sam produces a jeweler's loop and tucks it into his left eye socket like a monocle.

"You're going to . . ."

Cut my fingerprint into a different pattern. That sounds fun.

"Spin around and face the back."

I unbuckle and rotate around to kneel on the seat, facing the rear window.

"You're like Batman with his utility belt," I say.

"You're blocking my mirror, so watch our six." Six o'clock. Watch our backs.

I hold my right hand out in front of Sam. He brings up his right knee to brace my hand against, probably to keep it off the horn. I look away while Sam works. He squeezes the pad of my thumb, first using his left hand to hold mine, then his right. He must be alternating cutting hands, too, but that I can't feel. Outside the car, normal people arrive and leave, conducting the legitimate business of reasonable lives while Sam carves away my identity.

"What do you think Mom'll do about Monique punching her hand?" I ask.

"Probably take it out on you."

"That's what— That's exactly what Monique said."

"Then you're outvoted two-to-one," Sam says. "Enjoy your retribution."

I'm not sure my vote wouldn't be the same. "No arguing with democracy."

Sam blows on my hand like Geppeto blowing shavings off a brand-new wooden boy.

"So," I ask, "what do you think Mom will do *to me* about Monique punching her hand?"

"Maybe she'll kill your dog."

I know the Earth can't stop rotating, and that if it did then we'd all skitter across its surface like Sam's unused safety helmet crashing off the passenger seat. But it feels like everything stops, like the leaves are all stilled because the wind is holding its breath, like traffic halts and every head turns to look at us, waiting to see what the answer is to What do you say to that?

Which is nothing. You don't say anything to that.

"Relax your wrist," Sam says. I try. "Relax your hand." I try. Sam relaxes his grip on my hand, which gets me to relax. For the half second until Sam says, "Tell me the upside to killing your dog."

And what do you say to that? Nothing.

"Exactly," Sam says. "I'm not saying I wouldn't, but why would I? You have to think this shit through, Paul." Sam shifts his leg beneath my hand for the final few adjustments, then releases me. "Now that didn't hurt, did it?" It didn't.

"That's surprising."

Sam's hand darts out, drags the razor blade along the side of my neck and darts away again.

"Surprise! Ha ha. Just the back." The razor blade and the jeweler's loop are secreted away before I can change my underwear. "There are better ways to do that," Sam says, "but you didn't give me much lead time. This will only keep the count of ID points below threshold for a legal match. They'll still know it's you if it comes down to it. These fine ladies and gentlemen are going to take your picture, too, so you picked a great day to not wash your hair."

Inside, the testing is boring by comparison. Paperwork's no problem. I remember my name and numbers. I get a hundred percent on the knowledge test. Outside again, the car checks out mechanically, and the examiner lady likes that I know all the hand signals. On the road, I talk myself through some of the maneuvers ("Back window for backing up"), but the examiner's yesses and uh-huhs suggest that she's reading that as me trying to express my intent rather than me just being a spaz attempting to hide my incompetence. (I keep my Oh, shit; oh, shit; oh, shits to myself. And I don't touch her hair, though the way the sunlight brings out the red highlights in her auburn—Ignore her hair, Paul.) I do get points off for driving too slowly, but otherwise do what I'm supposed to do where I'm supposed to do it and soon enough, we're done and done.

They take my fimqerplint and my bad hair day picture and in four to six weeks I'll get my permanent license in the mail at an address that Sam wouldn't let me see.

"I'll get it to you," he says when we're back in the car, me holding my paper, temporary-but-very-real drivers license in both hands like it's going to try to get away. It's real. It's not a permit; I don't need another licensed driver in the car with me. It even includes a black and white image of the digital picture they took and my hair doesn't look completely retarded. Best of all, soon it'll be permanent.

"Thanks, Sam."

"Don't thank me yet," he says, easy-easing us out of the parking lot, presumably to head home, but, you know, Sam, so not so much. "Oh, you'll thank me, Paul-buddy, but right now you and that card are headed downtown to pass one more test."

## Chapter 13: But She Breaks Just Like a Little Girl

"A strip club? Sam, I'm 13."

"You're 18, Jimmy Jim Jim, and 18-year-olds try to get into places where you have to be 21. Like a *gentlemen's* club."

"I'm closer to kindergarten than to 21." No, I guess I'm equidistant. Still.

"Give me your license," Sam says. I can't see inside. It's either really dark in there or all the windows are painted out. I put my face to the glass and cup my hand over my—

Sam grabs my upper arm like he did in the dining room last night.

"Give me your license before I take it from you."

I opt to live. Sam paper-clips a wad of bills to my brand-new license just before he pulls me through the door—where, hello, we immediately meet our first gentleman, a shall we say "substantial" Samoan fellow occupying a rather disproportionate percentage of the establishment's vestibule. Good day, sir.

"Hey, Karl," the man says to Sam.

"Hey, man."

The end. That's the exchange.

Mister Man looks at me, then looks at me some more, getting used to the idea of my existence. Techno music seeps through the curtain leading inside. Nothing says party like the middle of Tuesday afternoon.

Still looking at me, the bouncer asks Sam/Karl, "What is this bullshit?"

"Remember that guy I never told you about? This is him." Sam/Karl hands the bouncer my real/fake ID. The bouncer looks at the date, my would-be age. A frown would be an expression, and Mister Man doesn't do expression. He turns my ID over to meet the eyes of never-President Benjamin Franklin, and Benny's twin brother(s?).

"Picture don't look like him."

"He's had a cold. We're here to cheer him up."

"Karl."

"We'll sit by the back door. I'll get him out fast if anybody shows up."

Mr. Man looks at me, looks at Sam/Karl, then back at me before throwing his gaze through the curtain to the rear of the building. He hands me my license, lighter than he received it, saying, "Don't order no alcohol."

That, sir, is a double negative.

He turns away to face the front windows, which are in fact painted out. There's nothing at all to see through them. He's figuratively and literally looking the other way.

Sam pulls me inside, through a second heavy curtain. It's loud and everything's red; the curtains along the walls, the low-backed chairs clustered around tiny tables, even the lights. The room smells like if you filled a locker room with taffy and coconuts.

"Karl," a dancer on the move says when we step in. "Hi, sweetie." She air-kisses Sam without fully stopping, giving my forearm a quick squeeze as she passes. "Introduce me to your friend when I get back. I gotta go pump. My tits are burstin'."

"Half of them have kids," Sam says over the music as soon as she's gone. "It's crazy." He's leaned in to talk, but he's not shouting because the music is actually only loud, not overpowering. "Sons," he says. "Their kids are all boys. They quit this shit if they have a girl."

He keeps talking, but, uh . . . uh.

There are boobs here.

The place is nearly empty, despite Par-tay Tues-day, but nearly everyone here has boobs and the ones who aren't wearing bikinis aren't wearing bikinis. I mean, not wearing their whole bikinis.

Boobs!

"This way," Sam says and drags me to a small table by a

hallway at the back, where he deposits me in a chair. The upholstery squeaks as I sink in farther than I'd expected. When I panic-grip the arms of the chair, my fingernails scrape across a strip of brass nail heads along the front edge, which strikes me as oddly formal for a big, red, stinky strip club.

So, yeah. Stage. Pole. Pole dancer. Dancing to the pounding 4/4 beat of the techno:

Nts, nts, nts, nts.

Bounce, bounce, bounce, bounce.

She's been doing some of the sit-ups too. What's bouncing is not a beer gut. Her stomach is taut, the muscles of her long legs and arms developed and well defined. Makes sense if she spends her time doing the athletic maneuvers she's doing now, gripping the pole, swinging those legs around, bending and twisting and arching her back, pointing her high heels in every impossible direction as she spins around, dancing and posing.

Sway, swing, shake, spin.

Nts, nts, nts, nts.

She has pretty hair too, light brown, gathered in a long, careful ponytail that accentuates the length of her slender neck. She's pale. Maybe the windows at her apartment are painted out too.

Nts, nts, nts, nts.

Shake, squeeze, stretch, spin.

Her ponytail whips around as she orbits the pole. The pole bends from the centrifugal force, making me wonder how securely it's attached to the stage and ceiling. There must be building codes about that. I'm not into politics, but those must have been fun city council meetings.

Gripping the pole, she lifts her legs over her head and does the splits hanging upside down. That would make me dizzy if I weren't already getting dizzy.

"Full nude in California," Sam says, I guess commenting on the fact that she's still wearing her bikini bottoms. And shoes. Probably nobody cares about the shoes. No shirt, no shoes, no problem.

Bounce, bounce, bounce, bounce.

Nts, nts, nts, nts.

Hands wide apart on the pole now, she slowly draws her feet off the stage, inverting her body again, arching her spine, craning her head back and slowly bending her knees to place the curved bottoms of her pointed feet on the back of her head, just to either side of the knot of her ponytail.

That looks hard.

She holds the position as she takes three slow breaths—I'm holding mine—her bikini's waistband bridging a gap of shadowed open space from hip bone to delicious hip bone as her abdomen pulls inward, releases, inward, out . . .

That looks really hard.

Speaking of which, my pants are tight.

The dancer lifts her feet off her head, straightens out her body and folds herself back into a standing position at the front of the stage.

There's a clumsy mix of heavy bass drum thumps as one song fades into what could be the start of the very same song, one indistinguishable 4/4 beat replaced with another. The DJ's terrible. Maybe he has to botch the transition so you know it's a new song.

"Let's give it up for Cinnamon," booms a voice over the P.A. from somewhere I can't see.

I don't notice there's one guy in the front row all by himself until he flings a wad of bills into the air over the stage, at/on/for the dancer. She does nothing as ridiculous as try to catch any of the fluttering bills, instead letting them fall to the stage for easy collection on all fours. She crawls around, folding the money into a neat stack in one hand while she smiles and waggles other body parts at the guy who threw the cash. For the final bill, still on her hands and knees, she turns away from him but looks back while she reaches between her legs, stretching to a bill way down between her feet, past her feet. Pressing lower, reaching now with both hands, pressing her shoulders and chest into the stage, she walks her fingers out, out, out, finally putting just her index fingers on the bill. She pauses, mouths, "Thank you," before she starts wiggling and slowly drawing the money between her legs—inducing another shower of currency from the guy up front.

I need to go home.

The dancer—Cinnamon—Cinnamon rolls onto her back, using both hands to gather the money, pulling it to the nearest point on her nearly-nude body, then from there—thigh, neck, breast—running the paper along her skin to stuff it into her tiny, tiny, lavender bikini bottom.

Ineedtogohomerightnow.

"Uh," I say to Sam, but that's all I can manage. Sam fills the gap.

"There's a place in L.A. called Jumbo's Clown Room," he says. How could that not be nice? "The strippers have to put their own quarters in a jukebox."

"Cinnamon!" the announcer announces.

Sam says, "They're open on Christmas."

One of the two dancers sitting together in the middle of the room stands up just before the DJ says, "Cayenne taking the stage." When we walked through before, I hadn't noticed there were two dudes sitting beneath those girls. "Let's give it up for Cayenne!"

Didn't we just give it up for Cinnamon? If we give it up for Cayenne, too, won't we risk running out of it for Saffron and Paprika?

"Cayenne now taking the main stage," says the DJ, with measured enthusiasm. Having put her bikini top back on during her eight-step journey to the (only) stage, Cayenne eschews the three stairs at the back corner, instead employing great focus and concentration in climbing over the lights and railing at the front of the riser in ten-inch platform shoes.

"Let's give it up for Cayenne!"

Maybe she's earned it just for walking in those shoes, or for surviving another whiplash musical crossfade from Cinnamon's cash-collecting song to Cayenne's heating-things-up introduction song, but either way, nobody's clapping or whooping or hurling wads of cash into the air, not even the guy whose lap she just vacated.

Cinnamon keeps her last bill in her hand and uses it to doink the nose of the now-seated money-throwing guy, smiling, and saying to him either Thanks, Sugar, or Thanks, Shifter, or Thanks, Shithead. She winks at Sam/Karl from the top of the stage stairs before descending and ducking behind a curtain near the back corner of the stage.

"She'll come out," he says.

Cayenne is already tugging at the knot of her bikini top.

Rosemary. I thought of another one.

Never mind. I'm really just trying to distract myself from a boner hard enough to cut glass.

I could build a shed without a hammer.

I could hit a ground-rule double.

I seriously might tear my pants. It's a legitimate problem.

Sam lied. The hard part is not done.

"Don't touch the dancers," Sam says. I hadn't noticed him stick his head next to mine this time. "Big no-no," he says. Sam/Karl asks me, "Got it?"

"Don't touch their hair," I say.

"Paul."

"No. I got it. Don't touch." Then I ask Sam/Karl, "Who's Paul?"

"That's my boy." Sam's eyes change targets to the back-stage curtain as Cinnamon steps through, now very modestly wearing 100% of her tiny, pale lavender bikini. "Here she comes."

She saunters across the room to our table. Oddly, the way she moves—long strides, slow and deliberate, but not overly so—makes me picture her wearing a flowing evening gown. I would say that my mind's visual overlay seems more exciting than what's actually presented (with zero imagination required), but I'm already pretty much redlined and heading for the trees. Whatever the etiquette is here, Sam and I stand because we've both been trained since birth to stand when a lady enters. Which is, you know . . . boner.

"Hey, Karl. Jasmine just took lunch."

Jasmine!

"You just missed her."

"We're not missing anything if you're here," Sam says.

Cinnamon hugs Sam/Karl and he hugs her back, so I guess that much touching is okay, at least if they initiate. Cinnamon's heels are less ridiculous than Cayenne's, but still fairly ridiculous, and tall enough to make us the same height, four inches taller than Sam. When they decouple after their brief clinch, Cinnamon looks me up and down, asking, "Who's your friend?"

"Jimmy," I say, offering my hand. "Pleased to meet you."

"We call him Babyface."

Looking thirteen years old or not, I feel my baby face twitch when I finally notice that Cinnamon has a black eye. She's not even trying to cover it with concealer. There's purple and dark mustard yellow, like, holy shit: Dijon.

"Look at you, so formal," she says, smiling and sweeping my hand aside to embrace me. She kisses me on the cheek on the way to wrapping her arms around me, pressing her whole body against mine.

"Oh," she whispers, holding me a little tighter, "you are pleased to meet me."

The word Sorry forms at the front of my brain and drops into my mouth automatically, but I manage to swallow it before it spills out onto her bare shoulder, because . . . she doesn't seem . . . I don't think she . . .

"Did I do that?" she asks, her lips brushing my earlobe. She shoves her hips against mine. With her long legs and the lift of the high heels, I'm not poking her stomach, I'm . . . My . . .

"Oh, you're just right, right there. I can feel you pushing against me."

I'm not exactly pulling away, but she's doing all the pushing. Beneath my hand at the small of her back, she actually starts rocking her pelvis.

"If I wasn't wearing these panties"—a hand in my hair now, cupping the back of my head, rubbing the side of her face against the side of my face while her breath pours hot into my ear— "you'd slide right in."

She drags her lips across my cheek as she releases me—

Not like that.

—taking half a step back and winking her good eye at me. Without letting go of my arm, she dips her head to listen to whatever Sam's whispering in her ear.

"You got it, Sugar," she says to Sam as she straightens up. Then she looks at me and grins. "How would you like to join me in the V.I.P. Lounge?"

Less awkwardly?

Much like dealing with Sam, I don't know what exactly I'd be accepting or refusing, so I don't give an answer. She doesn't wait for one anyway. She entwines her arm in mine, maximizing her body's contact with mine as she walks me toward the back hall.

"What's your name again, Sweetie?"

"I don't know."

She giggles. "You're funny."

Down the hall, there are two bathroom doors on the left across from an arched doorway on the right, the arch adorned with tied-back curtains, possibly velour, definitely red. At the farthest end of the hall, the green light of the emergency exit sign seems as out of place here as I am. Just this side of the escape hatch, there's a door marked "Talent Only. No Acceptions."

Yep.

Cinnamon squeezes closer—I wouldn't have thought it possible—as she guides us through the curtained archway into a much smaller, much darker room. Along the back wall, I can make out three empty booths, semi-circles of high-backed bench seating but with no tables in the centers. Opposite those are only two more like the others because tucked in the corner by the door where the sixth would be is the terrible DJ.

He's raised up on a sketchy plywood platform that does three things: gives him a view down onto the booths in this room, lets him look through a windowless cutout into the main room, and puts his head high enough to rub on the V.I.P. Lounge's drop-ceiling.

I'm pretty sure it was exposed ducts and pipes and conduit—well, exposed everything—out there in the main room, no drop-ceiling. Maybe this is supposed to make the V.I.P. Lounge cozier? Anyway, the DJ's got the big tile directly over his head popped out and slid over to lie askew in the dark dead space above the false ceiling. He wouldn't have to do that if he'd ditch either the heel-wedgie cowboy boots or the Mariner's cap. Just one. Not both. Don't give up who you are.

He gives me a 'Hey, man' head jerk, because that's who he is.

I chameleon his 'Hey, man' head jerk, because that's who I am.

He squints his eyes as he takes a hard drag on a stub of what at this point can only be burning filter. But then he darts his gaze to Cinnamon and back to me real quick, locking sure eye contact with me before he rolls his eyes so hard that I think he might fall upward through his little window. It's a warning. He's probably supposed to keep an eye out for trouble in here, but I get the feeling that he's spotted some and it ain't me. He takes the filter out of his mouth to light the next cigarette, jabs out the butt in an old-school black plastic ashtray on his windowsill, and turns his back to us.

I think of the emergency exit at the end of the hall.

Remember where the hospital is?

It might be me after all.

"James. My name is James."

"Let's go in the corner, James." Cinnamon guides me to the farther booth on the two-booth side and sits me down with my back to the DJ. "Scooch over," she says, moving me over from the end, before straddling my legs to sit on my lap facing me. "He can't see us here." Her knees on the seat, she lifts herself up, taking one hand off my shoulder to grab the top of the booth to look over. Her belly button is an inch from my face. My mouth.

"Nope," she says, smiling and lowering herself to again rest her full weight on my lap, but now squirming around. "We're supposed to wait until the next song starts," she says, "but you're so yummy." She sweeps her palms across my chest, smoothing out the fabric of my shirt. "I could gobble you all up."

But it's me who swallows, though my mouth is dry—and not from not ordering no alcohol.

"I guess Cinnamon is a stage name?"

"Uh, huh. Do you want to know my real name? James?"

Yes? No? I don't know. Do I? Do I *really*? Probably not. But before I can direct it otherwise, my mouth says, "Of course. If you don't mind my asking."

"Traci," she says.

I'll assume the i. I bet she—"Do you dot the i with a heart?"

"Maybe."

"You do."

"I'm not telling."

"You do. You totally do."

Traci pulls an imaginary zipper closed across her mouth, then immediately speaks. "A girl has to keep up some mystery about herself."

"That's a Yes."

"You don't know."

"I know."

"Shut up," she says, swatting my chest once and bouncing in my lap. Then, "Maybe." She palm sweeps my shirt again, rests her hands on my shoulders for a split second before stroking my neck. It occurs to me that she has maintained some degree of physical contact, usually a lot, from the moment she hugged me until now. I've read that people do that with horses—keep a hand on their side while you move around them so they know where you are and don't get spooked. I'm not sure what to make of being the horse in that scenario. Tiny brain, powerful body versus, well, me.

"What?" she asks.

"I didn't say anything."

Traci slips her fingers inside my shirt between my second and third button, flicks the buttoned button a few times with her thumbnail, but leaves it fastened.

"Sometimes . . ."

"Uh, huh."

"Sometimes I dot the i with a heart." Traci adjusts her knees, adjusts her . . . alignment as she nestles down. "For the right guy." Traci grinds her hips around in a quick circle, saying, "Oh, I can't wait." After the first circle, she doesn't quite stop gyrating. "When I came here from where I used to dance . . ."

"Uh, huh."

"There was another girl Crystal already, so I was all 'wah.' "

"Cinnamon is nice. It goes with your hair."

"Oh, thanks," she says. "You're sweet." I'm not sure stating objective fact is a compliment, per se, but whatever. "Do you like my hair?" she asks, arching her back as she reaches up with both hands to undo her ponytail. She puts the elastic band around one wrist before using both hands to shake out her hair, pulling it forward over her shoulders to hang midway between her breasts and navel. She collects a strand between her fingers, pulls it through from scalp to tip. "It won't do anything," she says, looking at me with her head still bowed. Her hair is dead straight and I'm surprised to understand that she means it won't hold a shape. Monique has the same complaint about her—

Do not think about your sister.

Paul David Stockton, James Tenor Drinbell, Jimmy Jim Jim, do *not* think about your sister while a bikini-clad exotic dancer wriggles around on your unit.

I'm ashamed to admit that despite a flash of Monique in my mind, the erection in my pants continues unabated, unrelenting, goddamn merciless. But one more bit from Monique before I find a nice compartment for her elsewhere in my mind, a stolen line about her hair:

It won't do anything; "It just lays there like an Episcopalian."

Traci laughs. "Oh, you *are* funny." She's twirling the end of a lock of hair around her fingers, but stops and gathers the strands near the end like a paintbrush. "It's soft," she says, brushing the gathered ends across the curve of breast above her bikini top until her nipple hardens under the fabric. "Oh," she says. She's saying "Oh" a lot. Traci raises her brush and skims it across my lips. "Soft." Slowly, gently, just hard enough not to tickle. "Soft," she says again as she brings her hair to her own lips, tracing around her mouth like she's applying lipstick, catching her finger on her bottom lip and tugging her lips apart. With her other hand she runs her thumb along my lower lip, easing my mouth open the same way, moving closer, pressing her cheek to my cheek to whisper, "Do you want to touch it?" She leans back, arching her back impossibly to keep her belly pressed against mine, her chest inches from my face.

"Is that allowed?"

"No," she says, shaking her head and making a pouty face, but also lifting my hand to the side of her head. "You're not supposed to touch me." Traci rakes my hand through her hair. "It's not allowed." Again. Her hair does feel soft. Still its natural color, the hair is healthy, undamaged, the strands sliding and rolling smoothly one over another.

"You have to stop," she says, as she starts our third pass. But now she entwines our fingers, digs in to grab a messy fistful of hair, and yanks—Oh, shit!—pulling, hard, back and down, cranking her head back. "Oh!" Her grinding of hips continues in time to the music as she leans back farther and farther, her other hand groping for my shoulder, neck, shoulder to keep from pitching backward.

She's strong, stronger than me. And any effort to pull her in with my trapped hand pulls her hair harder or pulls her crotch deeper into mine. She trails her bracing hand along my arm to seize my other hand. I resist, way less than I should, but soon enough we're mashing her breasts, yanking at her top, pulling it halfway off.

"Oh," she says. Just then the DJ jerks into the next song, the mismatched beats thumping bump-bump, bump-bump like a heart beat, racing. Traci says, "Ah!" matches the double-time pounding and it is on like Donkey Kong.

She lets go of my hands and throws her chest against mine. "You're not supposed to touch me," in my ear. Grind, grind, grind, grind in my lap. "But no one can see us." Leaning back, top undone, gone, then she's on me again. "So no one will stop you. Only—" Hand on hand in hair and yank. "Ah!—Me. Only me." Arching, grinding. "Oh, you're hurting me. I'll be good. I'll be good." Arching, grinding, her neck nearly pressed to my chin, the vulnerable curve of her throat out of focus just beyond my clenched teeth, her breasts compressing against me, her crotch grinding on my crotch.

It's awesome and awful at the same time.

"I'll be good. I won't try to stop you. I— I'll do what you want. Whatever you want. I—"

She stops, releases her hair, puts our hands on her neck as she says, "Put your hands on my neck." Traci clamps down on my hands with her own. "Oh!" Squeezes. Hard. "Whatever you want. I'll be good. I'll—" Harder. "You're hurting me. I'll be good. I'll—" Hardest. Hard enough to hurt my fingers. Her mouth says, Oh! with no sound.

Traci is crazi.

She leans back, her bare torso upright and writhing at arms length, breasts lolling. Grinding, grinding, grinding, grinding, she meets my eyes, her face already red in the dim red light, redder, redder, the veins of her neck standing out ropey above our fingers. Oh, again, her face pleading, tightens like she's trying not to cry, Oh, everything tighter, harder, faster, Oh, legs jerking, hers, mine, Oh, then, Oh, then, Oh, then she explodes and collapses on top of me. She pants into my ear, hips still rocking, methodically but gently, one hand rested on my cheek, cradling my face after she releases me.

Yes, like that.

"Did you—?" she asks, lifting her head to look me in the eyes again.

She smiles, feeling her answer shrinking between us, knowing that I did.

I have given it up for Cinnamon.

And having done so, now I want to run. Beeline for the back door. Vamos. But I don't want to be rude, to hurt her feelings, to take and be selfish without . . . I don't know.

She smiles more deeply, the purple and gold bruise crinkling at the corner of her eye before she lowers her head to nuzzle her face against my neck again, shoving her arms between the booth cushion and my shoulders to clutch me to her.

"You can put your arms around me," she says, tucking her knees up under my armpits without lifting her body off mine. "It's okay." She pulls her calves in tight to my sides, maximizing contact, shifting, adjusting, relaxing, melting her slender frame into mine. Monique breaks in again, an image of her on her yoga mat in this same position. You could do this one, Paul. Balasana. Child's pose.

"Please," Traci whispers, so quiet, so tentative, "please put your arms around me."

What she really wants.

What she'll give everything else to get.

When I try to stroke her hair, it sticks in the sheen of sweat on her back, so I gather it carefully to sweep it over her shoulder on the side where she's laid her head. Bent as I am to recline on the bench seat beneath her, I can see over her other shoulder, where a few stray strands cling to her skin, wild lines of wet-dark brown sectioning off patterns in the red light reflected from her back. As I gently collect those with my fingertips and work them aside, Traci coos and sighs in my ear.

Her hair draped off her back, I lay one arm across her shoulders to cradle the back of her head where it meets the length of her neck, my pinkie and ring finger arriving to lie just so, gently grazing the delicate curve of her ear. A tiny whimper. With my other hand, I stroke her back. I've blocked my view with my own arm now, but I can feel the bare skin is taut over ridges of powerful muscle, mid-back, lower-back. I close my eyes and trace the outline of her shoulder blades, the curve of her ribs, the cleft of her spine.

Traci has eased into shallow breathing like she's sleeping.

I run my fingertips along her side to the flare of her hip, over that curve to return to the indented channel of her backbone, slowly, slowly up, then across her shoulder blade to start another lazy circuit. This time Traci releases a soft moan when I press my palm against her back. Distracted by the sensation of her bare, slick skin gliding against mine, or merely widening the radius of my circuit, I reach farther around, halting when I find the softer dome of flesh formed by her breast where it's pressed against my chest. No protest, so I linger. Timid. Then less so.

I caress the curve. Gently massage the tissue. For a split second, equations pop into my head—for cones and parabolas and hyperbolae, for circles and spheres and ellipses, for density and coefficients of viscosity and elastic spring—math charging forward to make sense of my world. But numbers evaporate in an instant when Traci shifts ever so slightly, rotates to give me better access. My head empties of abstract numbers, overtaken with some deeper understanding, some fundamental discovery of flesh learning flesh. Supple skin. The unique give of her breast.

My fingertips find tiny bumps in the areola, a slight roughness to the nub of hardening nipple. Before I wear out my welcome, I move on. Slowly down the cleft of her spine, down, up, down. Where the indentation flattens out at her tailbone, there's a dimple a few inches to the side, another dimple mirrored on the other side. Returning my fingertips to the channel of her spine, my pinkie grazes Traci's bikini bottom. I freeze instinctively, timid again.

"Go ahead," she whispers. "You can do what you want."

Maybe people shouldn't always do everything they want.

Instead, I rest my hand on the small of her back. We breathe as the music trudges on and on and on at 140 beats per minutes.

Nts, nts, nts, nts.

The earth revolves.

Nts, nts, nts, nts.

The sun beyond the painted-out windows fuses hydrogen into helium.

Nts, nts, nts, nts.

Six hundred and twenty million metric tons a second. More than enough energy to light the V.I.P. Lounge until the end of time. I'm distracting myself again, but not from an ache in my pants.

Gently . . .

"Who hit you, Traci?"

She takes in a deep breath and lets it out slowly as she melts against me.

"Everyone."

Motionless except for our ever-slowing breathing, we lie together through a very, very long song. Or maybe the DJ manages—or chooses—to give us the gift of melding two together without the bone-jarring transition. I always try to accept a rare moment of peace where I can find it. Maybe Traci does the same. But eventually the next song herk-a-jerks in to murder the last, and our time together has drawn to a close.

Traci lifts herself, pausing above me with her hands on my shoulders and our faces just a few inches apart.

"Thank you, James."

"Thank you . . . Traci."

She climbs off me, seemingly somewhat reluctantly—at least slowly—and holds my hand as we leave the V.I.P. Lounge.

Sam takes one look at my face and starts to laugh. At me. Savage laughter, fired at me like shotgun blasts. Sam keeps laughing until Traci, with her long and confident strides, delivers me to our original chairs.

"Mazel Tov," Sam says, punching me too hard in the shoulder.

"I'll be in the car," I blurt to Sam. To Traci, I say, "It was a pleasure to meet you, . . ." but stall out on what to call her now—what she'd want me to call her out here, exposed.

Traci says, "Likewise," before I dart down the hall, emergency exiting, and running for the safety of Sam/Karl/Whomever's car, half-blind from the sunshine, hit at once by the hot July air and the alley stench it carries with it. I jerk at the car door handle, panic that I'm locked out, then toss myself in when I gratefully discover that I've only fumbled the latch.

Fuckin' hell.

My 13-year-old brain may not be done cooking, but I have burned this course for sure, scorched it so badly I may have ruined the pan.

Jesus.

Then out of the frying pan and into the—

Cop.

The car's in shadow from the building next door, and it's darker inside the car, but with my eyes still adjusting and the sun behind him, I can only tell it's a cop approaching the car by the movement of his silhouette: the wary turns of head, the arms held wide away from the bulk of the bulletproof vest, the purposeful but unhurried pace. Well, maybe I'm not really that clever. The baton is a dead give away, even if the holster isn't. Anyway, his trajectory clearly defines me as his destination, so I

Roll. Down. My.

"Good afternoon, officer."

"What are you doing here, son?"

My eyes are getting used to light with wavelengths shorter than red's 700 nanometers, and I can see him better now that he's close and casting his own shadow on me. He's an older guy, maybe forty, a bit of gray in his sideburns and temples. What are you doing here, son? Not Is this your car, son? I can't remember the last time I felt like a regular kid—and I doubt I ever will again—but I remember where I keep the costume. If you present as pure and innocent and pious, you can get away with a lot. Or at least discourage inquiry. Works for Dad all the time. I'm kinda sorta maybe going to throw him under the bus a little bit, but fuck him.

"I'm waiting for my dad, sir."

"Your father's inside?"

"Yes, sir. Inside the club." I reach for my backpack on the floor of the backseat, saying, "It's okay, I have my homework."

What I have is:

a wet crotch I want to cover up,

a backpack full of other people's homework that I secretly correct for my Physics instructor after he makes sure I got a hundred and tells me where I should have shown more work.

And what I have done is:

Presented a solitary police officer standing alone in the parking lot of a strip club with a heroine-thin suspect making a sudden move to put his hands where the officer can't see them. Genius move on my part. To the officer's credit, he only grabs his gun; he doesn't draw it.

"Hold it," he says.

"Sorry, sir."

"Slowly. Let's see some I.D."

In for a penny, in for the pounding of a lifetime.

"My name is Paul Stockton, officer, but I don't have any I.D. because I'm only thirteen. I have some school papers with my name on them."

Some nearly spilled out when I grabbed the wrong end of the bag, so I can now make a very predictable, non-threatening move to grab with two fingers the very corner of the top sheets, mine. I put one hand on the back of the driver's seat while I hand the officer my homework, put my other hand next to the first so they're both easy to see in his peripheral vision. Quick glance at the page. He bends lower to the window to take a closer look at my face.

"Whiz kid." He takes his hand off his gun.

His name is stitched on his pocket, but not his rank. His badge number is a palindromic prime number. The patch on his shoulder reads, "Service, Pride, Dedication." Over two flags and an eagle, there's a crest with four sections filled with Seattle semiotics: three killer whales, a jet airplane, the Space Needle, and a messy squiggle which I'm pretty sure is supposed to be an old-growth cedar like the ones my grand-pappy hacked down by the quad-zillions.

"Stockton like Senator Stockton?"

"Yes, sir."

"Your father's inside?"

"Not officially."

"I suppose not."

I'm deciding whether to make up something about Papa Douche ministering to the—Mom's words—"low women" inside, when the officer actually flips to the second page of my homework. Let the silence ride.

Clipped to his epaulet—another SAT study word I can spell and define but have never heard uttered—he has a radio handset connected with a coiled wire to a transmitter unit squeezed between black leather pouches on his over-crowded belt. Motorola. I wonder how many Watts they pump out. What's the range? Do they lose signal in alleys between two brick buildings? Do they bounce it to the car first for amplification? I note the model number to check it out later.

The officer interrupts himself turning to my third page of homework when Sam comes out the back door. At some point Sam must see the police officer, but I can't discern that moment. He doesn't pause or break stride. He makes no indecisive changes of direction or speed. If he looks over here, it's a less obvious glance than the officer's observation of Sam. Other than making the necessary two turns to walk around the building through the parking lot to the sidewalk, Sam does nothing weird except check his watch.

Because we are on a schedule.

"You shouldn't be here," the officer says, handing back my homework.

"I don't have a lot of control over my life."

I take the papers, very consciously decide to return my homework to the top of the stack, casually open my backpack and put the papers inside, align them just so before zipping the zipper to close the main compartment, flip the flap over the top, clip the plastic clip on the straps that secure it, taking my time, acting casual, like when I'm waiting for everyone to leave class before me, acting normal, acting like I'm just doing what I'm doing, going about my business, until that moment that somebody might interrupt this mundane, nothing task, say, Hey, Paul, have a good weekend, or We're getting together over at Alki Beach, you should totally come. Oh, sorry, were you talking to me? Love to. That'd be great. Pardon? Sorry, officer, I didn't see you there. What can I do for you? What seems to be the problem? I'm just waiting here in the car. Is there anything else?

I stare at his radio. We can't see radio waves, but they're no different from visible light or X-rays or heat or sound. Nts, nts, nts, nts. Energy radiating. Vibration. Even matter. Everything is just nothing vibrating very fast.

Sigh.

"You'll be okay here?" he asks.

"Yes, sir. I'll be fine. Thank you, officer."

He steps back from the car, glances around the parking lot before leaving the same way Sam went. Within a few seconds of the officer reaching the sidewalk and disappearing around the building, Sam appears at the window from god knows where behind me.

"How'd you play it?"

"Waiting for dad."

"Real Dad? Nice," Sam says, and only then does he get in the car. We flip around, take the alley not the street, headed in the opposite direction from the way the cop went. "Did you get his name? Maybe we should send him a nice letter on Dad's stationary." Before I get too deep into figuring out if Sam's serious or not, about what crazy angle might exist where we curry favor with law enforcement to exploit later to our—or probably just Sam's—advantage, he says, "Lay down on the floor boards or haul your ass up front. I'm not your goddamn chauffeur."

I drag myself over the back of the seat to sit up front with Sam. And starting with the first red light, for the whole ride home I'm careful to keep my hand over my seatbelt release button.

In the neighborhood about a mile down the hill from the estate, Sam pulls into an alley and parks his secret car behind the car that we usually see him drive to and from the house. I don't ask. I'm tired. My mind is fried. Dog, Driving, DMV, Dancing. It's been a long day and I'm just glad that Dinner will be a plate in my room. Sam drives us home, parks where he always parks, out of sight behind the main garage.

"I need a shower," I say.

"You need to follow me." I don't argue. He retrieves a paper grocery sack from the trunk, the kind with handles. It's double-bagged with a third plastic bag inside and there's something bulky inside, heavy like a holiday ham. I follow Sam into the garage where he grabs a shovel. He holds the tool upright against his shoulder like he's marching with a rifle as we walk around to the backyard.

"Is Mom in her office?" Sam asks me. "Don't be obvious."

"Yeah."

If I didn't see her head pop up and swivel after us, I bet I could still feel her stare. Sam and I eventually get to the far corner of the yard where I swear Gramps planted a row of evergreens just to block our neighbors' view. Sam sets down the paper bag and makes a production of getting ready with the shovel. He puts his foot on the foot-tab thingy where your foot goes and just as he *schooks* the blade into the ground for the first time, Mom yells, "Stop!" from up by the house.

We comply, by which I mean Sam complies because he's the one digging and I'm doing nothing. I'm not even sure what's going on. But here comes Mom, so en garde.

"Act casual," Sam says. He leans on the shovel while we watch Mom charge across the lawn. Judging by velocity and arm swing, I'd say she's at about 4.1, maybe 4.2 on the Stockton Rage Scale™. Another thing I don't know is how women do that. She's wearing three- or four-inch heels but they're not slowing her down a bit.

Act casual. I act casual. I put my hands in my pockets. Where I— Pot. A hundred bucks worth of pot. Ihavemarijuanainmypocket. Be cool, man. Act fucking casual.

Mom stops far enough away from us to let her semi-shout without it seeming weird. To her. Or maybe she's staying out of Sam's shovel-swing range. Come to think of it, I should back up. I should fucking run.

"What exactly do you think you're doing?"

"Terry got loose and got hit by a car," Sam says. What the what? He picks up the grocery sack and starts to reach inside as he tilts the open end toward Mom.

"I don't need to see that," she says. Her face is already pinched and sour. If she disapproved any harder her skin might crush her skull.

I was in physics class for one hour before Sam picked me up. He's efficient and effective at executing a plan, but could he— Don't say execute.

"I'm helping Paul bury her," Sam says, setting the bag down between us, then moving it to his other side when I lean over to look. "He was really brave when we found her. Strong. I was proud of him."

Mom doesn't need to see that either. There's a cracking noise from her cranial sutures when she squints at me. "You have glitter on your face."

"Birthday party in class. I must have—"

"Not here," Mom says, turning back to Sam, turning back to the burial. "Do *that*," she says, swirling a finger in the general direction of Sam's shovel and bag of mystery, "somewhere from which you cannot see any of my windows. Understood?"

"Yes, ma'am," we say. Sam adds, "I'll find a spot by staff parking."

He's halfway through "staff" when Mom spins away from us

and starts toward the house. There's no wobbling of ankles as she strides up the gradual incline. The split knots of each calf look like an anatomical drawing intended to show how the calf muscle is actually two separate bundles.

"Mom has stripper legs," I say.

Sam snorts. "Don't make me laugh. *This*," he says, imitating Mom's swirling finger, "is a very somber occasion."

We wait to hear the door slam. We wait.

"That's not Terry," I say, willing it to be true. Sam returns the bag to the ground between us. Three bags of flour. I feel my shoulders relax, which maybe Sam knew would happen. Know what will give you away. "She could call about the birthday party."

"She won't," Sam says. "Not this week."

"I should have said 'at school' or 'in the cafeteria.' More vague. Specific but vague."

Sam confirms by not answering. Mom's up to about 4.4.

"Stripper legs," Sam says, shaking his head.

"Nts, nts, nts, nts."

4/4. Right on the next downbeat, Mom slams the door.

"And that," Sam says, "is how you not dig a hole."

She won't check behind the garage because she won't go over there, this week or ever. We could napalm any part of the yard that guests can't see from the driveway or Mom can't see from her windows and she wouldn't give a shit unless we tracked burning cinders into the house.

I say, "We should bug out before she—"

"Double time."

We break for the garage, but there's no real hurry. The staff inside will be more convenient targets than us outside. And she's got to get ready for dinner out anyway. We are on a schedule, I remember Sam saying. Now I wonder how many people We comprises. I wouldn't have guessed Mom was included. Soon enough, though, I see Sam's purpose. He doesn't turn the lights on in the garage this time, so I wait outside. But when I hear him drop the bag into the trash, I realize that if Terry had run away, Mom would never leave it alone until I found Terry and brought her back. Stocktons don't lose. Posters. Rewards. Calling shelters and vets and animal control.

But now, now I *can't* bring her back. Sam did kill my dog. Or helped me kill my own goddamn dog. Now she can be dead, but now she has to be dead. Sam makes no sound returning the unused (but highly effective) shovel to its rack before he emerges from the dark garage to stare at me, arms crossed, waiting. Have I learned a valuable lesson?

"If I become—"

"Don't say the name out loud."

"If . . . If Paul goes away," I say, feeling the regular weirdness people feel about talking about themselves in third person, but feeling more strongly the very real distance opening up between myself and myself, "then Paul has to stay away."

Sam nods.

I have learned a valuable lesson. I could get away from Mom and Dad, and Sam, too, yeah, but then I'd have to stay away—

"Even from Monique," I say.

"And school and your teachers and your scholarships. Everything dies with Paul." Sam lets that sink in for a while. "And you can't just vanish. If you're missing, they're looking. We'd need more than three sacks of flour to fake your death, Paul. I can do it without a body, but you'd need to be dead-dead. I can help you with that if the time comes, but make no mistake: it's a send-off, not a step-one. It's a one-way ticket on a solo voyage. You think you feel isolated now."

I can't believe I'm going to breathe these words, but, "Thanks for saying you'd kill me, Sam."

"Anytime," Sam says. "But think it through. All angles. For one, think about it from Monique's point of view. You kill Paul and you kill a part of Monique too."

"I hadn't—"

"That's what I figured. A big part. You starting over would be hard as fuck, so it's not a pussy way out, but it's still a real dick move."

So there it is. Faking your own death is officially a dick move. Hard to argue. Sam's not wrong. I want out so bad. So bad. But I don't want to hurt Monique. And certainly don't want to never see her again. I want what I want, but all the what's that I want can't exist at the same time. Schrödinger's cat is alive and dead at the same time until you look at it. Stockton's dog is alive and dead at the same time but I'll never see her again. I want my dog curled up under my arm when I manage to fall asleep in my bed. I want my sister to be able to sleep through the night without screaming. I want my brother at some safe distance where I can see him coming and what he's got in his hands. I want to wash the glitter off my face and the confliction off my soul.

I want, I want, I want.

Sam waves his hand in front of my face. I blink, refocus on his steady gray eyes.

"You're a weird kid, Paul."

"I know." Would it be easier if I didn't?

"Think it through. We don't have to decide anything right away."

We. "Thanks, Sam."

"I do want to move some of that money around tonight."

I nod my assent.

"Alright, kid," Sam says, walking away from me now, not toward the house, but toward his car. "Hit the showers. You smell like spunk."

I take a shower, eat a grilled-cheese sandwich with the crusts cut off, take another shower, tuck my jammied self into bed, skip my actual homework to re-read 11 pages from "Cannery Row" and skim 92 pages of "The Origin of Species," before Mom and Dad and Uncle Kenny make it back from their funddrainer dinner to begin the ritual slamming of doors. Car. House. Dens and bedrooms.

Well, you have to. The house is so big, how would you know people were home?

Monique is still out.

Charles Darwin is the single most misquoted human being ever to have eaten a banana. He never said "fittest." Not one time. Not ever. He's what non-sciencey people call longwinded. Facts, figures, data. Silly scientist, being all precise and thorough and shit for 502 pages. 'Twas Herbert Spencer, old chap, old chum, old boy, what came up with the catchy "survival of the fittest" phrase, like five years later. Good marketing. Not so great science. Fit*est*? One? How's that going to work? It's not fittest. It's fit. Just good enough to not die—if you'll excuse my split infinitive. Fit. Adequate. With the bar set that low, there's a metric ton of room on the shady side of the bell curve for some pretty savage mediocrity.

Okay, I'm an idiot. Chapter Six. "Survival of the Fittest." I was totally fucking wrong. Stick that in your pipe and—

I have pot.

Only today would I forget—twice—that I bought weed from the stinky leprechaun who lives in the bushes at my school. Out of bed! Between showers, I rinsed off the outside of the baggie and stashed it on top of one of my tall bookcases. Mom searches our rooms, but I'm pretty sure she won't stand on a wheeled chair to look up high. Retrieving it now, I can already smell the pot before I crack open the zip-lock. Funky, even without the spunky. I'll have to do something about that. Another whiff—it doesn't smell like anything else I've smelled before. Unique smell like the unique feel of Traci's—well. There's a bit of give when I gently squeeze the dense flower. Day of firsts, I needs me a pipe.

As much as I hate it here, living in a museum does mean I won't have to change out of my jimmy-jams. There are some old pipes in the Let's You Guys Build Us A Railroad exhibit down in the Minority Exploitation wing. I just need to avoid the guards.

Because I'm always very patient and careful, I wait until everyone goes to bed so I can work quietly, under the cover of darkness, with no chance of getting caught.

Right.

I leave immediately with no plan.

And as I discover when I grab a disposable lighter from the stock in the pantry—no pockets. I tuck the bic into the waistband of my tighty-whiteys. The cheap plastic sort of sticks to my skin, too, so that seems fairly secure.

I travel on, taking care not to thump when I walk, shaking no cabinets, rattling no dishes, avoiding crashing into the antique chairs and couches and statues and lamps and tables and writing desks that line the dimly-lit corridors. Don't touch that. Don't sit there. I said don't touch that. Didn't I just say—? How many times have I told you—? Actually, it'd really help me out now if they'd just gone the extra step and roped all this shit off with some red velvet barricades. I float on, treading lightly as a ghost. But I should have worn shoes, because now I'll have to circle around outside to avoid slinking past Dad's office.

But, soft! What shit from yonder doorway flows? It is my dad and uncle being pricks. They're talking to each other a way I'm sure Dad and Uncle Kenny don't usually get talked to. The tone is clear, but I have to get right up to the door before I can make out what they're saying.

Uncle Kenny yelling, something, something, "your backward goddamn state."

Dad: "Fuck you, Kenny. Shaw is your asshole," the emphasis on *your*, the contention that Shaw *is* an asshole, uncontended. "My people wouldn't have fucked this—"

A dragon bites me—head turned sideways so one row of molars lands across my mouth and one crushes down across my waistband. No, it's Sam, now simultaneously squeezing the air out of me and sealing off its escape route. He lifts me off the ground and backs us both into the shadowed alcove where he was hiding.

I stop squirming.

"Quiet?" Sam whispers in my ear, loosening his grip enough to let me nod. He sets me down.

"They know about the money," I say. I sense more than see Sam nod his head.

"What are you doing?"

"I wanted some chocolate milk. Before bed."

"Why don't I believe you?" he asks, but doesn't pursue it. "They're going to be gunning for somebody once they're done crucifying Shaw. So, put them on the defensive."

"Cut the checks?"

"Right now. Get your milk as a cover, but watch out for Mom. She's not in her study." We both listen, but there's neither yelling nor footsteps coming our way. Sam says, "Go."

I go. Stealthy, stealthy, creepy, creepy. I get my tall glass of chocolate milk, then figure out a semi-plausible path to get my other glass of chocolate milk, wink, wink. Hey, I'm wrong again. The pipes aren't Chinese; they're Inuit. That tribe's not from around Seattle. Alaska? Canada? Guess gramps did some north o' the border clear-cutting too. A little cardboard notecard next to one of the pipes reads "1885 - Qawiaraq," which I'd bet 30 beaver pelts translates to "1990 – Endangered."

Twenty-five centimeters of yellowed walrus tusk, covered with tiny black lines. Tiny stick-figure hunters shooting arrows at stick-figure reindeer. Fishermen jabbing a walrus with spears while another walrus oarf-oarfs, "Sucks to be you, dude."

Walri are not known for their compassion.

Another pipe, smaller, plainer, has a soapstone bowl and an unadorned ivory mouthpiece held on with plate copper, the hammered surface covered with a faint green patina. Its card reads "Inupiat," which I like because it has Pi in it—as does "pipe," come to think of it—and "Inupiat" without question translates to, "Steal me, Paul."

I grab the pipe.

"You really should lock this stuff up. There's kids around."

I close the case, take two steps, stop, reverse, open the case.

"Know what will give you away," I say to no one as I grab the pipe's ID card so the absence won't be so obvious and shove everything but the chocolate milk into my underwear. Oddly, not the most uncomfortable I've been today.

The pipe and the lighter stay put, and concentrating on not spilling my chocolate milk makes me move slow and easy and quietly through the house. On the meandering path back to my room, I see no one but Antonia, in the hall outside the old kitchen.

"Boa noite, Antonia."

"Boa noite, Paul. Have you seen your mother?"

"About this tall? Retractable fangs? Feeds on smoke and misery?" I don't say stripper legs.

"She look for you."

"Shit," I say, "that's not good," because, Shit, that's not good. "Did Mom? Is Marisa okay?" Since New Girl Corina's risotto was perfect last night and Marisa wasn't around to supervise my perfect grilled cheese creation, I'm thinking Marisa is gone, daddy, gone.

"She fall on all fours," Antonia says. "Is left watching the ships."

Sometimes Antonia translates her idioms directly and it's like dereferencing a null pointer; that shit just won't compile.

Well, it'll compile, but it'll segfault.

Anyway.

"Perdão?"

"I speak by the elbows," she says, which means she thinks she's said too much already. "Marisa is gone."

"Sorry."

"Is better for her."

"Is better for her," I say. "Do you think she'd take me with her?"

Antonia frowns. She looks away for a second, then shakes her head like she's decided something. "Wait. I tell you now." Antonia pushes through the swinging door into the kitchen. The door swings back and forth, obscuring and revealing the kitchen like a slow camera shutter. Antonia in the kitchen. Empty kitchen. Antonia in the kitchen again, hands full. Antonia in the hall with the door settling behind her. She holds out a dustpan and a small, hand-held whiskbroom.

"She say you must do it."

"Okay." I accept the dustpan and broom, tucking the pan under my arm on the chocolate milk side and lifting the broom's bristle end up to my face. I don't know what the fibers are, but they're the stiff, old-school natural stuff like a witch's broom and they smell like a corn-maze I went to out in Carnation a few years ago. The maze was a total dud—simple right-hand rule wall-follower solution—but the field of stripped stalks, post-harvest, smelled great. I ask Antonia, "What am I supposed to do with this?"

"I speak by the—"

"Speak by the elbows. Yeah, okay. Boa noite, Antonia."

Antonia shakes her head. I touch the broom to my eyebrow to salute her, raise my glass toasty cheery style, then mosey on down the hallway.

Monique's car still isn't here. Her door's not locked or chair-braced or roped off, and she's not in her room.

But somebody's in mine. There's a giant thud on Monique's ceiling, accompanied by a crash of breaking glass. Like if you dropped a computer monitor on its face on my hardwood floor. And then another. And then another. And then another. I only have four monitors, so—crash. Oh, the old, one-piece original Macintosh.

Got to be Mom.

"Enjoy your retribution," I whisper. Everything goes better with chocolate milk.

A hollow metallic clang like you tossed a desktop computer onto a pile of busted monitors. And another. And a tower case. And another.

I chug my chocolate milk as I cross to Monique's window, leave the glass next to another empty on the windowsill outside. When did I leave that there? Whatever.

I'm guessing it's my laser printer that slams into the accumulating pile of debris as I tuck the dustpan into my T-shirt, followed by the heavier, dot-matrix printer when I position the whiskbroom in the cavity of the pan. I try to secure everything by tucking my shirt into my PJ bottoms, but the elastic isn't tight enough. I don't want to mess with the lighter and pipe in the waistband of my underwear, so instead I put the broom and pan against my chest on the outside of my shirt, bring the front hem up and hold that with my teeth while I climb out and climb up to my room, careful to avoid being illuminated by the light from my window.

A keyboard lets loose a spray of pieces upon impact, individual keys ricocheting around the room and scattering across the floor. I put the soon-to-be-rather-useful cleaning equipment on the roof between my dormer windows, then crouch on the window-ledge to peek my head around just as—Yep—Mom whacks another keyboard on the corner of an upturned CPU case. Another splash of keys. She raises the same keyboard again, the empty sockets in the frame looking like bites taken out of corn on the cob. She brings it down again, the cord whipping around following the same arc before it hits. Mom discards that in a crevice between monitor hulls before subjecting my flatbed scanner to the same corner.

Good times.

I doubt she knows she'd cut her hand if she tried to break a loose motherboard over her knee, or maybe she just doesn't want to mess up her clothes. She pauses (Checking for dust? As if.) before she bends to arm-sweep the table full of parts and components onto the heap of broken electronics. She snatches the modem off my desk, the power cord jerking out of the chassis when the cord reaches its limit. Maybe there's something wrong with me, but I think it's funny that the Ethernet cable is still plugged in to both the modem and the banged up computer at the bottom of the pile, like there's some signal passing through the dull gray cable. Hang on, little buddy. It'll all be over soon. She hucks the modem onto the pile and the funny part is definitely over.

My telescope.

A gift from Monique on my first rotten-teenager birthday.

Deep in the other dormer now, all I can see of Mom's wrestling match with my Celestron is her heels and the tripod's three rubber feet, spread wide in a defensive stance. The struggle lasts only a few seconds before it's confirmed that Stocktons don't lose. The empty, defeated tripod collapses on the floor while 23 pounds of precision-ground lenses and mirrors takes to the air, the short, fat tube of the C8 merely an orange blur until it embeds in the accumulated mountain of trash.

One boy's treasure is that same boy's trash once his mom is done with it.

The C8s are pretty tough, so there's a slight chance, a very slight—Nope. Mom snatches the tripod off the floor, snaps its three legs together into a single spike. The telescope's one 8" eye happens to be angled up at her, staring Mom down as she approaches, or looking for mercy. There's none to be had. She reels back and stabs my telescope like she's spearing a walrus.

"Sucks to be you," I whisper.

And that is that. She brushes off her jacket sleeves, straightens her skirt, and pulls out a compact to check her hair. Hmm. A compact would be good for looking into my room from out here on the roof.

Or for looking on top of my bookcases where the pot is.

Shit. Shitshitshitshitshit.

I might have to head her off.

Keeping my gaze on Mom and my head still so as not to attract attention with movement, I pull the lighter and pipe out of my underwear by feel and put them on the roof next to the dustpan and broom. Thankfully, the pitch here is slight: thirty degrees. In good weather it's actually kind of a great place to sit and watch the sun set. The bowl of the pipe stops it from rolling on the incline. I brace the lighter against it on the uphill side, eyes on Mom the whole time.

Don't see me. Don't look up high.

Focused on herself in the tiny mirror, Mom turns her head side to side. She makes no adjustments.

She glances around my room.

Don't see me. Don't look up high.

If she turns away from the window to check the jackpot bookcase in the corner, I might be able to hop in. I was hiding under the bed. I thought you were Uncle Kenny.

Don't see me. Don't look up high.

Finally, finding nothing needing snooping, nothing else to smash in misdirected retribution, and satisfied that she's looked good doing it, Mom snaps the compact closed and tucks it into her skirt pocket.

Silence.

Hands on hips with elbows out.

A satisfied, content look on her face. The buzz of abuse.

Silence.

Panic ebbing, fear receding, a wave of anger washes over me. I want to jump into the room and do something awful to her. Sam-level awful. But realistically, I think the worst I can do to her right now is rob her of the chance to deliver whatever bullshit "for your own good" lecture she's got loaded, deny her the pleasure of watching my face while I stand there and take it.

I stay put.

From the same pocket where her compact lives, Mom retrieves something else and places it on the edge of my desk. Small, flat, rectangular. She tugs once on the bottom of her jacket before leaving my room, killing the lights as she exits. I give her a solid hundred count before I grab the dustpan and broom and climb into my room. I sweep a little clean space to place one bare foot, sweep the next and repeat my way across to my closet so I can put on some shoes. Then, crunching glass and bits of brittle plastic as I cross first to the light switch then to my desk, I find that what Mom left for me is a platinum visa card. The Post-it stuck to the back, written before she came to my room, reads "one replacement," with one underlined.

Well, then, that makes it all okay, then, doesn't it?

Such a giving person.

Before I do anything else, I grab an old tube sock, stuff the pot and pipe and lighter inside, and stash the rig outside, triple thumbtacked up under the eave of one dormer window.

Okay.

Jesus.

Okay.

Mom isn't dumb, but she's ignorant, at least about destroying computers. I can probably salvage a bunch of parts from the CPUs. So those I stack on my newly-tidied work table for review later. The monitors are fucked, for sure. Hard to argue with broken glass. But because a cathode ray tube needs a vacuum to operate, they've actually sucked up most of their own tiny glass shards and dust when they tried to implode. Silver lining? Not so much. The CRT funnels around the electron guns are lined with lead, ionized and vaporized into the void over time by heat and emissions and now released to float free in the air. That's got to be good for my growing brain, too. Thanks, Mom.

I cover the cracks with masking tape and line up the monitors by my door. Technically, they're hazardous waste, so I can't just toss them in the dumpster in the garage, but that's exactly my plan. Until I think it through that the lead will get in somebody's water and that's shitty and some rules are good rules and that I can probably just call somebody to come pick them up and dispose of them properly and I can pay for all that with Mom's visa card so that's what I'll do. For now, though, they can slump against the wall like so many political prisoners, while the firing squad is off smoking cigarettes and joking awkwardly about who had real bullets and who fired blanks.

About *whom* had real bullets?

Could you second-guess yourself more, Paul?

Thanks for that, too, Mom.

I whisk, whisk, sweep, sweep, and clean the floor as I gradually make a pile of collected keyboard letters on my desk, assembling one set in QWERTY formation, arranging the second in DVORAK. But when I'm done dumping glass and plastic scraps into my bathroom wastebasket, and have picked all the glass out of the soles of my Chuck Taylors, I still don't have all the little plastic tiles. I'm missing a Z and an F2, but more importantly, somewhere under the bed or couch or easy chair or behind my dresser there's a lonely little horseshoe letter U hiding out, because using both sets, I'm still one letter short for

F_CK YOU MOM

and have to settle for

I HATE YOU MOM

which really doesn't seem like quite enough, until I figure out I can add

N DAD

But a surge of fear makes me scramble the tiles, re-collecting them into a single random pile.

Hmm. I could make fairly excellent passwords by picking loose letters from a fish bowl, bingo ball style. But my passwords are already unnecessarily robust, so never mind.

I climb down to Monique's room to see if vacuuming would bug her, but she's still not home.

I climb back up, grab my vacuum from the closet down the hall, vacuum my room just to be safe, return the vacuum, say vacuum out loud for no reason, climb down to check for Monique—Nope.—climb back up to my window but instead sit myself down on the roof between the dormers under the cold something of space. I forget the word.

The roof is warm through my pajama bottoms. Hey, what's this thumbtacked up under my eave? I sort of shred the sock unsticking it from the wood. I'll have to come up with a better storage solution.

Launching a projectile at 45 degrees from horizontal maximizes the distance it will travel over level ground, with $\sin(2\theta)$ reducing to 1 and the equation simplifying to $d = v^2/g$.

Loading a pipe is not rocket science. The only mistake I make is almost setting my bangs on fire with the lighter. Head held high and proud, I inhale gently, take the smoke deep into my lungs and hold my breath. In the afterschool specials that teach us how to do everything we're not supposed to do, the kids usually cough up a storm the first time they light up. I guess years of breathing Mom's second-hand smoke is finally paying off. So, Mom, really, thank you for that.

Wash, rinse, repeat. I exhaust the combustibles in the pipe's gumball-sized bowl. Nothing. I'm a tiny bit light-headed from repeatedly holding my breath, but otherwise nada. I knock the ashes into the copper gutter—checking first for dry leaves and pine needles because as much as I'd like to burn this place to the ground, that's not such a good idea. Well, it's a great idea, but when I leave here I don't want to go straight to prison.

Bowl two: spark, burn, hold.

Nothing.

Mari-what-the-hell?

Mari-where's-the-escapist-disconnected-from-reality-part?

Mari-why-aren't-I-blissfully-unaware-of-my-surroundings?

No, marijuana, I'm not mad at you. I'm just disappointed. We were all hoping you'd choose to be part of the solution.

Thumbtacking the kit back in place, I figure I won't have to come up with a better way to hide this stuff after all. I lie back on the roof and look up at the night sky. Light that left Proxima Centauri when I was 9 years old hits my 13-year-old retinas. Tucked down where I am in the canyon between the dormers, I can block out the moon, but I can't see all of the vast Andromeda Constellation. I look back in time to see what Alpha Andromedae looked like in 1893 and what M31 was up to when Homo Habilis picked up the first stone tool, circa Par-tay Tuesday 2.5 million B.C.

That's some old light.

That has experienced no passage of time since leaving its creator star.

An ancient photon lands on my retina. An electron absorbs its energy to jump up a shell, causing the excitation of a chemical compound in a rod or cone, which in turn reacts to generate an electro-chemical signal that travels along my optic nerve to my brain, where my mind creates images that are everything we see, but which are really just constructs that have precious little to do with what's actually out there in the universe.

If we changed those chemicals, could we see light outside the visible spectrum? We'd need special glasses to physically focus the longer wavelengths through a lens system not evolved to see heat. Provided proper prisms, though . . . I bet we could pop a pill, throw on some Coke-bottle glasses and become night-vision ninjas. Different pill, different chemical sensitivity, and we could see all the invisible ultraviolet patterns that flowers evolved to entice the bumble-birds and humming-bees.

Bee goggles.

Oh, hello, pot. You kind of sneaked up on me there, didn't you?

I should be used to being sneaked up on, with Sam—

Shit, I have to get online to push those checks out in Turks and Caicos to make it look like Uncle Kenny's screwing Dad and Dad's screwing Uncle Kenny. I'm off the roof and back in my room before I wonder if I should be worried about being careful getting off the roof and back in my room.

To have an operable keyboard, you don't really need the plastic keys, just make connections by pressing down on the membrane underneath. Well, okay, that membrane's partly torn on one keyboard. But, cool, the other chewed-up corncob of empty sockets looks good. I plug that and a mouse into a loose motherboard that has a good shot of being viable, add an I/O card for Ethernet, slip in a video card with a regular RCA TV out, yellow plug yellow plug to cable that to my (unscathed!?!?!?!?) television, power the motherboard from an otherwise empty case, juice the case from the wall, affix modem, insert tab A into slot B. The pot is making me think really, really, really fast. Faster than usual, even. After what feels like five hours but has actually only been about a dozen or so minutes, I have Frankensteined together my very own ugly-but-thoughtful computer monster.

"Please do as you're told," I say as I turn it on. "Asked. Please."

Worst case, I could get Sam to drive me to a computer lab at U-dub, or Monique when she gets home, or I could maybe try to drive myself over there. U-dub. U. I could steal a giant U from one of the University of Washington signs. Ohhhh, all giant letters.

YOU STIN_ MA.

YOU FRIGHTEN WINOS.

U R TINY SHIT.

U SWINE R TINY SHIT.

U GOOFS—

The computer boots up. "It's alive!"

Using this as a dumb terminal again, I really don't need much on this end to connect to— And connect through to— And I've already got everything preset to— Done. Done and Done. As I disconnect and shut down The Incriminator 6000™, two suspicious checks are queued to print half an hour after the banks open in Turks and Caicos, starting good people looking for bad people up to no good.

Now I should dismantle my monster in case Mom comes back, but first, since Mom never really leaves, I'm not going to keep anything important in my room anymore. No data on a hard drive, no projects, no programs.

Won't be keeping your dog here any more, either.

Shit, that's a shitty thing to say. Why do I do that to myself?

I shank all the hard drives out of the busted machines, slave them to my new monster, and make sure I've got everything I had before. I'm a lucky boy. And because I'm also a sneaky boy, I've already got a bunch of places on offsite servers where I can stash my stuff so nobody will ever find it. Mainframes are more fun to play on anyway. Ten hours or two dozen or so minutes later, I've got multiple backups streaming away to the safety of away-from-home.

It's on autopilot, and I've got an auto-correcting auto-co-pilot watching, too, so now I have nothing to do. I tap my fingers on my desk like when I'm waiting for some system query to come back that I don't think should be taking as long as it's taking. I'm antsy. But I should stay put. I should really just sit here and stay out of troub—

I return the whisk and dustpan and get another glass of chocolate milk.

I really, really should just sit here and—

I should take the monitors down to the trash.

"Wait here," I tell my glass of chocolate milk.

I grab a busted monitor and head out, humming the Mission Impossible theme. And I quickly figure out that I don't know very much of the Mission Impossible theme. Once I get to past the doodle-doo, doodle-dooooo part, I kind of have to just start over. That's gotten old before I'm back in the house after dropping off the first monitor. So, for the second, third and fourth monitors, I do it once in the hall and call that good, warning my milk to behave before each departure.

"I'm watching you."

"Don't try anything stupid."

"You're just going to make it harder on yourself."

Which may actually be what's happening. Down the driveway, the gate opens as I carry the last monitor across the turn-around circle. The driveway is long, but not so long that I'd have time to go hide behind the garage or to run back into the house. I freeze. Well, that's a lie. I stop. Then I twist and jerk and generally spaz around trying to decide which way to go, ultimately going nowhere. But, maybe they won't notice a six-foot dork in stripey pajamas breakdancing in the middle of the driveway with a busted monitor clutched to his chest.

## Chapter 17: Who Goes There?

The car kills its headlights as it pulls through the gate, idles up the drive toward where I'm standing traffic-cone style in the middle of the lane. I either manage to stand still or fail to move. As the car drifts past me, Monique waves, frowns at the broken monitor in my arms. I follow her to the garage and dump it with the others next to the Dumpster as Monique shuts off her engine. Coming around the back of the other vehicles, I wait by the big open door until she steps out of her car.

"Mom trashed my room."

"Nighttime voice, Hon," she says, barely above a whisper.

"Yeah. Sorry. Your room's fine. She smashed up all my computers. I built one though, from parts, so we could do that thing with those guys and that stuff at that place? Sam said go ahead, so I did it. It's done. I can't undo it."

"You, my friend," she says, reaching back into the car to retrieve her purse and a crinkly, medium-sized paper bag that almost certainly contains no part of my dog, "have had too much chocolate milk." Instead of slamming the car door, Monique pushes it most of the way closed, then bumps it with her hip. She leaves the big garage door open, too, when we step onto the driveway. There's more light here, which we duck out of almost immediately.

"You got your hair cut," I say. A trim.

"Just a couple of inches," she says, handing me the paper sack.

"Looks good."

"Thank you," Monique says. She'd paused at the appropriate distance, but now one moonlit eyebrow twitches and she leans in close and smells me. "Where else did Sam take you today?"

"You don't want to know."

"You should take a shower."

"I have the stink?"

"You don't want Mom smelling you smelling like that."

Mari-what-you-been-smokin'?

"Okay. Is this . . ." I ask, redirecting our attention to the bag of at most a single pound of flour, opening the sack and knowing the smell before she says—

"Artisanal—"

"Mac and cheese! Yum. Capital Grille. Did you have a date?"

"Mmm. Business meeting," she says, which explains the crisply pleated pantsuit—dark blue or black, it's too dark out here to tell.

"Gracias," I say.

"De nada."

We hug the shadows around the outside of the house, sneak up the back stairs and head straight for my room, Monique depositing her purse on my bed and her person in my easy chair on the far side by the window.

"This town is hell on shoes," Monique says, kicking off her heels. I see now that they and her suit are black like her hair, her blouse French blue. "The rain ruins flats and the hills destroy heels." She stretches her legs out straight in front of her, wriggling her toes and gripping at the empty air. Monique has stripper legs. Yoga legs? Legs that I can say, respectfully, and without it being weird despite her being my sister, that guys not related to her would find sexy.

And one creepy guy who married our Mom's sister.

Monique's shoes dropping on the hardwood make me wonder, "Do I thump on your ceiling?"

"I like knowing you're there." She takes off her jacket and lays it on my bed. While she's twisted sideways in the chair, she pokes the spines of the closest stack of books on my nightstand. "Great, great, boring, great, overrated despite being great, tech—" meaning she's not going to read it—"tech, fair, great, tech, meh, great, super great, tech."

There's a plastic fork in the bag with the food. I dig in to my mac and cheese. My computer minions have finished secreting away all my important files, so now, apart from my sister, everything I care about is outside this house. In search of something she hasn't read, Monique gets up to pad across my room in bare feet.

"I got all the glass," I say, my mouth still not just full, but overfull. I'd be unintelligible to anyone but Monique.

"I know," she says. "So, how'd it go at the Department of Licensing?"

"Sam has another car."

"Sam has a lot of cars. Drinbell?" she asks.

"Yeah. I passed. Sam cut my fingerprint. On my thumb. With a razor blade." When Monique turns to look, I hold up my thumb and wag the first knuckle. She turns back to the bookcase.

"He wouldn't prep until you asked yourself. I had an adhesive rubber film." Monique wags her thumb at me the same way without turning around. "Gwendolyn Elizabeth Nielson," she says. "Everybody's middle name was Elizabeth in 1970."

"Especially the girls."

Monique snorts. Then she glances where my telescope used to be and says, "Hey, where's your— That fucking bitch."

Monique shakes her head and turns back to the bookcases. She pulls out a book, flips to the first page before snapping it closed and sliding it back into its vacant slot.

$1990 - 1970 = 20$ now $= 18$ two years ago. G. Elizabeth N. would have been 18 two years ago when Monique was 16 going on 40. She could have—Two years ago, she could have gotten out.

"Why didn't you leave," I ask. Monique doesn't answer. She tugs a book to a 45-degree angle, shoves it back. "I can keep a secret," I say. Nothing. I add, "It's kind of a Stockton family superpower." Monique continues poking and fondling book spines, but when she tilts down the same book, I can tell she's not reading titles any more. "Monique?" Her hands stop moving, but she doesn't turn around.

"You were eleven." Monique finally turns around, her eyes hard, but glistening. "You were eleven."

"Did you get into Stanford?"

"I'm going to U-dub."

"But you got into Stanford." Stare. Stare, stare, stare. "Didn't you?"

"Don't."

"Are you not going away to—"

"Paul, don't."

—"a much, much better school because—"

"Please." Streaks are forming on the front of Monique's shirt, dark, whatever color French blue silk is when it's wet. "Don't."

I get out of my chair and go into my bathroom for a box of Kleenex. On the way out, I catch myself in the mirror. I don't look 13 or 18; I look 1,000. There are streaks on my shirt too that I could not have told you were there. But I walk over to Monique and hand her the box of tissues.

"Thank you," she says, her voice quiet.

"Thank you," I say, my voice quiet. "Thanks for not killing my sister."

When eventually I can turn away, my gaze tracks across the shelf of books. We've both reread last year's *Seven Habits of Highly Successful People*, looking for a way that Win-Win can exist when winning means the abject destruction of your foe. But this . . . I pull down a corner to tilt out Tufte's brand new *Envisioning Information*.

"Lots of pretty pictures. No politics." I leave the book tilted and head for the bathroom, adding before I close the door, "Nobody dies."

We have an industrial water heater like at a hotel and it takes a really, really long time before we run out of hot water. I'm full-on pruney before I get out. Monique's asleep in my easy chair with the book lying open across her chest. I grab the blankie off the back of my couch to lay over Monique. Blanket, man-boy, blanket. I cover her feet and legs, drape her torso, and start to pull the hem up around her shoulders when Monique's eyes pop open, her hand shoots out, and the blade of her stiletto catches the quickest glint of light before disappearing under my chin.

I freeze.

Monique blinks, then retracts the blade as she pulls her hand away.

We both say, "Sorry," at the same time.

She closes her eyes and tugs the blanket up under her chin. I go to my desk to curl up in some remote server. I have a quick debate with myself (Do you think— No.) about going out on the roof again, but soon enough everything is quiet and I'm snuggled in here, my mind far, far away, and finally throttling down after the weirdest fucking day in a lifetime of weird days.

I doze along. My hair is still damp when I first scratch my head. My hair is dry when I rub my temples and my eyes. All the while, the earth hums through space, turning slowly on the tilted axis that this time of year leans the northern hemisphere toward the sun that holds us captive. In the wee hours now in Seattle, it's technically Independence Day, the $4^{th}$ of July. Still the $3^{rd}$ in Honolulu. On another island on the other side of the globe, it's been the $4^{th}$ for a while now, but the banks won't be closed today in Turks and Caicos.

I want to break in and take a quick look to see what's happening there, but that's not the best idea. I'm congratulating myself on my own self-control, when I have to cut myself short because I do it in spite of myself. Sigh. Anyway. Good. The transactions are flagged. Investigations are underway, with the proper authorities, not with robber barren rulers Dad and Uncle Kenny, who— Speak of the devil.

My doorknob jiggles and begins to turn slowly. The knob stops turning and the door creeps inward, at least until it clears the jamb. When it'd be clear that my lights are on, the door swings open like it would if a normal person opened it. But it's the opposite of a normal person. It's Uncle Kenny, standing in my doorway wearing sneakers (appropriate) and shiny matching sweatpants and zip-up sweatshirt (questionably appropriate, depending on intent. He's still maintaining his you-can-believe-I-played-football-in-college physique, but I don't think he really runs much any more with the limp and all. But, the baggy pants have an elastic waistband.)

"Lose something, Uncle Kenny?" I ask loud enough to wake

Monique, who's already awake—and armed. So serving that purpose was moot, but I've inadvertently served another. I don't realize until Uncle Kenny does a little double-take at me and my TV-as-computer-monitor that "lose something" could also mean the money that he has actually lost, or has had misplaced on his behalf, by me. Whoops. Know what will give you away *before* it gives you away. I stoneface in time to hide my noticing him noticing.

"Looking for me?" I ask. "You were awful quiet. Didn't want to wake me?"

"Good evening, Paul."

"It's night. It's after midnight. It's night."

"Past your bedtime, I'd imagine." I don't have a bedtime. I don't have a curfew. A standard rule would rob Mom of too many opportunities to tell me what to do. Uncle Kenny shifts his gaze from me to Monique. "You should be in bed."

"A lot of people aren't where they should be," Monique says. She's still leaned back in my easy chair, but now she's pressing her open book across her chest. At some point while I was zoned out before Uncle Kenny arrived, Monique must have tossed the blanket on the bed. (My AC doesn't work as well as hers.) Her right arm outstretched, she's lain her hand palm up on my nightstand, her stiletto held in a relaxed grip. The blade glints in the lamplight when she schoooks it out from the handle.

Uncle Kenny looks from Monique's face to the knife and back to Monique's face. Then he shifts his gaze somewhere that makes me want to hand Monique another book. Uncle Kenny licks his lips. Monique slides in the chair to sit up straight.

"Water," I say. "You need water for your run." I pick up the phone and dial. "I don't think Monique's going to join you on your moonlit stroll, but you'd better stay hydrated. I'll have the staff get you some."

I dial Antonia's number as Uncle Kenny says, "That's not necessary."

"Hi, Antonia. Sorry to wake you. Could you bring up a couple of bottles of water for Uncle Kenny? He's in my room with Monique. Yes. Actually, send Marisa. She's already fired."

I watch the gears turn behind Uncle Kenny's humanoid mask. Fired means Marisa's super pissed off about all things Stockton and waaay less inclined to keep quiet about shit she's seen.

"Abrigada," I say to Antonia, which means 'thank you,' but only if I'm a girl. "Abrigado." Boys say 'abrigado.' It's hard to learn when no one ever corrects you.

Which may be why Uncle Kenny keeps trying to rape my sister.

"Two minutes. Have a seat," I say, pointing to my couch but hoping he'll stay standing because he won't want to take an order. That works, but probably only because he wants to move around my bed to get closer to Monique. When Uncle Kenny gets to the foot of my bed, Monique drops the book, plants her feet squarely on the floor. She's still seated, but not much weight is on the chair. The plastic fork I ate the mac and cheese with won't do us much good. I wonder how fast I could get to my toilet lid, and if I could lift it. Monique's ready to spring the second he comes around the corner. And that's where he stops.

As she stands up, Monique asks him, "How's the knee?" She's got her left foot forward and her left hand slightly raised, the knife back by her right hip, protected, her stance like I've seen Sam stand when he practices kicks in the backyard.

Uncle Kenny doesn't answer. He purses his lips like he's licking them without opening his mouth. He looks Monique up and down. His gaze lingers where it shouldn't linger. Monique's chest rises and falls with each purposeful breath. Uncle Kenny's mouth stops contorting when his lips come to rest in a grin—half excited, half satisfied, fully evil.

Then he leaves. He doesn't say anything, doesn't nod, doesn't gesture. He just turns and walks out the door, closing it behind him like just another day at the office.

Monique clicks the blade of her stiletto back into its handle and collapses into the easy chair. She let's out a giant sigh and says, "Fuckin' hell." I don't know what to say. Monique turns away and stares for a while out the open window to her left. She turns back and says, "Thanks for calling the cavalry, Paul. That was quick thinking."

"Should I get Sam? I think Sam has guns." I know Sam has guns. I'm pretty sure he's not old enough, but, well, Sam. Either way, I don't want to be pushy about it. Monique ignores the offer, or rather responds instead to the implications. Maybe just the situation in general.

"I might have to kill him."

That hangs there in the room long past when one of us should have objected.

"Do it soon," I say. "Midnight tomorrow you'd be tried as an adult."

Monique snorts another laugh and her eyebrows cycle once up and down as she shakes her head. She uses her pinkies to pull her hair behind her ears, then relaxes into the chair, laying her head back against the cushion. Then, looking at me again, her bright-blue eyes well with tears and a deep sadness—a mourning—washes over her face.

"What?" I ask.

She smiles, pauses, but just shakes her head. "Nothing."

"Something."

"Nothing I can change."

It's quiet. Monique turns and looks out the window. I look out the window.

From my vantage at my desk I can only see the black silhouette of treetops against the near-black blue of the night sky. The occasional porch or streetlight sparks in the dark blankie of trees as they shift in the gentle breeze. Above them, stars in the endless field of sky.

From her angle and with her wider view closer to the window, Monique would see the moon setting over the city, the Seattle skyline full of brightly lit empty offices. I've often sat where she's sitting and tried to find patterns in the lighted windows—codes, sequences, some meaning from the strings of Off or On, Zero or One, Dark or Light. But no matter how long I look or how hard I try, like so much of the rest of my life, nothing ever adds up to make any sense.

Suddenly three things happen at once: There's a quick rap-rap on the door, the door opens, and Antonia says, "Mr. Paul?" She actually steps back with her armload of bottled water, making room in the doorway for Xerxes, our hard-to-read but also rather sizable chauffeur. His reason for being here would not be lost on Uncle Kenny if he hadn't already made his escape.

Xerxes looks around the room, looks left into my empty bathroom, and asks, "Is Okay?"

Not really. Not as bad as it could be. Not as bad as it probably will be again soon. But I guess, now, for the moment, is okay.

We celebrate Independence Day as slaves and puppets and props.

We're in the limos before dawn to get to the outskirts of nowhere for a Boy Scout pancake breakfast, followed by a Kiwanis pancake breakfast, followed by a Rotary Club pancake breakfast. At each successive location, we're allowed to eat no pancakes and succeed only in circling around closer to the official middle o' nowhere. Money can't do everything. There are a lot of votes you buy with your face, thus our being invitold to participate. Speeches happen, but there's a laugh-clap-laugh-clap-cheer rhythm that's easy to pick up on so we don't really have to listen. And Mom leaves us alone if we keep smiling and remember where we are and who's paying for our uneaten pancakes when we spout our lines to the press.

"[This event's sponsor] has long been an important partner in serving [town's] community."

"[This event's sponsor] has long been an important partner in serving [town's] community."

"[This event's sponsor] has long been an important partner in serving [town's] community."

It's an honor to be (for ten minutes each) at the breakfasts that become brunches that become early lunches that become lunches. Some of the local sponsors repeat. Dad and Uncle Kenny change shirts every two hours. Mom's clothes wouldn't dare wrinkle. Every time Uncle Kenny slimes by, Monique smiles brightly and stabs him in the tricep with a giant corsage pin. Deeply. Rapidly and repeatedly. She has spares. By the time we're eating catered lunches in the cars, he's stopped flinching, but also stopped "checking in on you kids."

Fortunately, as lunches become late lunches become afternoon barbeques, as we get closer to dinner and closer to home, the events and dignitaries get more important and we kids get pushed deeper into the background. No more microphones get shoved in our faces and we're farther and farther from the podiums and centers of pictures. By 5:30, we've exhausted our usefulness and been jettisoned from the motorcade entirely.

Sam vanishes as soon as we're home. Monique checks her watch, then makes me the pancakes I've been craving all day before she vanishes too. I've probably got a good five hours before Mom and Dad and Uncle Kenny get home. I hook up my TV for a sec to quadruple-check on the vanished money, and spend the rest of the time unwinding on my roof making a bunch of pot vanish and reading until I lose the light.

The nearly full moon rises a minute before 7:00 p.m. The sun sets nine minutes after 9:00. With equally predictable disregard for the show's advertised start times, fireworks erupt all around me. Elliot Bay, Seattle Center, Gas Works Park to the west. Kirkland, Bellevue and Sammamish across Lake Washington to the east. Mercer Island to the south. Like thunder and lightning, I count seconds after the flashes to see how far away they are. Observations match known data. The world makes sense. I know little enough about the chemistry of metallic salts to let the fireworks just be fireworks. The air is warm, the night is clear, the sky is alive with color and all is right with the universe.

Until Monique screams.

## CHAPTER 19: WHAT GOES UP

I'd swear the scream came from off the right, not down in Monique's— She's in the attic next to my room. I'm on my feet before I know it, gripping the dormer and spinning my semi-disembodied body around to hop back in through my window. No. The stairs to the attic are at the far end of this wing. There's no door from my hallway on this floor. I'd have to head the wrong way, go down a flight, run back across the whole wing before I'd get to—

Monique shrieks again, angry, scared.

I bolt along the ledge, trying not to think about how high I am. Stoned, yes—high as fuck—but I mean like up high above the ground. Three stories if you hit the patio. More if you miss and catch the hill. Before that can psych me out, I get past my other dormer, past the chimney and find the first attic window. I yank it open and drop into the attic with a dusty thud, putting my foot straight through the rotted cane seat of an ancient chair, and crashing sideways into another old chair, starting it rocking, none of which does anything to help my sister. The back of the rocking chair tinks into the corner of a small wire birdcage hanging from a rafter, sending it spinning on its chain. I get to my feet. Get my bearings.

Monique grunts. They're in the next dormer alcove.

I hop my leg free of the chair frame, circle one-eighty around the mound of old crap piled against the wall and find Uncle Kenny holding Monique's right hand twisted behind her back, pressing her legs against an old dresser. His left fist is full of her hair, and he's got her head cranked back, stretching her neck and keeping her off balance and under his control.

Stuck in a rafter above their heads, Monique's knife reflects the popping oranges and red of the exploding sky outside the window behind them. I can't tell if anyone's cut, but he somehow got it away from her.

"Have a seat, Paul," says Uncle Kenny. "I don't mind an audience." He yanks Monique's head back to look at her face. "You don't mind if Paul watches, do you, sweetheart?"

"Fuck you."

"Precisely the idea, my dear little girl."

Torqueing her neck and twisting her arm, Uncle Kenny pushes her face down, forcing her to bend at the waist, bending her over the dresser. He drops his upper body on her arm, pinning it with his body weight so he can seize her flailing left arm. He's stronger than Monique—probably stronger than both of us put together—and he muscles her other arm behind her back too, tucking it underneath him, crushing his weight down on top of her. All that takes half a second. And now his left hand is free. Monique squirms and kicks as he reaches for the front of her jeans, but he's quick and they're undone and down to mid-thigh in another split second.

I start toward him, but he stops me ten feet back with a quick, "Eh!" and a glance at the knife still stuck in the rafter above his head, clearly within his reach. Not within mine. Not within Monique's.

Uncle Kenny lets Monique up just enough to reach around and grope her breast.

"Titties came in nice."

I lunge forward, but stop again when Uncle Kenny yanks the knife out of the rafter, straightening his arm like a fencer, pointing the stiletto at my chest across the open space between us. He holds the blade motionless. I step toward him, one step, two, closing the distance from eight feet to six. But I freeze when he lowers the blade to Monique's face.

I feel my weight shift from the balls of my feet, sink back onto my heels.

"There's a good boy."

Uncle Kenny slowly draws the knife away from Monique's

face, angles it my way for three pounding heartbeats, then stabs the blade into the wooden beam above their heads. A sickening thud when the tearing fibers absorb the force and the blade can't sink any deeper. Outside, heavy, resonant thumps of fireworks exploding, the violent power muffled at a distance.

"Do you want to jerk off while I fuck your sister? This won't take long. This one is so tight." He draws out the 'so' as he brushes the hair off her face. The fury in Monique's eyes. "Not as tight as she used to be," he says, reaching for his own zipper now, "But so—"

I'm running. Hard. Directly at Uncle Kenny. Sam's voice in my head—"Hit him low." And I do. As he straightens to reach for Monique's knife, pulling away from her, I ram my shoulder into him, hitting below his waist, below his center of gravity, lifting with all my might, charging, pushing, driving, to get us up and over the windowsill, through the glass and out.

But it doesn't work. I'm not heavy enough, or fast enough, or whatever enough, and I misjudge the angle, too, and drive us not out into the fiery red sky but into the hard edge of the window frame. One pane of glass breaks from my elbow or Uncle Kenny's elbow or who knows, but that's it. All I've done is break one pane of glass. And my collarbone. The ragged ends grind together, a mortar-and-pestle sound conducting through my body. Failure. Wreckage and failure.

Ah, but Monique.

Monique.

As I twist away from Uncle Kenny and drop on my ass with my back against the wall below the window, Monique is in his face with the stiletto. Well, she's on the way to his face by way of his larynx, the edge of the blade across his carotid and there's no way she's losing the knife again.

"One word, you die," she says. "Move anything, you die." To his credit, he doesn't jerk forward onto the blade when she knees him in the groin. Twice. She says, "Take it," the third time her knee comes up to his balls. And the fourth. And the fifth. He has his head back and his eyes closed. He grunts, clearly not in pleasure, and does as he's told.

For the even half-dozen, Monique steps back, says, "Take it, you little bitch," and wails one hell of a kick squarely into Uncle Kenny's nuts. His eyes open and immediately roll back in his head. He collapses onto all fours. Monique bends over him to put one hand in his hair and lay the blade across his neck again.

"So good," she says, drawing out the "so."

Monique seems to be elsewhere for a split second, then she looks at me, then at the window, then back to me.

"Were you trying..." Monique says. "Jesus." The hardness fades from her eyes for a moment, then returns before she focuses her attention on Uncle Kenny again.

"We're going downstairs," she says to him. "Are you going to try anything stupid?" He doesn't respond. "I'll take that as a no." Monique bounces away from him, stands next to me. She's ready with the blade, but Uncle Kenny doesn't do anything more exciting than make his shaky way to his feet. He takes a tentative step toward the attic stairs, then another. We follow.

At the top of the stairs, Uncle Kenny stops. He doesn't turn around, but he actually chuckles and says, "Nobody is going to believe you." He lets that hang there, then, "Cry all you want. Nobody is ever—"

Monique trips him—kicks one of his feet behind the other and gives him a shove. Uncle Kenny tries to catch himself on the banister, but the move spins him around and he tumbles down the full flight, all twenty-three steps. He lands in a jumble at the bottom and lies motionless, face down, head by the last step, feet almost to the door in the circle of light from the overhead fixture.

The utility room below us is still and quiet. The attic behind us is still and quiet. Monique takes a long, deep breath and lets it out. For a while, we just stand. Then Sam steps silently into view below us. Called by the broken glass? A sixth sense for the presence of violence? Sam looks up at Monique and me at the top of the stairs. He steps over to Uncle Kenny and places two fingers on his neck, checking for a pulse.

Sam's barefoot.

That's a weird thing to notice.

"Is he dead?" I ask.

Sam doesn't answer, but he grabs Uncle Kenny by the shoulder and rolls him onto his back. Sam kneels on the floor behind Uncle Kenny, gets him into a sort of seated position and hooks an arm under his chin. It's not until Sam cups the top of his head that I realize he's about to break his neck.

"Wait," I say. "We kicked him in the balls. A whole bunch." That won't pass muster on an autopsy. Know what will give you away. Sam sighs like he's disappointed, doesn't kill our uncle, and lowers him back to the floor. He checks his limbs, presumably for breaks, and doesn't find any. He zips up Uncle Kenny's trousers and brushes the dusty footprint off his crotch. Sam comes up the stairs, stops a few steps from the top.

He scopes out the attic from just above floor level, then says, "Your collarbone's broken."

"I know."

It's actually pretty obvious, with my left shoulder riding up so high, but Sam doesn't mean it like, That must hurt, are you alright? It's just one more variable in whatever equation Sam's calculating. Sam reaches for Monique's stiletto and she lets him take it. I jump at the loud shwook when Sam presses the button that retracts the blade. Eyes still on Monique, Sam slips the knife into his pocket without looking to make sure the blade retracted, trusting the weapon.

"Did he fuck you?"

Monique looks back at Sam for a long time.

"Not this time."

Sam doesn't say anything, doesn't nod, doesn't smile or frown. He just reaches over and grabs a cardboard box from the floor next to Monique's feet. We move down the stairs, Monique and I stopping a few steps up from the bottom. Sam lifts Uncle Kenny's torso and puts the box underneath him. Sam sits down hard on top of Uncle Kenny, crushing the cardboard box beneath him. Uncle Kenny groans, but does not regain consciousness. Might even just be simple bellows action. Who knows? Sam stands up and looks at Monique.

"Here's the play," Sam says. "Paul and Uncle Kenny were helping you move out."

I sit down because I have to. I knew. Monique certainly didn't hide it, but she didn't rub it in either. I must have known. But now it's real. Now it's now.

"Paul?" Sam's snapping his fingers in front of my face. I guess he's been talking to me. "Paul? There he is. You," Sam says, pointing to me, but looking down now at how he's arranged Uncle Kenny at the bottom of the stairs, "missed a step, tripped, and hit your collarbone on the banister." Sam bends one of Uncle Kenny's legs just a little bit more and looks at how he's lying. "Uncle Kenny tried to catch you, but fell." Sam lays Uncle Kenny's hand on the first step. "Show me where you hit your collarbone, Paul." I twist around to point to the bannister. "Higher up," he says. I point higher up. Sam nods.

"What about the window?" I ask.

"That window's been broken for a long time," Sam says, and despite the fact that I myself broke it only a moment ago, I believe him. "Mom won't have any trouble thinking the housing staff isn't paying attention." Sam stops for a second, standing over Uncle Kenny, staring down at him. "Ha," he says. "I almost forgot he's left handed." Sam moves Uncle Kenny's right hand off the first step and instead lays his left arm in the same arrangement with the wrist against the corner of the tread. As soon as Uncle Kenny's left arm is in place Sam stomps it and the arm folds in a way people's arms do not normally fold.

Uncle Kenny groans. I say, "Holy shit." Monique looks at me but says nothing.

Sam produces Monique's stiletto and sits down on Uncle Kenny's chest again. He doesn't extend the blade, but holds the handle with about half an inch protruding from the bottom of his fist. With his other hand, Sam curls back Uncle Kenny's top lip. Then with one precise, robot-like strike, Sam knocks out one of Uncle Kenny's front teeth. Tock.

Sam retrieves the tooth and holds it up. The goo catches the light from the overhead.

"No," Sam says. "Uncle Kenny didn't try to catch you like a hero. He lost his footing trying to jump out of the way when you fell." Sam looks up at me. I nod. Sam turns his attention back to

Uncle Kenny. "A good dentist could have saved the tooth. Reseated it. Would have been good as new. Almost. Some things can't be undone." Sam drops the tooth into Uncle Kenny's mouth, pushes his jaw up to close his mouth, then clamps a hand over his lips. "Too bad we couldn't find it. Maybe you—Awww" He strokes Uncle Kenny's throat for a few seconds until his swallow reflex kicks in.

Sam resets, lines up the knife handle with the other front tooth. He's still and quiet for a few seconds, then he's whispering. I can barely hear him. "You know you like it." Tock.

Holy shit. Uncle Kenny and *Sam*?

He looks up at Monique. A moment passes between them. And is gone.

Sam holds up this tooth to examine it as well, then wraps it in a cloth he takes from one of his pockets. The cloth—and the tooth—go into his pocket.

Sam sweeps the fabric smooth over Uncle Kenny's chest before he rises. He stands over him, watching Uncle Kenny breathe. We all watch Uncle Kenny breathe. Slow, deep breaths. Timed with the nadir of an exhale, Sam drops onto Uncle Kenny, TV wrestling style, focusing all his weight and momentum on the point of his elbow, pounding that force into that patch of smooth fabric like a sledgehammer.

Sam rises again to stand over Uncle Kenny.

"A ruptured spleen will kill him in a few hours if the 'holes won't take him to a hospital."

There's a win-win: dead Uncle Kenny or public embarrassment of Mom and Dad.

Sam turns his back to us, digs in his front pocket—

No, Sam is peeing on Uncle Kenny.

His stream is aimed just so to make it look like Uncle Kenny let loose his own bladder, though I suspect there's way more to it than that. More than I'll ever know. When Uncle Kenny is sodden, but before anything starts to pool or run on the floor, Sam stops and zips up.

"I'll go to the hospital to keep the ball busting out of the reports," he says. "Some people pay for that freaky shit. 'I'm sure you can understand, doctor, that both our family and his would be eternally grateful for your discretion in keeping Uncle Kenny's 'eccentric' sexual practices from besmirching the fine record of a respected public servant.' Won't even cost money."

Sam checks his watch. "Give me a minute to be in the shower." Turning to face us again, he lays Monique's knife on the third step with great care. "Then, Monique, you go for help." Monique picks up her knife as Sam rolls Uncle Kenny into his face down position again on top of the box. "Be there when he wakes up," Sam says, then saunters out of the room with a little wave. "Toodles."

The crushed cardboard box sticking out from under the ruptured spleen of unconscious, piss-soaked Uncle Kenny is split down one seam, the contents squeezing out like toothpaste from a cracked tube. In an hour and a half Monique will be a legal adult, fully free and emancipated, no longer in forced residence at the Stockton Family Penitentiary. But before getting sprung, Monique skipped carving her name on her cell wall and instead risked the attic.

For a box of my baby clothes.

"Come," Mom says when Monique knocks on Mom's study door. But I suppose she's expecting Antonia, or someone else she didn't give birth to, because as soon as we step inside she says, "No." Monique moves forward anyway, stepping through the brightly-lit furniture showroom, stopping behind one of the chairs in front of Mom's desk.

"Paul broke his collarbone."

Mom sighs like How is that my problem? and finishes writing whatever sentence she's writing on the mauve stationary she uses for Thank You notes. There's a stack of sealed envelopes to her right, a stack of empty envelopes to her left, a stack of blank pages in front of her blotter ready and waiting to be part of her not-at-all-calculated gratitude. Mom eyeballs Monique while she blows on the drying ink of her Joan Hancock.

"Come over here where I can see you."

Standing lamp, end table, six-butt puffy leather couch, end table, standing lamp, dance floor, Monique. Mom folds her note in half, uses what looks like an ivory cigar to teach the crease who's boss. She looks me in the eye for a split second, ignores my misplaced shoulder and looks back at Monique while she peels an envelope off the stack, entombs her kindest regards and lifts the envelope's flap to her pie hole. With the forked tongue working both sides of the glue strip at once, I'd expect the licking to be done lickety-split. But the grandfather clock rocks out one, two, three, four, other side, six, seven, eight, nine. I do appreciate her tidying all the envelope corners when she adds this one to the stack.

"Are you sure your collarbone is broken?"

I don't know how I'd get my shoulder where it is otherwise. "Pretty sure."

Mom slips a blank piece of paper off her stack and aligns it before her.

"You may call the doctor," she says as she commences gracious salutations.

Monique waits until Mom lifts her pen.

"He should have X-rays," meaning the under-the-radar house-call won't cut it.

Mom starts on the body of her essay. I'm going to tell you what I'm going to tell you, then I'm going to tell you, then I'm going to tell you what I told you.

"Should he?"

"I'll take him."

No means No, and Maybe means No, and Ask me later means No, but the little "shoo-shoo" double-flick of Mom's hand means Fine, go do that if you've convinced yourself it's absolutely necessary.

We stand silently while Mom finishes telling [that event's sponsor] what she told [that event's sponsor]. Sign, blow, fold, abject domination of crease, stuff, lick, stack, align.

"And why exactly are you still here?"

Monique manages not to grin while she does it, but it's like Mom's got a foot-wide red button on her forehead and Monique's pushing it with the index finger of a giant foam "We're #1" hand.

"Uncle Kenny is unconscious."

Mom leaps to her feet, shouting, "Oh, for fuck's sake, Abigail."

"Monique," we say.

Mom charges for the door. We follow, but our enthusiasm does not match Mom's. "What happened? Where is he? Take me there. What did you do to him? Move! Now!"

"He was helping me pack to move out."

"Where?" Mom shouts. I wonder first where Monique is moving to, but my second thought is that Mom would give zero fucks about that and only wants to know—

"Attic next to my room," I say, and now Monique and I have to hustle to keep up as Mom races through the house to the scene of the slime.

He's moaning, semi-awake. A string of bloody spittle stretches from the floor to Uncle Kenny's mouth when he rolls himself onto his back. The broken arm is no help and neither are we. Monique, Mom and I stand at Uncle Kenny's feet and do nothing more than watch his eyes roll around, trying to focus on us one at a time.

He uses his good arm to scooch back to lean against the first step.

Uncle Kenny says, "Huck."

Yeah, Uncle Kenny. Huck you.

When he looks at me and I'm pretty sure he knows where he is, I say, "I fell and hit my collarbone on the bannister." I point up high on the staircase where Sam told me to point. Uncle Kenny turns his head and squints like *That's bullshit*, or *What the fuck?* or *Hey, where's all my toofers at?* but Mom's too busy losing her shit to notice.

"You knocked him down the stairs?"

"No," I say.

"He tried to jump out of Paul's way," Monique says, pointing at our squirming uncle. "Lost his footing."

"Missed a step."

"Hit most of the rest of them."

Uncle Kenny smacks his lips, sticks his tongue through the space where his front teeth used to be. He looks at me again and I lock my gaze on him like I'm holding his eyeballs with tongs.

"We were helping Monique move out of the house."

He looks at Monique. He looks at me. A tiny, tiny nod.

"Hell," Uncle Kenny says, then makes a concerted effort to get that hucking F in there. "Fell."

Mom says, "Thank God all the press events are over."

Can always count on Mom to find the bright side.

Uncle Kenny uses his good arm to clutch his chest.

"Heart attack, Uncle Kenny?" I ask.

"Need a heart for that," Monique reminds me.

Me: "Right. Pancreas?"

Monique: "Gall bladder?"

Me: "Kidney stone?"

Monique: "Throat cancer?"

Me: "Colon cancer?"

Monique: "Stomach cancer?"

Me: "Knuckle cancer?"

Monique: "Lung cancer?"

Me: "Lunch cancer?"

"Will you two shut up?" Mom says.

Ahhh, I feel like we almost got a please at the end of that.

"I'm sure it's not as bad as it looks," Monique says. She turns to Mom, takes half a step forward to get right up in her face. "The lighting in here is really not flattering." Monique darts her eyes up at the overhead light, squints to engage the Stockton Scrutiny™, and focuses her gaze—hard—on various parts of Mom's face, finally lobbing the tiniest frown.

Mom flinches like she's been stabbed.

Monique is #1! Monique is #1!

Mom plays it casual, but steps back out of the light before turning to me. "Go get Antonia."

Uh, my collarbone?

"We'll tell her on the way to my car," Monique says. Everything means No, so no response means Yes. Monique collects the crushed box of my baby clothes, stepping over Uncle Kenny's feet like he's not there. "Did you say 'lunch cancer'?"

"Snack cancer?" We head out, but I stop in the doorway to drop the cherry on this sundae. "Actually, I learned in school that a ruptured spleen could be really serious. Like life threatening." Mom looks at me. Uncle Kenny looks at me. I point to my chest. "Thpleen."

I'll be honest; I do not make things easier on myself. In Monique's words, I do myself no favors. But if it—Life, whatever—is going to be a suck storm anyway, why not trade a notch or two of incremental shittiness for a bit of fun? In this case, I'd be wise to leave thpleen enough alone and just bolt before the murdering can begin. Instead, I immediately visit retribution upon my own damned self.

I say, "Toodles," which is all well and good and fun and funny and neato, but the accompanying wave? Wrong hand. Pain shoots in every direction from the two brand-new ends of collarbone where ragged bone grinds on ragged bone.

Sometimes I'm just stupid.

## CHAPTER 21: POLICE ESCORT?

When Monique lets me stop by my room for her birthday present before we leave for the E.R., I don't miss the opportunity to also take the four extra painkillers in my jacket pocket from the other night. Doubling the dosage brings instant relief to all three of my collarbones. (Not so much.) In the car, Monique's shoulders relax as we pull through the gate and off the estate. Mine do too, like always, but tonight they don't quite even out to normal alignment. I'd say, Oh, well, and shrug, but that would hurt. At least the passenger-side seatbelt lies across my good shoulder. Small blessings.

Another is that the hospital is close, so it shouldn't take too long to get there, despite Monique having to drive the speed limit because on a big drinking day like the 4$^{th}$ of July about every dozenth or so car is a police car.

As we ease to a stop at a red light, Monique asks, "How are you doing?"

"Eh. How are *you* doing?"

"Eh."

I want to ask her about Sam. I want to ask her about Not this time. Sometimes what you imagine or assume is worse than the reality. Sometimes it's not.

"Where are you moving?"

"Ah! A cute little place right by school. No view, but you'll like it. Good kitchen. Small, but laid out well."

"Two bedroom?"

"Yes, but, Paul."

"I know." In Washington we can be emancipated from our

parents at 16—with parental consent; explain that one to me. You can still get it if you fight, but if you're fighting who we get to fight? Stocktons don't lose, especially to lesser Stocktons. It was a non-starter for Monique. It's a non-starter for me.

"I know," I say again. "Maybe weekends?"

"Hopefully. You're welcome any time. I'll give you a key so between classes you can—"

As soon as the light turns green and we start accelerating, a siren whoops one whoop and the surrounding street becomes a post-fireworks, red and blue light show. The sweeping red and blue follows us to the curb as Monique pulls over. She turns on the interior light and puts her hands on the steering wheel. I lay my hands on my knees. I don't know where we learned this stuff. Maybe Sam, but I don't remember.

"Taillights?" I ask.

"Nope. Five will get you ten it's Mom." Monique watches in the rearview mirror, takes her hand off the steering wheel for just long enough to push the buttons to roll down both our windows. Warm air pours in, supplanting Monique's wintry air conditioning.

"Police escort?"

"Fat chance."

Two flashlight beams, one from each side of the car, sweep over us as the officers approach. Rather slowly. And not all the way.

"Passenger!" yells the guy on my side. "Put your hands on the dashboard."

That's gonna hurt. Yep. I whisper to Monique, "Do they have their guns out?"

"Not yet," she says, "But they're ready."

The flashlight beams continue searching inside the car during the slow advance.

"Mom called it in stolen."

"Fuck," Monique whispers. "You're right." As much as possible without letting go of the wheel, Monique turns her head to her window. She shouts, clear and loud, but in a matter-of-fact tone, "Officers, my name is . . ." There's the briefest pause, just long enough for me to imagine *Fuck you, Mom*, for making me say, one last time, "Abigail Stockton. My passenger is my brother Paul Stockton. We are both minors. This vehicle is registered to our mother." Mom has a name, but Monique doesn't have to say it before the two flashlight beams drop in relaxation. Hardened criminals are one thing; a couple of kids in Mom's car . . .

"Stay in the vehicle, please," says the guy on Monique's side.

If they have the same radios as the officer at the strip club, it's Motorolas I hear crackle back and forth, punctuating their chat with Dispatch. I've had about as much dashboard time as I can stand, so I figure I'll risk sitting back. No shouting. No gunfire. No problem. Monique keeps her hands on the wheel.

When they again approach, they come all the way to the windows and are much more relaxed. The guy on my side still wrecks my night vision with a blast from his flashlight—"Ow, that's bright."—but at least he's hitting me with photons, not the foot-long flashlight full of D batteries.

"Good evening, officer," Monique says to her guy. "What can I do for you?"

"This vehicle was reported stolen."

Sometimes I hate being right.

"Can you just arrest me quickly and drop him off at the hospital on our way to jail?"

"Kid's got a broken collarbone," my officer says. I'm surprised at how fast people pick up on that. The other officer looks where his partner shines his light.

"I'll go quietly," Monique says.

"I don't think we need to waste anybody's time with that." He and Dispatch have already decided Mom's call is bullshit. I can hear it in his voice. Something just this side of resentment. Like me, he doesn't appreciate being used in somebody else's power play. Unlike me, he might actually want to be spending the holiday with his family. Five will get you nothing, the APB— which is moments old and probably included the route we'd take—has already been softened or reprioritized or whatever designation means it'll be ignored by other officers with better things to do than be the thumb Mom's trying to keep us under.

The proceedings now have a formality feel.

"Can I see your drivers license, please, Miss?" Monique is purposeful in predictably opening her purse at 75% speed, retrieving her license and handing it to the officer.

Meanwhile, at the Daytona Speedway: an engine not quite as deeply rumbly/throaty as Sam's secret hot rod, but still obviously a big V-8, roars up behind us. The officer at Monique's window straightens up and steps closer to the car as Mom's notorious limo screams by at 200% of the speed limit. I can't see either of these officers' faces now, but I suspect that all four of us are just watching Mom's taillights get smaller. Watching and fuming.

"Officers," Monique says, "I apologize for our mother's disrespectful behavior."

The officer returns his attention to Monique's license, shines his flashlight on it for a split second, flicks the corner once with his thumb and immediately hands it back when Monique is who she says she is. Well, who her drivers license and Mom say she is.

"Would you like to see the registration?"

"That won't be necessary. Do you know how to get where you're going?"

"Yes, sir."

"Keep it slow like you were driving before. You're free to go."

"Thank you, officers," Monique and I say in unison, jerking our heads back and forth like idiots while we each try to thank both of the officers before they disappear from our windows.

I believe I have learned another valuable lesson: you can be wrong, and get away with it, as long as someone else is wronger.

Monique bows her head and rubs her face several times with both hands before she raises our windows and pulls into the lane to drive us to the hospital.

We hit some lights, but make good time.

We see more police, but nobody stops us.

We travel in silence, but at one point Monique says, "Cunt," without realizing she said it out loud.

Ever been to an E.R.? This one looks like that. We check in. We sit. We wait. But the hospital's fully staffed for a busy 4th of July night, so I'm pretty sure I'll be next in line after this guy.

"Ouch," I say.

Monique follows my gaze to the wobbly-legged man being shoulder-crutched through the automatic doors by A) his best friend, B) his least-drunk friend, C) the guy at their party with the fewest outstanding warrants, or D) all of the above. D) is shirtless and heroically sunburned.

"Hang on, Mikey." Mikey's right hand, held up in front of his face, is a giant, bloody wad of what must be a whole roll of toilet paper.

"Let's hope that's a fresh roll," Monique says.

"Dr. Stockton," I ask, "have you ever seen a more aggressive case of fist cancer?"

Mikey's friend tells him, "We're there. We made it."

Well, Mikey almost makes it. As soon as they reach the reception window and stop moving forward, and just as the nurse behind the glass raises her gaze to Mikey, he drops onto the linoleum like that was what he planned to do all along. His buddy lets him go down, but somehow keeps hold of his wrist to keep the wound elevated.

America's Least Wanted Friend of Mikey just says, "Little help?" but the nurse, and another, are already bursting through the double doors that lead to Back There.

"He got his hand caught in a machine," I say.

"He's not going to get to tend them rabbits."

Mikey responds to smelling salts with a mighty, "Corndogs," which makes as much sense as anything today. Six undamaged hands spot him as he shakily self-mounts a gurney. Then the excitement's over and nothing so medically interesting happens with the treatment of my simple, closed fracture of the transverse clavicle. (It's so textbook and boring that I had to add transverse in there to make it sound like anything.)

X-rays, weight, height, double-check height—Yes, I've been checked for everything; I'm just tall—blood pressure, temperature, pulse, doctor will be with you in a moment. And she is. A pretty, redheaded doctor walks in holding the films up to the overhead lights. She pokes here and there. What should hurt does, and what shouldn't doesn't. I don't even get a cast, just a sling with a waistband and a lot of Velcro. The only hard part is not being obvious while smelling her hair when she stands close to adjust the fit of the sling. She has one freckle at the top of her ear. Luckily nobody takes a second reading of my pulse.

Picking up an Rx pad from the counter, she drops onto a wheeled stool and starts writing as she asks, "Are you on any prescription medications?"

"I took a couple of Midol before we left the house." The doctor smiles as she glances over at Monique, who shrugs and shakes her head. I say, "It's not just for the ladies."

"No, it's good stuff. That should handle your bloating. This will do better for the pain," she says, snapping off the top sheet and handing it to me.

"Thanks."

"You can fill that down the hall. Unfortunately, there's not much else we can do for your clavicle." She checks her watch. "I have a couple of minutes before the next car crash arrives. Anything else we should look at?"

"At this height, I've been prodded pretty thoroughly the last year and half."

"Fair enough," she says and rises to leave, adding almost as an afterthought, "You seem fine, but for certain injuries in the E.R. we're required to ask if you feel safe at home."

The right answer, or at least a less suspicious answer, would be one that isn't preceded by my head jerking backward, then a giant, awkward pause in which I say nothing and instead look to my sister to try to get a sense of how to answer.

My doctor lets go of the doorknob and turns to face me directly.

I look at her, look back at Monique. Not safe would mean police, child protective services. Foster care? At least temporarily. Out of the house is out of the house, but . . .

Monique reads my mind. "That's thermonuclear."

The doctor crosses her arms and says, "This shouldn't be a hard question to answer."

"You're not wrong," I say. "Is she covered by my doctor-patient confidentiality?" I ask, indicating Monique with a nod of my head. "As my agent, or my caretaker, or at least my ride on this particular occasion?"

"Doesn't work that way, but that doesn't matter. If I think someone is hurting you, I have more obligations to protect your body than your privacy."

"I did this," I say. "Technically, not a lie. Technically, I hurt myself while trying to keep someone else from hurting my sister."

"Careful," Monique says.

The doctor's pager buzzes. She ignores it.

"Just now, our mom reported the car stolen so we'd get stopped on the way here. Yesterday, I gave away my dog because I thought our brother might kill it. She," I say, pointing to Monique, "is moving out of the house in about six minutes when she turns eighteen."

The doctor's pager buzzes again. We're well into car crash time.

"Where I live, the name on the mailbox is the name on one or more of the special care units upstairs. Do I feel safe? Not there, not here, not anywhere. Safety is a foreign concept. But there's nothing you, or I, or anybody else can do about that tonight."

Her pager buzzes again. She turns it off by feel.

"Go," I say. "You can help those people. Go. I'll be fine."

She goes.

## CHAPTER 22: LIKE A HOT ROCK

Monique is patient, a planner, and a pleasure delayer.

"Not yet," she says when I pull out her birthday present after the doctor leaves. We make good our escape from the exam room and E.R. and are in the pharmacy when the last seconds of Monique's last day of childhood click away to her official,

"Happy birthday!"

"Thanks," she says, and smiles her real, eye-crinkly, no-plastic smile. But she won't take the little velvet box out of my hand. I start to open it, which is kind of a fumbley exercise in my current state, but Monique puts her hands over mine.

"Not yet."

"It's your birthday."

"Not here." Same story in the parking lot. "Not here." Same story at some random spot she drives us to downtown. "Not here."

Belltown's not too sketchy, but I'm not going to be waving the jewelry box around. There are more people than I'd expect to be on the street after midnight, but there's a good mix of restaurants and bars and apartment buildings around, so I guess it doesn't not make sense. We got the only open parking spot in sight, and probably just because it's not really a parking spot—red paint, fire plug. You don't need a fake drivers license to know that means no parking. Monique hops out and I join her on the sidewalk next to the hydrant to stare across the road at an old, three-story brick jobbie. We're nowhere near the university, so this isn't Monique's new apartment.

"Where's here? What's this?"

I can't adopt her fists-on-hips pose of triumph because of the sling.

"When I was eleven, Mom and Dad put this in Abigail's name as a tax dodge."

"Only your—"

"Only my name. I've got a buyer lined up to sign final papers in the morning. Easy to move product at twenty percent below market. After commissions and capital gains, one point nine mill."

"You're fucking those fuckers."

"I am totally fucking those fuckers," she says, working her jumble of keys in her hand. She gets the car key off the ring and steps into the street, stopping in the bike lane. "And they can't do a goddam thing about it."

Monique hucks Mom's car key into the storm drain.

When I stop laughing, Monique is still standing in the bike lane. She lifts the key ring up in front of her like Mikey's bloody mess of hand, presses a button, and behind her, parked across the street, a new-ish Camry flashes its headlights as the doors unlock.

"Now let me show you *my* place."

It's awesome, and Monique's boxes of stuff are already neatly piled in the living room, along with a new couch and a small dinette set in the eating area between the attached kitchen and the big window facing the street. Bedroom with bed, bedroom with desks. Full size tub, neutral tile. Well lit, no horrible fluorescents. It's great. The landlord thumps like a linebacker up the stairs to Monique's floor of the duplex, but turns out to be a tiny, thousand-year-old woman, Tricia, who likes to stay up to watch Late Night. Their negotiations and transactions are old news; it's just a binding signature from a real, legal adult she needs now that Monique is one. Easily accomplished during the commercial break she's allotted for the task. Done and done. Tricia squeezes Monique's upper arm on the way to the door, saying, "Welcome, sweetie." For me, she becomes Yoda. "A looker, you'll be," then winks at me as she eases the door closed. "Already. And smart?" She fans herself with one hand. "Watch out, ladies." She thumps down the stairs like half a dozen bowling balls.

"Isn't she a hoot?"

"Adopt me, she can."

"She might be up for that. She raised six kids and has love enough for a hundred more."

Monique glances around the main room and smiles before taking a big, huge breath, raising her shoulders and crossing her hands over her chest. She blows it out, swinging her hands down and out, throwing them out like she's stretching her wings.

"Okay. Now."

I'd like to joke about Now what? but I am neither patient nor a pleasure delayer. I meet her in the middle of the room, and finally get to give Monique her gift. She cups the fuzzy, little jewelry box with both hands like she's making a snowball, and brings her hands up to her face, touching her knuckle to her lip before lowering her hands a few inches.

"I know I'm going to love it because it's from you."

"I hope so."

We stand there, in Monique's living room, a foot apart, saying nothing, doing nothing, and while I am anxious for Monique to open her present, I begin to understand not just a peaceful moment devoid of noise or trauma or alarm, not just a calm or quiet moment stolen between inevitable, perpetual crises, but a perfect moment, a moment complete in and of itself, suspended in the now. This moment. I learn simply to be. I learn to savor.

But then, holy crap, I can't take it any more.

"Are you going to open it?"

Monique opens her hand, holds the box between us. She cracks open the lid, but keeps her gaze fixed on me, her eyes shifting back and forth as she looks me in one eye then the other. Eventually, she pops a single, quick glance down at the earrings—probably just long enough to register the simple teardrops, sapphires set in platinum—before she returns her gaze to meet mine. Tears pool on her lower eyelids, but her cheeks stay dry until she smiles, when tears pour down her face from both eyes like matching waterfalls.

"They're perfect." No jerking sobs, just quiet weeping. "Thank you." She gives me a ginger hug, then stares at the earrings with her other hand over her mouth while I sit down on her couch. "Oh, my god. They're so beautiful."

"I'm glad you like them. Happy birthday."

"It is. The best birthday yet."

"Try them on."

She does, inclining her head to one side then the other, then smoothing her hair behind her shoulders on both sides with a quick sweep of her hands.

"Well?" I don't have time to say they look great—They do.—before she spins around and skips into the bathroom. "I have to look." Pressed to describe the sound from the bathroom, I think I'd have to say, Squeeee!

She's in there for a long time. I take off my shoes. The anticipation over, and the hospital meds starting to work their chemical magic, I'm going down fast and hard. I lay out on the couch, but fight to keep my eyes open. Here is a place I actually want to be.

There's a streetlight directly in front of the building, shining through a deciduous tree, casting a faint shadow on the wall next to the dinette table. I'm too tired to turn around to look, but based on the rounded, heart-shaped outlines of the individual leaves, I'm going to guess Katsura. In the fall, that tree will smell like cotton candy. Now, the leaves drift and sway in the warm, gentle breeze.

Drift and sway. The neighborhood is quiet. Drift and sway.

When I wake up on Monique's couch in the morning, most of the boxes are already flattened and stacked by the door. She's asleep, the earrings on her nightstand next to her watch. I don't do anything as loud as try to cook breakfast, but there are some staples in the fridge, including chocolate milk. I have some cereal, do some extra credit work in the pain management department, and go right back to sleep on the couch. Monique (wearing the earrings) wakes me up making pancakes, which may be the greatest thing that's ever happened to me.

I sleep most of the morning on Monique's couch while she

unpacks and decorates and goes out to sell that building and turn in the paperwork for a legal name change. I help her put some stuff away up high, but figure out she's going to get it down by standing on a chair, so she could have put it away by standing on a chair, so she's just making a point of including me. We try paint chips for the living room, shady side, sunny side. We paint test squares in patterns. We walk around the neighborhood. We talk about school. We watch paint dry. We shop. We cook. We eat lasagna and French beans and roasted cauliflower and baked pears with blackberry sorbet and it's the best meal I've ever eaten and the best day of my entire life.

And then it's over.

Time to go.

Monique's quiet on the drive back to the house. About a hundred meters from the keypad control she cranks her Camry off the pavement. She won't even pull all the way up to the front gate. We grind through the gravel until the sedan stops with a heavy scrunch, the weight of the vehicle sinking in, rocking gently and settling. Monique cuts the engine and the lights.

Out my window the nearly full moon hangs low and large across the deep, cold waters of Lake Washington. The moonlight flickers in a wide, broken line across the dancing, black water. They say water seeks its own level, like it has a choice. But the tides are the moon's gravity pulling the oceans toward it. And the sun tugs in its direction while the earth relentlessly pulls down. Gravity always wins. It's what stopped our moon turning, leaving it orbiting now with the same blank face staring down at us forever. That face glows now in the last rays of the sun setting behind me to the left, behind Monique, behind the monstrous house looming at the top of the hill.

I unlatch my seatbelt and feel the mechanism retract the nylon strap off my body. The buckle thunks against the door and rattles into the narrow crevice where it lives. I can't look at Monique. If I look at her, she'll say, "We're here." But we're not here. Only I'm here, only I'm stuck in that big empty house. Monique's not here. Monique's leaving. Monique's gone.

The engine ticks and ticks and ticks as it cools, as all the heat leaves its heart, as all the intricate, interdependent parts contract and shrink, as entropy dissipates energy from order into chaos, an undeniable, immutable, unbreakable law of the natural universe.

I'm looking to science to comfort me, but it keeps grabbing my chin and cranking my face toward the pain.

I turn. Blood red light bends through our atmosphere to silhouette the house. If I was lucky, there'd be a comical arrangement of lit windows making a smile or a winky Santa out of the Stockton family estate—even a horror mask would humanize the place—but it's a black hole.

Monique picks with her thumbnail at the seam around the center section of vinyl covering the steering wheel.

"We're here," I say.

She matches my gaze when I turn to her. She pulls out slack on her seatbelt, slides a knee across the leather as she rotates to sit sideways, but she leaves the safety belt buckled. The shoulder strap cuts across her neck, so she ducks out of it.

"I'm sorry, Paul."

"No," I say. "You had to leave." And she did. I can't, but she did. "I'm glad. Really."

Monique lifts her hand from her bent knee, lowers it again. I have the urge to offer my hand, but with my left arm in a sling that's one more thing that's impossible.

"You can visit anytime," she says.

"I'm going to be grounded forever for helping you move."

"Well, when you get a pardon from the warden."

"Probably no time off for good behavior. I'm not a model prisoner."

I'm unlikely to muster up the good behavior to trade, partly because that too is impossible. Say jump and I'll ask, How high? But who said you could land? Gravity always wins. So I'll suck it up. Bread and water and no TV; straight home from school and a month in the hole; hard, hard time that I'll have to find a way to bear without Monique to stand with me against the screws.

"Whenever. Anytime," Monique says. "I'll give you a key."

"I'll lose a key."

"I'll get a number pad. You won't lose a number. Speaking of, do you remember my phone number?" she asks. I rattle it off. Monique expels a quick, semi-laugh. "Wait." She digs a piece of paper out of her front pocket. "Say it again." I say Monique's phone number. She reads along. "Yeah."

"Okay," I say.

She says, "Okay."

And then, for the first time ever talking with my sister, I don't know what to say. And I have no idea what I'd want to hear that wouldn't be taking something away from her to give to me. She lifts her hand again and rests it on my upper arm. I put my right hand over her hand on my arm. Monique's lips tremble into a smile. I squeeze out the best smile I can, and then I can't take it anymore. I say, "Happy birthday, Monique," and I launch myself out of the car.

In my hurry, and not wanting to slam the door, I don't push it hard enough, so it doesn't close all the way. Inside, the overhead light stays lit. Standing right next to the car, I can't see Monique, just my empty seat. I bend my knees to put my hip against the round of the door and shift my weight. My push rocks the car *ever* so slightly, like the tidal pull of the moon. The door latches, cutting the overhead light, throwing the interior into darkness. I should go now, but instead I just stand there for a few seconds. I want to climb back into the car. I know I can't, I know I might anyway, so I have to force myself to start moving.

I walk. The gravel crunches beneath my feet as I trudge toward the gate. The road next to me pounds heat into my face, radiating back the sun's heat the asphalt has absorbed all afternoon. Jasmine. Night blooming Jasmine. It's really hard to grow here. Somewhere down the hill a Barred Owl hoots its dog-bark-ish call. A Great Horned calls, "Hoo, hoo, hoo," nearby and the wise old Barred is smart enough to shut his pie hole. Crunch, crunch, crunch of the gravel.

Behind me, Monique hasn't started the car. My crazy math thing kicks in and I count steps to the gate. I'm good with distances—literal distances. I run the calcs, figure it's 97 steps all the way. My eyes start to water at 23. By half way I'm taking jerking breaths that sound like hiccups and stab pain into my broken collarbone. At 97, I'm glad it's dark so Monique won't be able to see my face when I turn to wave goodbye. Before I do, I punch in the code. Some hidden motor whirs, clunks a gear against a heavy chain, and the giant, iron S on the Stockton front gate cracks down the middle and separates as it pulls away.

I take a deep breath and turn toward Monique parked down the street. I can barely see the car. I wave. Monique clicks on the interior light with one hand and waves three quick waves with the other. Almost immediately she flicks the light off again, and I can't be sure, but I think she wipes her cheek before the car falls dark.

The engine turns over and thrums quietly. Monique doesn't blind me with the headlights. She eases through a perfect, three-point turn, drifts partway down the hill before filling the trees with light. I watch until she disappears.

The driveway's blurry, the lights along the sides bursting into spiky stars like one of my migraines. But my eyes don't hurt. My head doesn't hurt. Even the ache of my broken collarbone is just background static in the storm of real pain in my heart. I step off the driveway onto the grass, take the long way around the garage to pass the never-dug grave of my not-dead-but-long-gone dog, and slink around to the back of the main house.

Despite the broken collarbone and lack of light I can still climb the outside of the house to my bedroom window. I've thought that I could probably do it with my eyes closed and now I do. As my conscious mind implodes in on itself, my disembodied hands and feet run on autopilot, find every outcrop and trim piece and drainpipe, and I'm on the roof opening my dormer window before I know it. But as I crawl into my bedroom, numb, exhausted, broken, I realize that without Monique, home isn't home, and I am, for the first time, alone in this house with nothing secure to hold on to.

Three years minimum.

Three to five.

Hard time.

CHAPTER 23: UNEXPECTED VISITOR

I wake up on my back on the floor in the middle of my room when somebody knocks on my door. Lightly.

"One second," I say. I roll over and push myself up with my good arm, shake the sleep out of my head. I've slept past time for more pain meds. When I open my door, it's Sam, stepping toward me and swinging a claw hammer down toward my head.

"Just kidding," he says as he walks past me. He flips the hammer around and points at the door with the handle. "Close that." He's also carrying a lunchbox, a bright red, vintage, kid's metal lunchbox. Nancy Drew Mysteries. "I was going to get you Hardy Boys, but it looked a little faggy." He sets the hammer and the lunchbox on my desk. "Check out that mouth." I was checking. Nancy Drew, supple lips parted in surprise or about to kiss some unseen boy, hardy or otherwise, definitely draws the eye. I mean, it's a cartoon, but still. Sam lays the lunchbox on its back and snaps open the little clasp. The interior perfectly fits three 4" stacks of twenty-dollar bills.

"Wow."

Sam pulls a few bundles off one of the neat stacks, waggles them at me, holding them at one end.

"You'd draw attention spending hundreds, so this is only about fifty grand total."

"It smells gross."

"It reeks," he says. "Money is filthy."

I take the bundles from Sam's hand, take a good whiff. "Touched by so many commoners," I say, mimicking our mother's practiced disdain.

"It's obscene," Sam says, joining in, but quickly getting back to business. "You can have more than this. Just let me know. But don't buy anything pricey the 'holes would see. You understand?"

"Yeah."

Sam takes back the bundles of bills, returns them to the lunchbox and closes it. With both hands, he holds it by its sides in front of his chest, then presses it to mine. I grab it by the handle with my good hand. It's heavy. The bills are packed in there and must weigh two kilograms, at least.

"Okay," Sam says. "Mom's coming. You have twenty seconds to hide this. Where do you put it?"

I look at my bookcases. The lunchbox is too big. I try to get a hint from the hammer, but that doesn't spark anything. My bathroom. My cleaning stuff. Mom wouldn't—

"Short term, under the sink in my bathroom."

"Long term."

"Probably outside."

"I thought you might say that." Sam picks up the hammer and points again with the handle. "Window." I'm not sure he means all the way out until he opens the window and actually climbs onto the roof, headed for my hideaway spot. Oh. Yeah, that makes sense. I climb out after Sam, and sit down next to him between the dormers. "Hold this," he says, handing me the tube sock with my pipe and questionable combustibles. He retrieves a rather long nail from one of his pockets, and first presses it into one of the thumbtack holes I made before, way up high under the overhang of the dormer's eave. The nail stays in place while Sam aligns the hammer. He takes out a tiny flashlight, holds it in his fist so just a pinpoint splash of light spills up under the eave.

"If you bang, bang, bang, people can track the sound." With expert aim and considerable strength, Sam gives the nail one good whack. He turns off the flashlight. "But if you hear something once, and don't know what it is, you'll listen for a few seconds and go back to what you were doing. You can't get a good direction, and the pattern of the activity is disrupted, so it's harder to figure out." He waits a few seconds. Flashlight on, whack, flashlight off. "That should do it." Sam reaches up and tugs on the nail, finds it satisfactory.

"Fifty grand in twenties weighs about five pounds." He takes the lunchbox out of my lap, hooks the handle over the nail, and slowly lowers his empty hand. "That should hold." He takes the lunchbox down again and opens it. "What I don't trust is this cheap latch. Weed?" Sam holds out his hand to receive my paraphernalia. I'm too dumbfounded to do anything other than hand it over. He stuffs it into the lunchbox, closes the lid, then dangles the box from its handle, rattling it, though not too briskly.

"You're not . . ." I start to ask, clearly about the marijuana, but I trail off. Not going to kill me? Not going to rat me out? Not going to beat the crap out of me? It appears he's going to do absolutely nothing about it, because he just waves his hand once and stays focused on the best method of secure concealment. Using a knife from one pocket, he cuts a short length of cord from his supply in another pocket. It's the same cord he used on Monique's door.

While he lashes a loop around the closed lunchbox, he asks, "Do you know what a Pelican case is?"

"No."

"Look into it. I should have gotten you one of those. Rugged, waterproof. On the heavy side, so test that nail before you trust it. If a Pelican case full of cash fell off the roof into the yard, the case would survive but you might not."

"Okay."

Sam returns the lunchbox to its hanger and the whole rig is now hidden under the eave. His task completed, he sits back and looks out toward the lights of Seattle. The moon's nearly full, too, so we can see the contours of the hills falling away around us, the topography of the treetops paralleling the undulations of the ground below.

"This is nice," he says, then falls quiet again. Eventually he asks, "How's your collarbone?"

"Hurts. Not too bad, but I'm late for my pain meds."

"I'll let you go then," he says, rising, tucking the hammer into a loop on his pants. Sam turns. He doesn't head back toward my window. Instead he stands there in the moonlight and lays his hand on my shoulder. He's chosen my unhurt shoulder, but he's also gentle.

"You took it to him, Paul. You did good." He pats me once and lets go. "You did well and you did good." Starting up the slope, Sam says, "More than I did at your age," and disappears over the crest of the roof.

CHAPTER 24: UNEXPECTED HOST
*or* M. IS FOR MONIQUE
*or* MISCIBILITY
*or* WHAT'S THE WORST THAT COULD HAPPEN?

There's no light under the door of Mom's study, and I'm pretty good about not making noise when I close the door behind me, so I jump when Mom says, "Hello, Paul." Shit.

She's nearly invisible in the darkness, only her hands illuminated in the small circle of light from her desk lamp, and the cherry of the cigarette in her mouth. I'm going to need a cover story tout de suite. I'm here? to steal? your liquor? Double shit. She places her pen in its stand, stabs out the cigarette, and rests both hands on the lavendery, creamy paper in the circle of light.

"Couldn't sleep? That's surprising after such a big day."

"Monique made lasagna. I guess the carbs have me kind of amped up."

Mom says, "Hmm," neutral. But she ripples the fingers of her right hand, pinky to index, the perfectly manicured nails tapping lightly against the paper. She says, "Monique." This too is neutral, but it's an acknowledgement. It's also only the second time I've heard her use Monique's chosen name, the first time intoning "Monique?" half like she was asking if she heard right, half like somebody just dropped a turd in her mouth. Neutral is progress. Huge.

Mom reaches up and snicks off her desk lamp. This leaves the giant room lit by maybe 40 watts from the floor lamp at the near end of one of the sofas. The bottom half of the wall of windows behind her is dark where trees block the view of our neighbors. Across the middle, the skyline of Seattle sparkles in the distance. Above that, in the far-distant distance, a few thousand stars throw light through our thin atmosphere. The nearly-full moon is low in the western sky now, a couple of hours from setting.

Mom's chair scrapes ever so lightly on the hardwood floor, and when she stands, her silhouette rises above the tree line behind her, her shoulders and perfect hair gliding across the window and disappearing again into the darkness behind the other couch. Like a shark moving silently through black water, I can't see her or hear her, but I swear I can feel the air move in the room, displaced by her presence. Sometimes that's all there seems to be of her.

Mom shunks on the floor lamp at the far end of the other couch, dimly illuminating the liquor cart parked there, brown liquids in clear bottles arranged by height in neat rows like a choir.

"Thirsty?"

She's still only lit from the waist down, so I can't see her face, but I don't think she's kidding. She sets down an empty tumbler glass she must have brought with her from the shadowy part of her desk. It makes the smallest sound of heavy glass on wood. She doesn't clink her glass against the other empty tumblers. She doesn't clink bottle against bottle when she extracts one from the line up.

"This whiskey," she says, "is older than you." There's a tiny, resonant pop in the darkness and the bottle tilts down through the light. Mom fills her tumbler. I mean she fucking *fills* her tumbler. Three inches, easy.

Then she fills mine.

Mom picks up both glasses and moves around the end of the couch to stand in front of the lit end next to the bottles. She gestures with my drink to the unlit end of the opposite couch and says, "Have a seat."

I discover that I've been squeezing the doorknob this whole time. My fingers ache when I de-clench to move to the middle of the room. Mom holds out my glass when I approach. It's out of the cone of light now, but the thick base glints with white highlights like the tips of her fingernails. I take the drink in my right hand, wait like a gentleman for the lady to sit, then ease myself down into the plush, over-padded leather.

Mom adjusts herself in her seat. She's obviously changed clothes since visiting Uncle Kenny in the hospital, because she's wearing one of her more casual, just-lounging-around-the-house formal skirt suits. Monique would be pissed if I said they looked alike, but my mother and my sister have the same blue eyes and the same angular face framed by black hair. Weird how you can get such different results from the same starting point, though. But I guess even a jack-o-lantern has two eyes and a mouth. Matters who carves what into it and with how much care. Monique minus compassion plus scorn plus derision plus two decades equals Mom.

Mom raises her glass out of the cone of light and says, "To Monique."

I raise my glass to toast, saying tentatively, "To Monique."

Mom's gaze stays on me as her glass finds her face and she takes a deep pull. I can't look away. I feel the edge of my tumbler touch just below my bottom lip. Slowly the cool, smooth glass slides up and over my bottom lip, touches my top lip and nestles into the parting there. I tilt my glass back, tilt my head forward, and take the tiniest sip of whiskey.

Fuck.

Burn, yes, but also an undeniable wash of heat and relaxation. The same wash of comfort I got from Mom's glass at dinner the other night. Profound comfort seeping into me.

"Why are you making that face?" she asks.

"It burns my throat."

"I know it burns. Why are you making that face?"

Mom watches me watch her take a swallow. I can practically feel the whiskey burn down her throat. But she smiles. She lowers the glass and smiles so brightly, so warmly, that for a second she looks like Monique. Then it's gone.

"Go on," she says.

Try it again. Hide the pain. Learn to act like nothing ever hurts. Stockton family secret.

I take another sip, a bigger sip, which actually doesn't seem to hurt as much as the first one, but maybe that's my imagination. I hold Mom's stare as I hold the fire in my mouth, then I scald my throat, all the while making sure my face doesn't betray me. I repeat the process, and though Mom certainly isn't yelling "Bravo," I perform two encores. For her benefit or mine, I can't say, you'll have to read your programs.

Mixed reviews. The audience seems satisfied, but this critic has seen better. Mom drains her glass. She stares at me until I drain my glass. At this point, I'm blinded by the spotlight and the cheers of the crowd, and I can't even say what hurts or doesn't hurt anymore.

Mom nods when I lower my empty glass. She puts her tumbler on the cart next to her as she slides forward to hold her hand out for mine. She fills both—quickly, neatly, expertly—and returns my glass to me. She takes a reasonable sip and does something I'd swear I've never seen her do. She takes off her shoes. Knees together, she slips the first heel onto the floor with a clunk, then the second. She takes another sip and puts her feet up on the table. Unprecedented. Unbe-fucking-lievable. Mom *never* relaxes. Legs crossed at the ankle, she scooches forward, stuffs a throw pillow behind the small of her back, and takes another sip as she reclines against the cushy cushions.

"Put your elbow on the arm rest."

"My collarbone. That'll hurt my—"

"Pretend it doesn't."

Shit, shit, triple shit. I disconnect my face from the rest of my nervous system and twist the sling around to lift my elbow onto the arm rest. It hurts like—

"Don't lean. Do it properly."

I leaned away to my right to cheat the angle, merely sticking the point of my elbow on, well, the side of the armrest. To actually put my arm up top—my whole arm, what's she's actually asking for—I'll have to . . .

I take a good sip of my drink and transfer it to my left hand so

I can work the fingers of my right into the Velcro seam on the waistband of my sling. One, I'm buying a little time peeling the straps apart bit by bit. But two, I know in my bones—broken and otherwise—that I'll be criticized if I boorishly destroy Mom's serene atmosphere with a loud zhwook of tearing Velcro.

Mood is a subtle thing, Paul. Fragile. Care must be taken if one is to avoid shattering a carefully crafted ambiance.

The strap undone, my elbow is free and the unrestricted range of motion lets me raise my arm away from my side. I look over at the window, at the stars above the tree line, and they're joined now by new stars right here in Mom's study, sparkling in little constellations around everything I can see as I raise my arm to lay it along the overstuffed armrest. I extend my hand, dangle my drink over the edge, pinky casually tucked under the bottom of the glass. I cross my right leg over my left knee and actually lean into the side of the couch, lean into the pain.

"Seattle is truly majestic this time of year," I say. "The clean air and clear skies, the long, temperate days. Simply lovely, wouldn't you agree?"

I swirl the whiskey in the glass, let it settle, then bring it to my mouth and take a long, deep drag on that son of a bitch like it was what I was born to do.

Mom says, "Good."

I drain my glass. Ever the good hostess, Mom extends her hand to take my empty glass, but this time she doesn't sit up. Standing up to hand it to her would give me a good excuse to put my arm back where it should be, but she's not giving me that; she's making me stand to make me stand. So instead, I merely lean forward. Jury's out on whether pulling the break apart hurts any more or less than grinding the jagged ends of bone together. Does seem to throb a bit less. I'm careful not to grimace when I lower my elbow off the armrest to place my glass on the low, wooden table between us. It's way too big to have been used on a ship, but it has raised trim around the perimeter like they have to keep things from falling off in rough seas. With a flick of my wrist, I send my empty glass sliding toward Mom. It arrives with a gentle thunk as it hits the lip on the other side, about three inches from Mom's ankles.

While I wait for her to refill my glass, or to cut me off and call in my tab, I strap myself in and quietly secure the Velcro. Some things only make noise when you tear them apart.

Mom finishes her drink. She takes a different bottle off the cart—short and fat, bulbous. She peels the foil off the neck and squeak-squeak-pops out the cork. When her own glass is full again, she leans forward to put the bottle on the table next to my glass. With her foot, she gives my glass a little shove, then sends the bottle gliding along after it across the smooth, wooden surface. Both stop in front of me about an inch from the table's lip, the liquor swirling in the bottle, then finding its level.

THE GLENROTHES in simple raised lettering formed into the bottle. Founded 1879, 700ml, 43% by volume. If you pour 500 ml of ethanol into 500 ml of water, you only end up with 960 ml of liquid. The alcohol molecules are smaller and fit in between the water molecules, like pouring water into a bucket of sand. The bucket looked full.

I pour myself a drink.

"Monique," Mom says again, raising her glass. I raise my glass, too. Mom empties hers, remedies that. "Did she show you her birthday present?" Mom asks, then when I don't answer, adds the address of the apartment building Monique is in the process of cashing out below market value. I nod. I drink and I nod again.

"You know about that?"

"Paul, who do you think put that building in her name? It wasn't the goddamn Shriners, I'll tell you that. I know about that. Of course, I know about that. I'll tell you another thing. Here's something you don't know. Something Monique doesn't know. *I* am buying it. Third party, arm's length, secret, anonymous, double-blind, straw men and all the rest, but it is I."

"Why?"

"That property has always performed. Your sister would do better to hold the asset rather than liquidate it."

"No, why are you—?"

"Well," she says, "Not really for her birthday, per se. Not for that. Per se. For other things, shall we say? Compensation, for diminished value."

"What are you talking about?"

"No one gave me an apartment building, Paul. Nor my sister."

(Mom has a twin sister. It's a fucking horror show.)

"What are you talking about?" I drink. I refill my glass. I'm still behind Mom. I can't keep up. And I can't quite track where she's going.

"I did the best I could."

"Why are you giving Monique two million dollars?"

"She's earned it."

"How?" Mom doesn't answer. She drinks. I drink. She drinks. I ask, "Earned it how?"

"Lucky for you, your father became powerful enough in time not to need Kenny's support so desperately, by the time Kenny came sniffing around you, Paul."

What's starting to make sense doesn't make any sense.

"Monique gets that because you couldn't stop Uncle Kenny? Couldn't stand up to him?"

I'm all too familiar with that feeling—that standing up is like stepping in front of a train. You're not even going to slow it down. And the best you can hope for is maybe the paint on the iron will lessen the impact. But. What's starting to make sense only doesn't make sense because I don't want it to, because I'd dearly love to believe that no one would be—that no one could be this evil.

"You traded Monique for political favor."

"It's a great deal more complicated than that."

"Or not."

"Didn't that school teach you anything about the mighty Kings and bartered Queens of Europe, Paul? Alliance. Power. Dynasty."

Mom finishes what's in her tumbler. She sits up to fill it again, drinks half of it before topping it off and laying back. The abyss and I have been gazing into each other about as long as I can take, so now all I want to do is get as much scotch in me as quickly as I can and get me out of here as soon as inhumanly possible. I refill my glass. Four.

"Empire, Paul. We all have our purposes to serve. We all play our roles. You didn't think I wanted to marry your father, did you? Or that my sister wanted to marry your Uncle Kenny? My father sold us like cattle."

I empty and refill my glass. Five.

"And don't think he made Kenny buy the cow without trying the milk first. I was younger than Monique the first time. Not the first time with Kenny, but other ambitious, promising gentlemen."

I refill my glass. Six.

"Kenny said my sister wouldn't lose her figure after children." She drinks. I drink. "If you can call that vile brood of rat-faced vermin children. Hideous, the lot of them."

They do suck. I can't stand them.

She drinks. I drink. I finish mine, sit up straight on the edge of the couch and set down my glass. Maybe I can carpe the moment to make my exit if I let Mom have the last awful word and just go.

"Life is hard," she says, like I don't know that already. "It's a struggle, a fight, a war. Learn to endure."

"That which does not kill us?"

Shit. Shut up and go. Get out.

Mom asks, "Do you know anyone stronger than your sister? Present company excluded."

"She's strong as oak."

What. The. Fuck. is wrong with me? Firstly of all, Brazilian walnut is way stronger than oak. And second, What. The. Serious. Fuck? Getoutgetoutgetoutgetout.

Waiting, waiting, waiting. No, I think maybe I can go if I go. Go easy. I'm a little dizzy when I stand up. Hmm. That's a lie. I'm a lot dizzy. But I've been growing so much lately that my body's in a constant state of figuring out what the fuck is going on, so I guess it just figures this shit out too. Fucking hell. Roll with it. I let out a big sigh and head for the door, realizing how walking is usually more of an autopilot thing than it is now.

"Wait."

Without getting up from the couch, Mom rolls/leans over and

pops open the door on the cabinet part of the liquor cart. She pulls out an unopened bottle of the same stuff we started with, a standard-shaped bottle with a long neck. She lays back, rests the base on her stomach and turns the label to the light.

"The year Sam was born."

Still reclined, Mom extends the bottle out to me, holding it by the neck. I step-step-step back to step around the table to take it from her, but it takes me a second to figure out she's giving it to me. I look for the year of production, the year of Sam's birth, but it's dark and I don't know where to look and maybe it isn't even printed there anyway. Maybe she's just remembering something special.

"Thanks."

She answers with a sigh, then says, "I never drank when I was pregnant."

I guess I could thank her for that too, but she's kind of talking to herself now.

I head for the door again, slowly, carefully, trying not to thump while I walk, trying not to fall while I thump, trying not to Stockton while I Paul. As I twist the knob, Mom stops me again.

"Paul." I turn, look at Mom lying limp in the dim circle of light on the couch. Post sip, she lifts her index finger from her glass and taps it on her lips, making the "Shh" sign, and whispering past her finger.

"Your father will beat the shit out of me if he smells that on your breath."

CHAPTER 25: BABY'S FIRST HANGOVER

*or* HANG-OVER, HANGING-OVER, HANGED-OVER

*or* NO DOG, NO HAIR OF

*or* I SEE WHAT YOU DID THERE

*or* HOW DO YOU GET TO POWERHOUSE?


In the way-too-bright and who-knows-how-early, two blurry copies of American Gothic are hanging at the foot of my bed—business formal, no-pitchfork versions.

"Disgraceful," the moms say.

The dads leave without a word.

And that is how you don't stay out of rehab.

## Chapter 26: At PowerHouse I Learn Life Skills
*or*  Carrots & Sticks
*or*  Sticks & Sticks & Sticks & Sticks
*or*  $(x - \text{Paul})^2 + (y - \text{Paul})^2 = r^2$

My hangover is no worse than the headaches I get for less rewarding reasons than drinking too much, so there's that. Monique doesn't say I told you so about staying away from that stuff, she just picks up my schoolbooks and is first in line to get in the second that visiting hours start at 11:00. They don't let her in. No visitors, not the six days while you detox and get to know the program and the counselors and your "peers" and think about what brought you here. Uh, Mom? I mean, Xerxes drove us, but . . .

Anyway.

People bitch about not being able to use the telephone, or not being allowed to smoke in the building, or that we ain't got no ShowTime on the TEEvee. Nobody seems to care about being off-line. The general population is not as addicted to the Internet as I am. But honestly, that's the only thing I'm jonesing for. I'm not sure I'm using that word right. Jonesin', at least. Gs are for snobs. I do beg your pardon, but I am simply jonesing for some Grey Poupon. Might you be able to help a brother out?

Anyway.

I think in a single morning session, I've already seen a complete cycle of what goes on here. Complain, complain, complain, get called on some obvious bullshit, deny, admit, cry. And somewhere in there—probably between the crying and the heartfelt thanking of all y'all—healing happens.

According to the big painted lettering on the wall and the brochures and the counselors and the more enthusiastic residents, At PowerHouse We Learn Life Skills™. But I think a guy who I'd pegged as seventeen going on twelve, sums it up better: "Ain't nobody in here got a drug problem. They all getting glazed fixing some worser problem." Smart kid, turns out. But he hangs himself during the lunch break. He doesn't *die*. Nothing as dramatic as that. At this end of his long, uninterrupted chain of failures, he fucked that up too. He's back at 1:00, beltless and rubbing his neck.

Everybody's jealous of the pain meds that I get dispensed every four hours for my collarbone, pretty doctor's orders.

No, everyone is envious of my medications. I am jealous of them.

I have learned that I'm kind of a dick.

I'll let you know when I pick up a life skill.

Anyway.

So, around 2:30 we're deep in the deep, working out some heavy, heavy shit (that I seriously cannot relate to at all. Know-what-I'm-sayin'? No. Not at all. I have no idea what you're talking about. Sorry.) when I learn that if you make laws for a living, you kind of don't give a shit about rules. One of the orderlies, Jaime, a tall Mexican dude with kind eyes, steps up to our circle of chairs in the big common area, and waits patiently until the counselor leading us finishes listening to some deep, heavy, heavy, deep shit, and looks Jaime's way.

"Paul has a visitor."

Paul has been here about six hours, not six days.

Paul is going to have a hard time fitting in here, too.

The counselor looks passively at the orderly. The orderly looks passively at the counselor. They say nothing, which is to say that they communicate everything they need to.

"Back here after, Paul?" the counselor asks/tells me.

"Okay."

There are a couple of other meeting rooms and loungey areas, but Jaime escorts me back to the door of the room I'm sharing with one of the guys in the circle who hasn't found out yet that he doesn't have a private room anymore. Maybe I can smooth that over by getting us ShowTime.

"I'll be at the station," Jaime says, and heads down the hall to an admin/nurses/catch-all counter and desk area. The only computer I've seen here is there.

"Thanks." I put my hand on the lever.

Do I want this to be Mom or do I want this to be Dad? No.

It's Dad. Under the window, there's one institutional chair between the plain twin beds. Dad's occupying the whole room from there. It feels like I'm pushing through a hurricane gale to fight my way into the room, and I end up squeezed just inside the door with my back against the concrete wall.

"Hi, Dad. How's Mom?"

"Cut the smart talk, Paul."

"Just asking about—"

"Paul."

"Yes, sir."

"Have a seat," Dad says, indicating the wrong bed. I don't really want to get any closer to him, or to sit down, or to do what I'm told, but he's inadvertently given me the mildly-disobedient option of sitting on my bed instead of where I've been told, so I do that.

"This one's mine." He's about to start talking so I ask, "What's up?" just 'cause.

"We know about the money."

What money? Who is 'we'? What do you know? What do you *think* you know? I say nothing.

"You're going to need to return what you've taken."

Am I? *I'm* going to *need* to, or *you* already *want* me to? And how desperately?

"Do you understand, Paul?"

"Yes."

"Good," Dad says as he stands. It's unreasonable to think you can change the world, so all change comes about from unreasonable people. But then again, so does a whole lot of shittiness. Dad straightens his tie, before stepping to the door. I wait to speak until his hand hits the lever.

"You're dumb."

"What did you say to me?" He heard me right but his brain won't let that process.

"You think because I understand you that I'm going to comply." Sometimes I just get myself started, and just can't seem to—"That's dumb."

"You'll comply."

"Carrots or sticks? What are you going to give me?"

"You disappoint me, Paul. We were all hoping you'd choose—"

" '—to be part of the solution,' " I say with him. "I bet you were. So, nothing? No carrot? What's your stick? What are you going to threaten me with?"

"You're not going to win this."

"I don't have to win."

He doesn't quite make a face, but there's something in the blank look that tells me he's surprised, and surprised to be surprised. And with shields and cloaking devices already engaged, he's probably charging weapons.

"Didn't think of that, did you? What if the point is only to make you lose? At any cost? How the fuck are you going to win then?" I'm in it. I'm in it heavy and deep, and I know what I'm talking about. I put on my giant, foam, "Monique is #1" button-pushing hand. "I *am* smarter than you. You know that, right?"

He steps over to stand in front of me.

"You are out of your league."

I bat away the number three, the number of miles in a league, the distance a shorter-than-me, average-height dude can see out to sea at sea level at the sea shore. Always, but especially now, I'd love to be three miles away from Dad. I'd sign up for the full 60,000 miles of 20,000 leagues, but that's two-and-a-half times the diameter of the Earth and impossible.

"Maybe I am out of my league," I say. "Maybe I'm dumb. Maybe, 'cause I'm not real sure what league we're talking about? Senators who steal? In fact, I'm not even sure what money you're talking about? What money *are* we talking about, Dad? What money do you think is missing, Dad? Where did that money come from, Dad? Are there 'unrealistic restrictions' on how you spend campaign funds? So you had no choice really, but to appropriate them for blah, blah-blah, blah-blah, blah-blah. No, because then you'd have actually used some of it at some point to help somebody. Which you haven't, for years and years and years and years. So, no. You're just a common thief."

Dad backhands me across the face, hard enough that I hear a couple of vertebrae in my neck pop.

"That's what I thought," I say. Common would have worked on Mom, too.

Dad stands above me, the look on his face unchanged. No sorry. No forgive me. Also no threat that more's coming. No change in carrot or stick. Just his standard M.O. Just how he rolls. I'm not dumb enough to ask him if that's all he's got.

Instead, I ask, "Would you like to negotiate?"

"Would you like to see your sister again?"

"What, you're gonna kill her?"

I wouldn't put it past him. But like Sam's dog-killing math, there's probably no upside.

"You're a troubled young man, Paul. Your mother and I are starting to share the opinion that your sister has contributed to your maladjustments of personality and anti-social tendencies. We feel it would be better for your recovery, that she not be allowed to be a part of your life."

Dad starts pacing around, like a TV preacher or an overconfident, hack trial lawyer, that come to think of it . . .

"A fresh start requires a break from bad influences. A clean break. Total and immediate."

I believe 'cold turkey' is the term of art among practicing professionals.

"With a protective order in place, at such time that your sister were to entertain you in her place of residence, or transport you in a vehicle without my prior written consent, or should she make any effort to come within five hundred feet of your person while on or off campus, or should she write you a letter or call you on the telephone, then she will be subject to arrest for contributing to the delinquency of a minor."

Dad makes his way to standing in front of the chair.

"A serious offense that your mother and I would pursue to the fullest extent of the law, with the utmost of enthusiasm and tenacity."

Dad sits, resting his case. He crosses one leg over his knee. A silence descends on the courtroom like a cloud of stink from his river of bullshit.

"Oh! Sorry, I kind of dozed off when you opened your lie hole. Start again with the part where you pretend to care about what's best for me."

"You're trying my patience, Paul."

"Let's try this," I say and push myself up with my good arm. "I took your money. I left you just enough wiggle room to stay out of jail." Dad straightens up in the chair like he likes the admission, but doesn't like my tone or the fact that I'm right. "But if you want to keep wiggling, and if you want the money back—*some* of the money back—then, you are going to have to humble up and negotiate in good faith. And in the meantime . . ."

I kick my door as hard as I can. It's loud in here. It'll be loud in the hall.

"I probably don't want to press charges."

I kick my door again as hard as I can. Over here, everybody. Look over here.

"But I think it would be better for my recovery if my father weren't allowed back at PowerHouse."

And then fuck me if I don't slam my own goddamn face against the door as hard as I can. My cheekbone may or may not be broken, but I split the brow, because there's blood running into my eye, warm and salt-stingy. And I got the nose, that's for sure. That's for sure-sure. Blood's pouring over my lips like joyful tears from Monique's eyes.

The room's going blurry and gray when I turn to face my father, just an indistinct silhouette against the window—huh. Like Mom last night. Falling back against the door now, I manage to spray out a gooey, "Fuck you. Fuck you so much," before dropping my hip on the door lever and letting my dead weight push it open as I collapse onto the hallway floor.

I land on my back in a circle of PowerHouse staff, so many

credible witnesses. Beyond them: two concentric circles of PowerHouse residents, less credible, but irrefutably numerous. As the tunnel-vision narrows my view to the innermost circle, I luck out and find Jaime just before he fades into the darkness.

"I fell on the stairs."

## CHAPTER 27: THE VICE PRESIDENT OF LIFE

If I were in a spacesuit, floating around outside of the International Space Station at 416 kilometers above the surface of the Earth, I would not—because I have learned from experience—I would not be surprised if Sam appeared, lurking behind a solar panel or just idly picking the lock on a hatch.

Sam broke into PowerHouse.

"Nighttime voice," he says, his face six inches from mine when I open my eyes. From time to time, he's woken me up by putting his hand over my mouth and holding me down until I stop flailing around, but he's doing me a kindness not doing that now with my face all bashed up. Or maybe he just figures I'll cry out. Either way, he nods when I nod about nighttime voice, and makes no move to restrain me. "Do you believe in democracy?" he whispers. I nod, shrug, shake my head, then mouth What? Sam says, "You're the vice president of life. Get dressed."

While I suit up—which I'm already getting good at, even quiet Velcro opening—Sam eyeballs my roommate, Jebediah. Okay, his name's not Jebediah. Derek? Darren? Daryl? Whatever. He told me and I forgot and I was embarrassed to ask but I'll find out tomorrow at circle time. Sam stares at my roommate, willing him to stay asleep, or instilling the fear of Sam into him to make him at least keep pretending to be asleep.

"Do you have a red T-shirt?" Sam whispers. I nod. "Wear that." He pulls a small strip of paper from a pocket and lays it on my roommate's bedspread near the hem at the head. If he gets out of bed while we're gone, we'll know.

When I'm dressed, Sam looks through the narrow window in the door, then cracks the door and uses a compact like Mom's to peer left and right.

"Stay close."

I shadow Sam as he guides us down the hall, pausing before passing the admin/nurses' station, easing through a staff door, moving quickly then stopping to wait at an exterior door—marked "emergency exit" and "alarm will sound."

"What would make that alarm go off?" Sam asks.

"Breaking a circuit or closing a circuit—"

—"Nighttime voice."—

"—or a—" I adjust my volume. "—motion sensor signal or a heat sensor or a combination."

"Low rent," Sam says. (This place isn't cheap if you can pay, but it's actually a non-profit.)

"Breaking a circuit." Sam points to two plastic modules mounted an eighth of an inch apart, one on the door, one on the frame. "Reed switch," I say. "And a magnet," holding the reed switch closed, keeping the circuit connected.

Sam taps his nose twice like I got it right. He takes another plastic module out of his pocket, along with some duct tape, and affixes his magnet to the reed switch that's going to stay on the doorframe. Oriented incorrectly, it'd be easy to get the polarity wrong and cancel the magnetic field with the second magnet before you even opened the door. That'd be a fifty/fifty chance, but I think Sam knows what he's doing.

But this is a trick that makes it easy to bust *out*.

"How did you get in?"

Sam waves that off. Not on today's lesson plan. Sam eases the door open about three inches—no alarm—and braces it there with his foot.

"Look. See the path that goes to the parking lot? When I say Go, stay to the left of that path until you get past the bushes, then duck behind them and stop. Duck behind them means crouch down. Got it?"

"Left of the path, hide behind the bushes. Is there a camera? Sweeping?"

"Affirmative." Sam points above the door on the hinge side. The angle puts it about twelve feet off the ground. He holds his mirror in the three-inch gap up near the top of the door, angles it at the camera. "Seven, six, five, ready?"

"Yeah."

"Three, two."

"Wait."

"What?"

"Go on one or Go on zero? Three, two, Go, or—"

"Three, two, one, Go."

"Okay. Ready."

"Now we have to wait."

"Okay." Waiting. Ready to run. Left of the path. Hide in the bushes. Hide *behind* the bushes. Waiting. Waiting, waiting, waiting. Sam points at the hole in the doorjamb where the catch would engage if we weren't holding the door open. He points where the catch would protrude and runs his hand up and down along the edge of the door before tapping my hand. I run my hand down the edge of the door and feel the strip of tape that's holding the catch inside its recess. This door won't latch. I give Sam a thumbs up and we're back to waiting. Waiting, waiting, waiting. Slow camera. Seriously, shit. "How'd you get in? Sam, how'd you get in?"

"I climbed a fence you can't climb."

What? Monkey-boy can climb. That's bullshit.

"I can climb—"

"Quietly. I climbed a fence you can't climb quietly. Two, one, Go!"

We run, run, run, stay left, and hide behind the bushes, no problem. The only suck part is running with my collarbone, so maybe I couldn't climb a fence—probably I couldn't climb a fence, certainly not quietly. Sam hands me his little mirror and vacates the spot at the end of the bank of bushes.

"Don't bounce any light, but take a look at the camera. When would you go to get back in?"

I watch for a while, figure out where it was pointed when Sam sent us out the door, figure out when it would see us if we stood up from behind these bushes. It is a slow camera, but more so because it's also covering a lot of ground. They'd do better with two, overlapping coverage areas. Or two static, with one roving—

Anyway.

"Go when it's pointed at the edge of that exercise yard," I say. "Sweeping away."

"Good," Sam says. I try to hand him back his mirror, but he says, "Keep it."

"Okay. Thanks."

Any point in asking?

"If you killed the motor," I say, "not the camera, but the motor that rotates it, I bet that nobody would notice for a while. As long as the camera still worked. If there's even anybody watching."

"Destruction is escalation," Sam says, "and evidence, but that's good thinking if it came to it. Come on."

We duck-walk along the bushes until we reach a line of trees, then we just follow those out to the street where Sam's parked. He's got a Camry like Monique's, but not as new. "Urban and suburban camouflage," he says. "These things are invisible." It's not locked, so no beep-boop or flash of headlights, and he's got it rigged so the overhead doesn't come on when we open the doors. I'm not sure "fire's up" really applies to the four cylinders of sensible fuel economy under the hood, but Sam turns the ignition and we're off, me AWOL from PowerHouse—for now, unofficially. No, let's call it an impromptu field trip. I might still learn some life skills. It could happen. Of course, I know zero parts of the plan or even where we're going.

Turns out it's the hospital. Maybe I'll see my pretty, redheaded doctor. Or maybe that would be a very bad idea. We drive past the regular parking lot, park in the neighborhood and follow a path to the hospital that involves lots of cutting through bushes and avoiding of streetlights. We tuck ourselves into the shadowed corner of a fenced enclosure for dumpsters, where Sam's already stashed a backpack.

"Red," he says pointing to my T-shirt then his own. Here in the dark, it looks black or very dark gray or brown. In the light, it looks loud and bright and the dumbest color in the world to wear if you're up to no good. Or at least up to some sneaky-sneaking around.

Sam pulls on drab green scrubs over his other clothes, hangs a lanyard around his neck with an official-looking ID and keycard. He takes a second folding mirror out of the backpack before zipping it up, and puts that in his shirt pocket.

"Good shoulder," Sam says. He hangs the right strap of the backpack off my good side. The backpack is not empty. At least I don't have pot in my pocket.

"You don't know me," Sam says. "You're visiting your dad on four. He had a heart attack. You got lost and I'm helping you find your way back."

"Where do you work?"

"Depends who stops us. Cry if you have to. Best if we're not seen at all."

Crossing the loading dock, we don't see anybody, but we don't try to go in that way. Sam circles us around to a side door, a non-patient emergency door that's propped open with a big rock, presumably from the bushy area surrounding the four-foot-square pad of concrete the door opens onto. Next to the door stands a garbage can with an ashtray on top, the sand stuck with so many butts it looks like a tiny shag carpet.

"That's our danger point. No good story. No good view of incoming traffic. We're going in, and immediately right up the stairwell." We leave our bushes, cut across a sparsely landscaped area with little cover, cut through those bushes and up to the door. Sam starts talking as we step onto the concrete pad. "No, you're fine. You just got turned around. If your dad's on that floor, then—" He stops midsentence when we're through the door and find the stairwell unpopulated.

"Okay. Six flights up to seven. We're going to go up three and stop to assess. Above that, if we hear anybody, we head down and enter the floor."

"K."

We do the stairs, see no one, and the only hard part is trying not to thump when I walk. Like at PowerHouse, Sam uses the mirror to check the hallway on seven. I stay close and we move, pause, move, pause, until Sam opens a patient door and deposits me inside.

"Put these on," he says, handing me a pair of latex gloves. "Five minutes," he says as the door closes between us. Inside the what-a-hospital-considers-darkened room, I'm not at all surprised to find Uncle Kenny (asleep or unconscious) and very much surprised to find Monique (neither). Monique looks at my face, my broken nose and swollen eye.

"Jesus. What happened to you?"

"Dad."

"Jesus."

"No. Dad."

"Glad you didn't break your sense of humor." Monique brings her hands up to my face, but they have nowhere to land that won't hurt, so she puts them over her own mouth. "Oh, sweetie. We should think about the thermonuclear option."

"I think showing him I have the launch codes should be enough," I say. Not including myself, who didn't see a whole lot after the door, there were a bunch of credible witnesses at PowerHouse. I toss the backpack onto the guest chair. "Hey, how'd Sam get you here?"

"He said you'd need a ride home."

"Home away from home. Hmm. Is shithead really asleep?"

"He's out. I poked him."

"Did Sam—" I start to ask if Sam kept Monique's kickball score out of the sports pages, but realize I can check for myself. Then reaching for Uncle Kenny's chart, I find my hand already conveniently full of latex gloves. "Sam's crazy good at this stuff," I say as I put them on. Looks like he did. And he was right about the ruptured spleen.

Allow me to remark upon a remarkable commotion down the hall. There's a lot of beeping and buzzing and running and shouting, obviously very loud at a distance. It crescendos quickly and, for us, fades again into the background noise of a working hospital.

"That'll be a diversion," I say to Monique.

A few seconds later, one of the machines connected to Uncle

Kenny beeps once, and its orange, mono-chromatic screen starts flashing. He's breathing on his own, so that's either for the little clippie thing on his finger or the bundle of wires running under the blanket.

The flashing text reads TELEMETRY LOST, meaning it's no longer talking with the nurses' station or wherever this call would be monitored or recorded for quality assurance purposes. The text changes to PAIR W/ CONSOLE for three cycles and returns to TELEMETRY LOST.

Uncle Kenny is offline.

Sam opens the door.

"Did you just kill somebody?" Monique asks. She's joking, but she's asking.

"Nah, he'll be fine. Hundred percent. Good as new. Better than new. Right as rain."

"Collateral damage?" I ask.

Sam stops joking around. "No, really. He'll be fine. What's happening down the hall is a routine, nothing emergency that will have no lasting impact on that patient."

"Okay," I say.

"Nothing unusual or interesting. Nothing noteworthy. Nothing that will cause investigations or reports. What that is, is very purposefully a non-event. Do you understand me? I'm going to need you to focus all your attention right here. Both of you."

"Okay," Monique says.

"Out of your mind?"

"Yes," Monique says.

"Forgotten?"

"Sam."

"Okay." Sam pushes a button that starts Uncle Kenny's bed rising on the pair of scissor-lift supports that hold up the bed frame. Sam's already wearing gloves. Monique's not. "Have you touched anything?" he asks her, while the bed rises, whir-irr-irr-irr-irr. Monique shakes her head. Sam says, "Don't. Not even the door."

"I know."

"Did you come in the way I asked you?"

"And opened the stairwell door with my sleeve. Yes."

"Okay."

The bed stops. I don't know what medical reason you'd need to have the bed go up that high, gurney height or operating table height or whatever, but it's pretty high. Sam has to kind of throw the blankets over the bed to drape them over Uncle Kenny.

Wait, what?

Sam gets one heavy hospital blanket (folded in thirds the long way) draped over Uncle Kenny's chest, from neck to wrists, and another (folded the same way) laid across his legs, kind of groin to ankles. Sam tugs the blanket smooth over Uncle Kenny's chest and tucks the end under the bed, capturing it in the beams of the scissors-lift. He does the same with the blanket on his legs before walking around to the other side.

Now Sam pulls the blankets taut, making sure these ends are securely enmeshed in the beams of the scissors-lift before pressing the button to lower the bed, whir-irr-irr-irr-irr, gradually pinching the trapped blankets as the levers squeeze down. Sam stops to make an adjustment at about the height where the bed started, then proceeds, everything getting not necessarily tighter, but definitely locked in place as the beams nest together in the bed's lowest position. High was pretty high and low is pretty low and if Uncle Kenny wakes up, he is going nowhere with those blankets strapping him down. And he also can't hit anybody with his arm cast. And the IV on the back of his other hand won't get torn out because it's exposed between the blanket restraints.

Monique has her hand over her mouth again, but this time it's not covering a What are we going to do? face. We know what Sam is going to do. But he says it, in a soft voice that feels like it wouldn't even propagate all the way to the walls.

"I am going to kill Uncle Kenny. That is my intent. But we are going to take a vote."

Monique doesn't say, You're crazy.

I don't say, Stop, Sam, be reasonable.

Sam takes a large, clear plastic bag out of the backpack and lays it on the blanket.

Sam takes a roll of electrical tape out of the backpack and lays it on the blanket.

"There is a motion before this body," Sam says. "It is moved to execute Uncle Kenny, without delay, and leaving no evidence, if at all possible. Are you ready for the question? The chair recognizes Mr. Paul Stockton to speak to the motion."

"I yield the balance of my time."

"The chair recognizes Ms. Monique Stockton, née Abigail Stockton, to speak to the motion."

"I'm not doing that, Sam."

"Ms. Stockton moves the previous question and yields the balance of her time. As is his prerogative, the chair calls for a roll call vote. Mr. Richard 'Sam' Stockton, how do you vote?" Sam tells himself Aye, and gives Uncle Kenny a thumbs down. "Ms. Stockton, how do you vote?"

Monique doesn't answer. Sam's getting some of the procedural stuff not quite right, but that's obviously not why she's demurring. Sam waits. I wait.

Sam asks quietly, "Does Ms. Stockton wish to abstain or to vote for or against the motion?"

I say, "You can vote no, Monique."

"Mr. Stockton, you are out of order," Sam says, still in a low, even tone, possibly the least threatening I've ever heard him. "Ms. Stockton has the floor. Ms. Stockton, you are within your rights to vote against the motion." Softer, much softer: "The bag and the tape can go back in the knapsack and we can all walk out of here right now. If that's what you want."

They say in jazz—good jazz—it's the notes they don't play. Monique is laying out, bobbing her head with her eyes closed, listening to the other musicians with her eyes closed.

Sam asks, "Is that what you want?"

When Monique still doesn't answer, I whisper, "Mr. Chairman, will the speaker yield?"

Monique, barely audible, says, "I yield to the gentleman from Washington."

I say, "You should vote no, Monique."

We're all quiet, long after when Monique would have figured out what that means, what I'm offering.

Then she says, "I don't want you to have to choose to—"

"Let me. You vote not to, Monique. You vote to save his life. Vote for mercy. Vote for more than he deserves. Vote for hope and goodness and remorse and redemption. You can do that. You can give yourself that."

"I vote no," Monique says.

Sam pauses for a second. "Mr. Stockton. How do you vote?"

The Vice President of Life, casting the tie-break vote, extends his good arm, sticks out his thumb, turns it down.

"The Ayes have it and the motion carries," Sam says.

Sam is crazy good at this. He just gave Monique almost everything she wanted.

The rest is . . . Uneventful. Anti-climactic. Clinical, without the first-do-no-harm part.

Sam slides the plastic bag over Uncle Kenny's head, makes a careful fold at the neck to get a good seal, and closes off part of the seam with tape. The plastic moves ever so slightly in and out as Uncle Kenny breathes through the remaining opening.

"I can take him out with just the bag, and not leave marks, but then he'll be loaded up with carbon-dioxide, and we're shouting through a bullhorn asking for inquiries. I can choke him down to these two cubic feet of air and use a re-breather to scrub out the $CO_2$ so his body won't thrash around to wake itself up, but then we have to wait for him to use up the oxygen. And since we don't actually use up very much of it, especially just lying there like a piece of shit, we three end up sitting here with our thumbs up our asses waiting around for shallower and shallower breaths. Was that the last one? Was that the last one?"

Pfffff! Sam blows a raspberry, dismissing the ennui-producing, not-fast-enough murder of our not-much-beloved uncle. As Sam pulls a short piece of tubing out of the backpack, he asks, "Paul, is the glass half full or half empty?"

It's an engineering joke. The glass is too big. Or the glass is 100% full: 50% your liquid of choice, 50% ambient gases.

So I say, "Yes."

"Helium is groovy," Sam says, retrieving a cylindrical tank from the backpack. Metal, about two liters, with a tiny brass valve and pressure gauge, and a quick-release fixture that Sam mates with the tubing. I don't think this is something Sam whipped up in the last twenty-four hours. He probably could, but I suspect this falls under his philosophy of Don't get ready; stay ready.

"But Helium is designed for the guy *inside* the bag," Sam says. "We'll notice carbon dioxide building up in your system. 'Oh, no, oh, no!' But we're dumb as bricks when it comes to figuring out when there's no oxygen around. 'Doot, do, doo. Collapse. Die.' Still, too much waiting around for us. So, how shall we dispatch him with alacrity and aplomb?"

Professor Sam in any room at any time with any thing?

"Paul. Ninety-nine percent of the atmosphere is what?"

"Oxygen and Nitrogen. Mostly Nitrogen."

"Nitrogen," he says, holding up the little tank. He lays it on Uncle Kenny's chest and tapes the loose end of the tube into the last remaining opening in the plastic bag. "Three breaths of inert gas and the net flow of oxygen is *out* of the body."

Sam grasps the tank and the tiny, brass valve and makes eye contact first with Monique, then with me.

"Yes," Sam says, repeating his vote.

He looks at Monique. "No."

They both look at me. "Yes."

Sam turns the valve. The bag inflates slightly around Uncle Kenny's head. Beneath the taut blankets, his chest rises and falls for those first three breaths. Sam rides the valve, adjusting the pressure to keep the bag gently inflated while a small amount of gas vents around Uncle Kenny's neck. He started out unconscious. It doesn't take long before he's stopped breathing. Sam feels for a pulse, and soon doesn't have to. To be sure, he pulls a stethoscope out of the backpack, not part of his disguise for whatever reason.

Sam activates the bed, whir-irr-irr-irr-irr, and tosses the stethoscope into the backpack as the bed starts to rise. Tank shut

off, tape off the tubing. Into the backpack. He slides the bag off
Uncle Kenny's head, flattens and folds it in two quick motions.
Into the backpack. ID. Sam holds his compact mirror in his teeth
as he takes off his scrubs. Into the backpack before the bed's at
full height. Blankets off, folded, into the backpack.

Zip.

Done.

Sam starts the bed down, whir-irr-irr-irr-irr.

"Gloves," Sam says, holding out his hand. I peel off my gloves
and hand them over to Sam, who wads them into his fist and
captures them by turning his glove inside out over them as he
takes his first glove off. With his remaining gloved index finger,
Sam stops the bed where it started out, then pulls the last glove
over the first three. He jams that wad in a smaller pocket of the
backpack before throwing it over both shoulders.

"Ready?"

We nod. Monique draws her sleeve over her hand and pulls the
door open just enough for Sam to check the corridor with the
mirror. Sam goes. We follow, all of us walking normally, not
looking obvious by looking obvious. We see no one in the
hallway or the stairwell or the smoking area or the bushes or the
neighborhood. Monique takes the lead and Sam walks us to her
car.

Before he turns to walk away into the night, he says, "Be
surprised."

When we find out. Be surprised.

Act natural.

Traffic's light for a Friday night, though I honestly don't have
much experience with that. Monique drives the correct amount
over the speed limit, but it doesn't matter anyway, because we see
no police on the way back to PowerHouse. Unlike dropping me
off at "home" last night, neither of us cries when Monique pulls
over to drop me off at rehab.

"Thanks, Paul."

"It was the most I could do."

"Thanks."

"I better go," I say, cracking open my door. "But four days. Official visiting hours."

"Count on it."

I jog my lopsided, thumping jog along the line of trees, stay low behind the bushes and use Sam's mirror to time the camera swing. Inside, I remove the door tape and alarm magnet and pocket this small collection of items that weirdly adds up to a key to the free world. The piece of paper Sam put on what's-his-name's bedspread is still there, too, so I'm good. Nobody will know I was out. Picking up the tiny slip of paper, I find that Sam's low-tech roommate motion detection system is a fortune, a fortune cookie fortune.

傷心有多少　在乎就有多少

The eleven symbols means nothing to me, except for recognizing that the last three characters of each set repeat, and that the end ones kind of look like little sleepy drunk guys. But the six Lucky Numbers below the characters? The days and months of our birthdays, Sam's, Monique's, and mine.

I put the fortune in my pocket with the key kit before I get undressed, climb back into bed, and sleep the sleep of angels.

CHAPTER 28: 7/7/1990
*or* BLOOD MOON, STOCKTON BLUE
*or* READING SEMAPHORE
*or* DID THEY
*or* DID THEY NOT SAY 'NO VISITORS'?

My roommate's name is Doug and he's an okay guy. He's a good student in an age-appropriate grade for an almost-17-year-old. He likes to draw and paint and is interested in the optics and light theory I learned about in photography class. Both his parents are doctors, which is not great for him at home with them working all the time, but is pretty good for us both here because we both care about education and have been to Europe and don't have to be self-conscious when we use words like "lassitude" or "abstruse" or "postmodern aesthetics"—or "pretentious douchebags" when we start talking about abstruse postmodern aesthetics, 'cause we're still just a couple of dipshits who got themselves thrown into kiddie rehab.

On Saturdays we have Reflection Time instead of our weekday Circle Time, which means games or chatting or reading or anything but TV or napping. Reflection Time is wildly unpopular. Some of the kids are depressed, most of us seem a bit introverted or at least actively introspective, and if normal is the goal, aren't we all pretty much aiming for Standard American Sullen Teen? Maybe sullen teen is redundant. As a policy, we're encouraged to stay out in the common areas, but Doug and I adjourned to our room after breakfast because we were being too cheery and bumming everybody else out.

But about 10:30 we learn what amateurs we are at that, when an eerie quiet falls over PowerHouse.

Once during a freak snowstorm, the electricity at the estate went out in the middle of the night. When the wind died down, I actually woke up because it was so quiet. TVs, alarm clocks, radios, computer fans, hard drives, fluorescent lights, incandescent lights, light switches with a dimmer, HVAC, refrigerators, everything that's always—even when they're off—radiating some kind of electrical hum, was for once blissfully silent. I tripled up my blankets (ooh, that reminded me of Uncle Kenny), opened my window and just lay there listening to the quiet. It was so peaceful.

This silence is the opposite of that. This quiet is the hush of frightened animals, switched hard into flight, holding their breath while deciding which way to run.

"Shit, I think my Mom's here."

"One unsanctioned visitor isn't enough, Paul?" Doug says. "You *better* get us ShowTime."

I don't mention Sam's visit last night. Two, so far, and I hope that I'm wrong about—

Mom opens the door. Sometimes I hate being right.

"Hi, Mom. This is my roommate Doug. Doug, this is my mom."

Doug looks at Mom's boobs. Boobs, legs, boobs, lightning fast. I can practically hear the camera shutter going off in his head.

Mom steps in, glances at Doug just long enough to say, "Get out."

Like I said, he ain't dumb. He's out the door before the gentle hydraulic piston can ease it closed behind Mom. I hope he and I end up being friends, but I won't ever make the mistake of having him over to my house to play. And for his own good, not because he checks out Mom's butt in her tight skirt before the door latches.

She shakes her head and rolls her eyes at my broken face, but doesn't say anything about it. She sits in the one chair, crosses her legs and takes out a cigarette.

"You can't smoke in here," I say.

She sparks up, inhaling deeply. Mom holds the smoke in her lungs while she twists to slide open the big window behind her, then turns back before making eye contact with me and blowing all the smoke into the middle of the room. Tell me again what I can't do. She picks a flake of loose tobacco off her lip with her thumb and ring finger, flicks it onto the floor.

When I sit down on my bed, she says, "Your Uncle Kenny is dead."

"What happened?"

I was supposed to remember to be surprised. I haven't really blown that exactly, but the level of emotion Mom and I are bringing to bear, individually or in total, we could be talking about a really good cheese. Made with raw milk from grass-fed cows, aged a dozen or so months in limestone caves, Gruyere goes perfectly on a toasted ham sandwich, or try it chilled with candied walnuts and revenge.

"Your brother finally killed him," Mom says. So there's that. "Your father doesn't know and no one is ever going to find out." So there's that. Done and done. Mom takes a giant drag on her cigarette and holds it so long that no smoke comes out when she exhales.

"He was an asshole," I say.

"Don't speak ill of the dead," she says, with about as much oomph as, "Elbows off the table."

I get up to get a notebook from my backpack and tear out one piece of paper. Mom watches as I hold the paper to my belly so I can use both hands to fold the sheet into a little box—not at all some cool origami creation, just a half-ass container, open on one end. I hand it to her just as her cigarette ash reaches unmanageable proportions.

"Paper?"

"School stuff is infused with fire retardant."

She sets it on my bed and flicks her ash into the open top. We sit while Mom quietly smokes her cigarette down to a miniscule nub. She turns her ankle and stubs out the flaming cherry on the sole of her shoe before lighting another with her lighter. I watch her burn that one down, kill it, light another.

"Would you like to get out of here?" Mom asks casually.

"To go *home*?"

Mom shrugs and continues smoking.

Outside, two of the older kids appear through a door onto the paved exercise court past the lawn below the window, one dribbling a basketball. He half-heartedly breaks for the basket and lays it up for two easy points while the kid in the peace sign T-shirt ambles onto the court, failing even to attempt defense.

Code. I always see math and code. The peace symbol was made by superimposing the semaphore flag symbols ∧ and | on top of each other in a circle. I'd guess the circle is meant be the earth. I know the ∧ and | (N and D) stand for Nuclear Disarmament. Maybe that's why Mom is here.

Kid Basketball retrieves the ball, dribbles out a ways and shoots a predictable $y = t^2 + t + c$. The ball clunks off the side of the rim and smacks the backboard, setting it rattling and quivering in a tangle of disharmonic waves. Neither one goes after the loose ball. They suck. And it's already hot. They quit. They abandon the ball and the game to go back inside, final score two-nil. No more happy counting for Paul, no more amusing quadratic equations for Newtonian mechanics.

Mom was twisted around with her hand on the window to close it, but didn't and lets go.

She lights another cigarette.

I ask, "Did you know the peace symbol was built from semaphore flags?"

"Fascinating," she says, so neutral I don't think I can even call that sarcastic.

"Are you here for a reason, Mom?" Maybe I should worry that she's been tasked with presenting me an offer that she's choosing not to present.

"The funeral will be back east." Makes sense; that's where Uncle Kenny lived with Aunt Horror Show. "Sam's going," she says.

"Okay," I say. "Do I have to go?"

"Not with that face. We'll let you stay home."

"Or here."

"You'll be supervised, either way."

Not by you, either way. By Antonia or—Oh. Ohhhh.

"You'll never get Monique," I say. "Not in a million years."

"We'd like her to be there."

"But she already told you No." I know I'm right, and this time wouldn't hate to be.

"I believe that you could persuade her."

"Tell me why I want to."

"Tell me what you want," she says, putting me back in the losing position of first-person-to-name-a-number. Reading Monique's negotiation and business management books, it's pretty clear that right along we kids have been managed, not raised.

Handle your dog.

I have handled my dog.

"Sixteen," I say.

Mom cocks her head and stares at me. Sixteen is (to her) no obvious fraction or multiple of the dozen or so Super Large we took from Dad and Uncle Kenny, or of Dad's half, so she can't make sixteen be about the money, which it isn't anyway.

"I'm listening," she says.

"When I turn sixteen, I want you to give me zero shit about going to live with Monique. Official, on paper, legal emancipation, with no resistance from you or Dad."

Mom has a thousand ways to say No, but employs none.

She looks up at the ceiling, running her own calculations: dog rentals, furniture repair after sawing chair legs off inch by inch until I'm sitting on the floor, rhinoplasty if my door doctoring doesn't de-swell back into something presentably Stocktonesque.

"Weekends too," I say, "between when I get out of here and then," I say. Some almost-acquaintances at prep school had parents with the good sense to split up and split custody of their broods of rat-faced vermin. But I should define my terms. "Weekends means Friday mornings after breakfast 'til Monday after dinner."

Mom just continues smoking, until, "And the money?"

"Kenny's money is gone."

"I don't care about that," Mom says, waving smoke away from her face.

That's a little disappointing, but only because I just thought of a great, 'It's so far off the table it can't see the table from where it is,' line that I don't get to use now if she doesn't care. Moot. Oh, well.

And talk about not caring. Mom has a black belt in not caring. There's nothing legit about the cash, so Uncle Kenny's widow wouldn't have any of the normal legal rights, but still. That's her sister that she's looking out for in *no* way. Why would *she* want all that money? Flush it.

"Do you care about Dad's money, or your and Dad's money?"

"Your father's. I don't, no, not particularly. But he certainly does. The principle of it, you understand."

Somehow I know she doesn't mean the principle upon which interest would accrue but his Don't let anyone steal what you've rightfully stolen principle.

"I'll hold half of it until I'm sixteen, to make sure the deal goes through."

"You should hold all of it," she says. "I'll tell him you said all of it, and we'll go to half only if we absolutely need to."

All of a sudden Mom's on my side? Or all of a sudden Mom's showing me she's not entirely on Dad's side. Because, maybe not-so-all-of-a-sudden, she's not.

"Can you get him to take that?"

"Can you get Monique to the funeral?"

"We'll see. Write it up—the emancipation thing, not all the illegal—"

Mom's Oh really? face, her Are you the dumbest person in the world? look.

"Never mind. When you've both signed it, then I'll ask Monique. I won't mention it before. Notarized signatures. And no weasel-out clauses. No judgment calls, on anybody's part. You 'will' or 'shall' or whatever it is, all absolutes, effective exactly on my birthday—my *sixteenth* birthday. Simple language. Nothing tricky."

"You'll accept a faxed signature?" Mom asks. When I squint my eyes she says, "Your father has already returned to D.C."

I thought the sun was a little brighter today.

"Sure, that'll be fine."

"Anything else?" Mom asks.

"Can I use my third wish to wish for more wishes?"

"No," she says, proving she hasn't sprained her No muscle. But while I'm figuring out where this No falls on the Mohs hardness scale, she says, "I'm afraid I can't raise the dead either." Mom takes a giant drag on her cigarette, and adds, with smoke pouring out of her mouth and nostrils, "even if I wanted to."

"Can we fix this?" I ask, swirling my pointed index finger around my smashed-up face like she did around my ex-dog's fake funeral in the backyard. I'd bet a lunchbox full of twenties they'd require me to anyway, but now's the time to ask for what I want.

"We may have to wait until you stop growing—if you ever stop growing."

Anybody's guess about that, but with regard to my aforementioned atypical vertical situation:

"I don't want to go to basketball camp any more."

"Paul, you've *not attended* basketball camp."

It's true. I only went once—with a book—when Monique had a dentist appointment. They had to check the roster. And after watching me play for about two seconds, they let me read.

"I don't want to *pretend* to go to basketball camp any more?" I'm shrugging as I ask; I can feel it in my collarbone.

Mom rolls her eyes. "Fine."

I can't think of anything else to ask for other than unlimited chocolate milk, which I suspect I'm already getting the blind eye on anyway. But Monique's negotiations books again: don't let it get too lopsided or the other guy will feel squashed and be pissed off later. Mom's all about blowback, so I don't want to disgruntle her.

"Do *you* want anything?"

"What I would like hardly matters, Paul. But thank you for asking."

Monique got out. I'm getting out. Mom has nowhere to go.

"Just get Monique to the funeral?" I ask. She nods. I nod. "Can you get her in here to . . ." I bail out of the question, because it's stupid.

"Between lunch and dinner," Mom says. "You'll be here?"

"I'll be here."

Mom tamps out a half-smoked cigarette and drops it into the paper ashtray. "Very clever," she says, folding it closed and then crushing it in her fist as she stands up. She tucks her lighter into the cigarette pack's cellophane wrapper, and as she walks by, pauses to offer me the pack.

"No, thanks."

"Suit yourself. They do wonders for your nerves."

CHAPTER 29: ENDINGS & BEGINNINGS
*or*  DRAWING IT OUT, WRAPPING IT UP
*or*  KINTSUGI

Barely in the door and through security, Monique gives me just a bit more hug than my collarbone wants. My face hurting is my own fault for smiling, tightening muscles over the hairline fracture in my zygomatic arch, the butterfly bandage tugging at my skin. Monique whispers, "There's no way I'm not going to that funeral," before letting go (so I was wrong about that), then practically sings, "But if we don't tell Mom, I can come back tomorrow."

"I won't tell her if you don't tell her," I say.

"I won't tell her if you don't tell her," she says.

"I won't tell her if you *don't* tell her," I repeat, but she doesn't pick up the game. Monique's in a great mood, but silly will have to wait.

"Give me the two-dollar tour," she says.

"I'll owe you a buck seventy five. Not much to see." I flourish my good arm game-show style at the PowerHouse slogan painted in three-foot, purple letters along the hallway: AT POWERHOUSE WE LEARN LIFE SKILLS. "Self-explanatory." It's actually too big to read from any one spot in the hallway, so as you walk by it's kind of like you're sounding it out. At PowerHouse ... Okay, learn what? Oh! Life skills. Cool. Still, this hallway's shorter because of security/intake, and before my lips stop moving as I read along, we hit the main room.

"Here's where we learn life skills in a big circle. Four hundred eighty ceiling tiles." An adjacent conference room. "And there's where we learn life skills in a rectangle. One hundred ninety-two ceiling tiles." Hallways branch out from the main room. "Guest rooms. Guest rooms. Down there is where nobody learns culinary skills," but is also Sam and my unofficial exit.

"Food's bad?" Monique asks?

"Food's not *bad*."

"The *food's* not bad."

"Can you stay for dinner?"

"Yeah, if they'll let me."

"I think you can do whatever you want."

So. The quiet in the main room now is not everyone eyeballing Mom and fearing for their lives, but rubbing their eyes and wondering how she's age regressed two-dozen or so years since this morning.

"I'm down this way."

Strolling along my hallway, Monique says, "I got their contract for springing you at sixteen. My *lawyer* said it's solid. Contingent only on my appearance at Uncle Kenny's funeral and associated press events."

" 'Associated.' That's where they're going to try to screw us."

"No, there's a specific list. A long list. Mom's been busy."

"Addendum A?"

"B, actually. A is wardrobe. I have to wear a skirt, black, plain, below the knee, et cetera, et cetera."

"Mom didn't mention that to me. I didn't—"

"I know. It's fine," she says. "I don't mind looking good when I take my final bow out of public life. And they're responsible for transportation to and from, so it's on them if I miss curtain at any of their melodrama productions."

"Hiss the villains, cheer the . . ."

Monique laughs. "Yeah, cheer nobody. But we're good. It's solid. It's signed. We're good."

"Cool. You want to go? You *want* to go? *You* want to go?"

"Would. Not. Miss it. Watching Mom and Auntie A-hole try to outdo each other making it about themselves? That is going to be amazing. I'd hire a camera crew to film it all if that wouldn't make them happier. I've already booked my flight."

"This is me. A hundred and twenty-six ceiling tiles. One roommate," I say, pulling the door open and holding it for my sister. "Monique, this is Doug. Doug . . ."

. . . is frozen, eyes wide, jaw slackening as his mouth falls open. Not sure if it's ever exactly polite to stare, but his gaze is intense and he's clearly transfixed by Monique's face—So, yeah, staring as politely as possible, not scanning boobs, legs, boobs. (Doug said, "Don't take this the wrong way, Paul, but your mom is hot." I didn't say wait 'til you see my sister, but when he drew Mom in his sketchpad—really, really, *really* well—when he drew Mom, he didn't have his Soul Chewer pencil, so she ended up looking more like Monique.)

"Easy, killer," Monique says.

"I'm sorry," he says, climbing off his bed. "You probably get stared at a lot. Sorry. Mea culpa. I didn't mean to be rude. It's a pleasure to meet you. Paul won't stop talking about you. It's a pleasure to meet you in person, Monique."

Monique shakes Doug's hand when he offers his. I think, Don't kiss the lady's hand, but like I said before, he ain't stupid. Three distinct up-and-downs, very businessy, and a nod and smile—from both of them.

He asks, "Do you guys want some privacy? I'll clear out if you'd like."

I guess we've already concluded our actual business, so we'll just be visiting, so . . . Through my bruises and bandages, Monique reads my face telling her the call is hers.

"We're just hanging out," she says. "You can stay if you like."

"Thanks," Doug says, and offers her our one chair. "Please." He waits for her to sit.

And we hang out. Like real people. We hang out while the earth rotates in space, slowly angling the basketball hoop farther and farther away from the sun, gradually lengthening the shadow its support pole casts across the corner of the court. We chat about school, and life, and nothing and everything, about hurting his knee skiing and getting hooked on painkillers after surgery, about his good parents and our bad. We leave out the more rapey and killy bits, but otherwise it's nice just to relax and connect and spend a quiet, summer afternoon sharing Reflection Time.

"Are you drawing me?" Monique asks.

"On the outside," Doug says. "I'll have to get to know you better to really draw you."

Monique is not a giggler. But she does get a little twitch-twitch in the corner of her mouth when she's trying not to smile. As corny as I thought that sounded, maybe she didn't. Monique is— despite being tough as diamonds and my own private superhero—still just an eighteen-year-old girl, who wants to be loved, just like everybody else does.

And why wouldn't I want that for her? She's my sister. She's *my* sister.

Doug holds his sketchbook out at arm's length, angled so Monique and I can both see. Monique puts her fist over her mouth. On the page, Monique just before a laugh, eyes crinkling, unselfconscious, joyful, every detail just so, right down to her birthday earrings. Doug sees her, sees Monique the way I do, but maybe a way that Monique is only now starting to be able to see herself.

"Dibs," I say.

"Huh?" he asks.

"Dibs on that. Can I have— Is that acid-free paper? I want that drawing."

"You can have it," he says. "Sure."

"It's amazing," I say to Doug. To Monique, I say, "Wow." She nods.

"Graphite," Doug says, and begins gingerly tearing out the page. "On acid-free paper. It'll last forever if you take care of it."

Which means if it never sees the inside of our parent's house. Doug and I lean forward so he can hand it across to me. I look for a bit, then hand it to Monique, asking, "Will you keep this at your place?"

"Try to stop me."

As we talk through the rest of the afternoon, we end up having to lay the drawing face down because Monique and I can't stop looking at it. And not like the way I can't keep my eyes from tracing around the window frame and following the seams between cinderblocks. This picture's thousand words are poetry set to music.

Monique delicately rolls the paper when it ends up that they won't let her stay for dinner. We walk her out to security. For our good-bye hug, she splits the difference between just-right and her just-a-bit-too-much greeting. Doug isn't pushy about hugging Monique, though I don't think she'd mind.

"Rain check on dinner?" he asks.

"*I*," she says, "will see *you*," sweeping the tube in front of us both, being purposefully, playfully vague, "tomorrow."

If we're counting one day at a time like we're supposed to, today has been a good day. One in a row. And without getting too far ahead of myself, I think tomorrow could be too.

"Mañana," I say as Monique turns away to get buzzed out through the big front doors.

She pauses in the open doorway, awash in sunlight streaming in from outside, pressing against the door's hydraulics with one hand, cradling her portrait close with the other. Pauses in the sunshine and birdsong. Pauses, but doesn't turn around. Monique is not a look back kind of girl. She lets go and steps out into the world. I wouldn't notice myself taking a deep breath, but filling my lungs pushes on my slinged arm and grinds the jagged seam in my collarbone. Everything's connected, what's intact and what's busy scarring over.

## THE END

## ABOUT THE AUTHOR

Lawson Reinsch lives in Kirkland, WA, with his wife Judy, one feline allergy bag, and two of the most ridiculous six-pound dogs on the planet.

*Uncle Kenny's Other Secret Agenda*, won first-place in the Pacific Northwest Writers Association's literary contest (mainstream category). If you'd like to spend more time with Paul, Monique, and Sam, check out the thriller *PowerHouse*, available in print and electronic formats.

For more information about the author and his work, visit LawsonReinsch.com.

## ACKNOWLEDGEMENTS

Epic love and gratitude to my wife Judy. She fills my days with joy and laughter, and amazes me with her patience and generosity of spirit. So much of what I do and who I am would be impossible without her.

Thanks again to my longtime critique partners Lia Kawaguchi and Jean Miller for all their encouragement and feedback while this book came together. And a special thank you to Charis Himeda for challenging me to improve the ending. I was happy with it; now I'm happier with it.

And thank *you* for reading. If you had a good time, please share this book with someone you appreciate.

Made in the USA
San Bernardino, CA
18 October 2017